Wagons Westward

I continued my leisurely rounds on Hawkeye.

WAGONS WESTWARD

THE OLD TRAIL TO SANTA FE

WRITTEN AND ILLUSTRATED BY

ARMSTRONG SPERRY

DAVID R. GODINE, *PUBLISHER*

BOSTON

For
MARGARET
who listened so patiently

First softcover edition published in 2000 by
David R. Godine, Publisher, Inc.
Post Office Box 450
Jaffrey, New Hampshire 03452
www.godine.com

Library of Congress Cataloging in Publication Data

Sperry, Armstrong, 1897–1976
Wagons westward : the old trail to Santa Fe /
written and illustrated by Armstrong Sperry — 1st softcover ed.
p. cm.
Summary: In 1846, fifteen-year-old Jonathan Starbuck
sets out from Independence, Missouri, on a journey
along the Santa Fe trail.
ISBN 1–56792–128–0 (alk. paper)
1. Santa Fe National Historic Trail—Juvenile fiction.
[1. Santa Fe National Historic Trail—Fiction.
2. Frontier and pioneer life—West (U.S.)—Fiction]
I. Title
PZ7.S749 Wag 2000
[Fic]–dc21   00-029376

First Printing March, 2000
Printed in the United States of America

CONTENTS

CHAPTER   PAGE

I.   WHERE THE TRAIL BEGAN   1

II.   I MEET PIERRE LEROUX   13

III.   OLD CHIEF THROWER   21

IV.   "THE GRASS IS UP!"   33

V.   WEST WITH THE SUN   45

VI.   PIERRE TAKES A HAND   56

VII.   COUNCIL GROVE   68

VIII.   THE FATE OF THE COOPERS   77

IX.   MANUEL DISAPPEARS   87

X.   BUFFALO AND INJUNS   101

XI.   MESSAGES IN THE SKY   116

XII.   CIMARRON CROSSING   127

XIII.   THE ATTACK   139

XIV.   THE JOURNEY OF DEATH   149

XV.   CAPTURED   160

XVI.   THE LONG ARM OF ARMIJO   172

XVII.   MAGOFFIN'S GOLD   178

XVIII.   VICTORY   192

    TRAIL TALK   199

LIST OF ILLUSTRATIONS

	PAGE
I continued my leiurely rounds on Hawkeye	FRONTISPIECE
A man pulled up with a flourish	11
My home — a cabin in the clearing	23
A strange glitter shone in Roybal's eyes	43
I, Jonathan Starbuck	53
We faced each other, eyes flashing	65
I was alone with the thundering herd	107
Behind us came the high yells of the Indians	112-113
Suddenly the half-light was alive with racing figures	138
We rode on, wordless, tongueless	153
The Comanche pony fell	162
I compelled Armijo's eyes with my own	185

CHAPTER I

WHERE THE TRAIL BEGAN

LET ME introduce myself. My name is Jonathan Starbuck. I was fifteen years old on the third day of April, 1846, and I stood five-feet-nine in my moccasins. The runt of the litter, my father called me, meaning by "litter" the whole tribe of six-foot Starbucks. But runt though I must have seemed to a man who topped six feet four inches, I had been blessed with a strong body, toughened by a boyhood spent in the open. I had, moreover, a quick finger on the trigger and an eye that could see straighter than most.

The Starbucks were plagued with the urge always to see over the top of the next rise. Wherever danger's bright eyes beckoned, there they fought their way. Breaking with Eastern precedent and custom, they turned their backs on the seacoast to hew a new world of their own out of wilderness. What need had they for ruffled shirt or claret waistcoat or fancy snuffbox? Leave such "fofarraw" for the chicken-livered who stayed at home; but give them the ax and the rifle, deerskin for their backs, and a buffalo hide for a bed.

Of such fiber was Grandfather. In his youth he won a fine girl from her family. With her at his side, and ax and rifle to his hand, he set forth from peaceful Virginia to dare the wilderness that was Kentucky. There his wife of a year molded bullets all of one night during an Indian attack and on the next morning gave birth to a son — my father.

By the time my father grew up and married, the family had moved from Kentucky into Indiana, through Indiana into Illinois. There my own mother died when I was nine years old. My father,

broken by her loss, sold out our homestead, loaded a few possessions into a wagon, and we slogged the raw, westward miles from
Illinois to the booming frontier town of Independence, Missouri.
You see, Illinois was getting pretty civilized by that time, too. And
when the settlements grew so thick that the Starbucks could see the
smoke rising from their nearest neighbor's chimney, then it was
time for them to pull stakes. They'd had a bellyful of civilized fixin's.

And now that you know who I am, and how I came to be living
on the frontier, let me get along with my story.

The winter of 1846 had been a hard one in Missouri, if you will
recall; and at the beginning of April patches of late snow still lingered in the bottom lands. But on the particular morning that old
Lanky Lewis and I cantered down out of the hills toward the
town, I knew that at last the blighting dullness of winter had been
shaken off. The sky was as blue as a babe's eye — a wide sky washed
clear by the spring rains. Cottonwoods and box elders waxed
bright with their first shoots. Freshets leaped and sang as they fur-
rowed their way to the Big Muddy. I saw the first flock of geese
against the sky, flying high with the south wind, and on the top
rail of a snake fence a squirrel arched his tail along his back to
cock a suspicious eye at the rifles slung across our saddle horns.

On such a day it was good to be fifteen and astride my roan;
good to know that Mother Applegate would have breakfast waiting
for me: hominy grits and spoon bread and hash fried to a turn —
all the things that my own mother had cooked for me when I was
a cub. But best of all, this was Sunday, and Sabino Roybal — may
he fry in his own fat — never opened his saddle shop on the
Sabbath. In this respect he differed from the other shopkeepers of
Independence, who lost no opportunity to extract a copper from
a population that was here today and gone tomorrow. You see, I
had been apprenticed to Sabino Roybal to learn the saddler's
trade. From daylight till dark I labored under his relentless eye.
Sunday was the only day in which I could draw the full breath of
freedom.

Lanky and I reined in and let our animals nibble at the road-
side. The town lay in the valley below us, back at a safe distance

from the caprices of the river. Independence — a settlement flung
down on the outermost edge of civilization, fighting the wilderness for survival, the jumping-off place for the white-topped wagons on their westward venture. The bluffs along the Missouri were
dotted with the dark bulks of the wagons, their osnaburg tops
shining white as snow in the early-morning sun.

The wagons had begun to come in by the middle of March,
straggling at first. Lean, hard-looking men marched beside those
lumbering wagons, men grim about the lips but with a vision blazing in their eyes. Their women were brown and lined and horny-
handed, clad in homespun and sunbonnet, riding the high seats.
Children peered from under the tops of the Conestogas with
wide, scared eyes.

They came from all the States that lay to the east — from neat
villages bordered with elms; from farms that had been lost to the
landsharks. They came, some of them, to evade justice or to seek
it. They came up the river by boat, by wagon. They came on
horseback or covering the raw miles on foot. They came, lean-
ribbed and in rags. They came. All day long the wagons creaked
and rumbled through the town, oxen straining in the mud, men
shouting and cursing to the crack of the bull whips. They spread
out along the banks of the river for two miles or more, and the
fields and bottoms overflowed with them. By night a thousand
mess-fires glowed in the darkness, and by day the air resounded
with the clamor of the bullwhackers, the lowing of the cattle, and
the shrill squealing of the unbroken mules.

Something about it, far beyond the reach of my own memory,
set the blood racing in my veins. The swing and smell and stir of
it never failed to lift me in its grip. This — why, this was where the
West began: raw, violent, dauntless. Why shouldn't I have warmed
to it? It was but a scant six years since my father and I had struck
this frontier, driven by the selfsame urge that drove those men down
in yonder valley. And each year since then it had been the same:
I had watched the great caravans gathering on the banks of the
river in the early spring, making their preparations for the hazardous journeys to Santa Fe or Oregon. Then when the magic cry

sounded, "The grass is up!" and grazing for the cattle on the prairies was assured, they'd be off. Each spring I had watched them roll out, wanting, more than anything in the whole world, to be riding with them toward that mysterious West. You would have thought that I'd be used to it by this time, but each spring it seemed harder to watch them pull out.

"They'll be moving any day now, Lanky," I observed.

The old trapper shot me a quick look and nodded his assent. "Yep," he grunted. "The grass orter be startin' on the prairie by now. The wagons'll be rollin' out any time, shore 'nough." He lifted his old head and sniffed at the untamed wind, as if it brought him some half-forgotten message from the plains; a grim nostalgia written on his craggy face.

Involuntarily I glanced at the stump of his left leg where it had been amputated above the knee. Lanky had been a trapper for the American Fur Company when, in a brush with the Blackfeet, he had stopped an arrow in the foreleg. The wound had turned gangrenous. Many times I had listened while the old trapper related the gory details of that episode in plains-surgery: how four men had held him down while a fifth cut through the flesh above the infection with a skinning knife. Then the saw through the bone, and the red-hot king bolt that seared over the arteries, and the tar from the wagon hub plastered onto the stump.... Today, for the first time, I realized just what that accident on the plains so long ago had meant in his life. Lanky would never again see the buffalo herds surging in full flight or watch the bighorn scampering up to rocky heights or hear the bugle of the bull elk when the first snows flurried.

As he sat his pony on the hilltop, watching the activity of the distant wagon camps, I suppose that to some he would have seemed a comical figure with his one good knee high from shortened stirrup, the stump of the other gripping his pony's belly; the tail of his coonskin cap swinging idly in the breeze, while his beloved fiddle (from which he could scrape the most enticing tunes) was tied to the cantle, bumping against his thigh. Yes, comical he was, perhaps, but his heart was as tough as an old he-badger's and he owned a spirit to match it.

"'"Tain't no pleasure trip whar those coots is headin','" he observed laconically, nodding his head toward the distant camps. "Every Injun tribe from here to the Rio Grande is on the warpath 'count o' the scercity o' buffler. Don't know's I blame the red devils! The buffler is meat and coverin' fer the Injun, and it's gittin' scercer and scercer every year. Why, when I fust crossed the Plains in '23 we raised our fust buffler as fer east as Cottonwood Crick, and now they say eff you sight 'em this side o' Little Arkansas, yo're lucky. I recollect ridin' through one herd fer three hundred mile! They opened up to let us pass and closed in behind us, and the calves was so thick you had ter pry 'em out o' the spokes o' the wheels! Never seed the like this side o' Santy Fee. Wagh!"

"What's Santa Fe really like, Lanky?" I questioned, for probably the hundredth time.

"Hmph!" he snorted. "A mud town, that's what it is. Looks like a huddle o' brick kilns. Full o' greasers an' fleas an' other varmint."

Probably, I admitted with reluctance, Santa Fe *was* like that. But I knew that the country cradling that mud town must possess some splendid magnetism to draw men and their families away from the ordered security of their homes, out across a thousand miles of wilderness. Look at them down there in the camps! Making ready — for what? Old people would die on the way. Babes would be born. The luckless would lose their scalps to the wild-riding Comanche or the Pawnee. Their wagon wheels would break or be mired in quicksands. Their stock would be stampeded or die of thirst. But no man or woman would think of turning back. And if they should fall by the way, cut down by hunger or thirst or arrow, they would fall face-forward toward the Rio Grande, a fabulous land whose valleys were rich in black earth and whose mountains were of purest gold!

Some day, when my apprenticeship to Sabino Roybal should be at an end, perhaps I would follow the westward trail — trap the beaver in hidden streams, watch the trout and the grayling flash through some clear mountain pool, and know the thunder in my ears of the buffalo herd. The wander-urge of the Starbucks sang its song and would not be denied. I must go! But even as the wild

hope crossed my mind, I thought of my father in the cabin in the clearing, crippled. And I knew that while he lived, the Trail would never be for me.

It was a heavy thought, one to sag the mind beneath its weight. I dug my heels into Whitefoot's ribs, and the roan leaped forward.

"Come on, Lank!" I shouted over my shoulder. "I'll race you to the edge of town!"

A blood-curdling whoop from behind warned me that the old trapper had taken up the challenge. Neck and neck we tore over the rutted ground, the horses lifting and surging beneath us; foam from their mouths flying back into our faces.

"*Ai-a-ai!*" I yipped, Pawnee fashion, and dug my heels into Whitefoot's ribs and lay forward, flat over her extended neck.

"*Ai-a-ai!*" came Lanky's answering whoop, high-pitched and strident, as he pulled abreast of me. Neck and neck, shoulder and shoulder, eye and eye.... Lanky had closed up on my get-off and now he held it; neither of us able to pull ahead of the other. Over the rough ground we raced, hell-bent for leather.

At the edge of town we drew up laughing, the horses breathing gustily.

"You're gittin' soft, ole hoss," Lanky roared, giving his pony a whack on the flank. "This white man's kentry ain't fit fer an Injun pony, any ways you look at it. A buffler hoss like you orter be able to show his rump to any old nag from Kaintucky!"

Hawk Eye flung up her head, stung with the insult. Mark her well, Reader, for Hawk Eye has a part to play in this tale of mine. Just another spotted Indian pony wearing the split-ear sign of the Comanche. Hard winters and scanty pasture had robbed her of fat and flesh; but if you knew a horse from a hitching rack, you could have seen at a glance that her legs were well set and her withers as fine as a deer's. True — she'd never been stabled, curried, or shod; a veritable mongrel of horseflesh. Yet she could climb a precipice with the assurance of a goat or plunge down a rocky slope with the wild indifference of a buffalo.

"Git yore ole fleece along thar," Lanky cried, giving the animal another dig with his good leg. "See eff you cain't make town without goin' under, do ee hyar now?"

The clock on the church was striking the hour of six as we rode into the town. There was a pack train moving down the street toward us, weighted with buffalo hides and Mexican silver and beaver plews. A lean, grizzled man at the head of the procession detached himself from his companions and rode to meet us, his leathern face cracked into the semblance of a smile. I recognized Joe Meeker, an old Mountain Man famous along the frontier. His long body slouched easily over the saddle horn, rifle crosswise before him; buckskins daubed with blood and grease until they looked like polished leather.

He raised an arm in salute and hailed Lanky. "How thar, ole coot!"

"How thar, Joe!" Lanky shouted back, vastly pleased at this meeting.

"What's sign?"

"Fair. What's beaver sellin' fer up to Taos?"

"Dollar a plew."

"Wagh! *That* don't shine!"

Joe wagged his head sorrowfully. "The days when a good plew fetched six dollars, beaver or kitten, is over," he grumbled. "The beaver trade's rubbed out, Lank. The danged Yankee that invented silk hats orter have his guts ripped out."

"Beaver's shore ter rise," Lanky put in hopefully.

"Got ter," came back Joe's answer. "Tain't in man's nature not to trap. Hell's full o' high silk hats. Wagh! What they gittin' fer powder hyar, Lanks?"

"Two dollar' a pint."

There came another throat-scraping "Wagh!" and Joe Meeker spat his contempt of store tenders and traders. "Got a chaw of bacca 'bout ye?"

"Have so." Lanky proffered a wedge of tobacco which the other fell upon, tore off a sizable hunk, and rolled it into his cheek. "Reckon you must be hungry fer State's doin's, Joe," Lanky chuckled.

"Yep – half froze fer punkin pie and light bread. Got a thirst, too! How 'bout a drink over to Uncle Wood's?"

"*That* shines!" came Lanky's ready answer. "Uncle's got some Blue Ruin that'd make a jackrabbit spit in a rattlesnake's eye!"

The two old Mountain Men ignored me as a stripling too insignificant to be invited to drink with trappers. As they moved off in the direction of Smallwood Noland's hotel, I looked after them and my ears caught Lanky's question:

"Come through the Blackfoot kentry, Joe?"

"Not this coon. I like my ha'r right whar hit's growin'. 'Member the time Broken Hand killed three buffler with one bullet down to the Platte, Lanks?"

"Do so. An' that time we was ambushed up to Spanish Peaks. . . ."

As long as consciousness remained and their tongues wagged clear or otherwise, these two old cronies of the Trail would live over the many hair-raising times they had had together. I was half tempted to follow them, then remembered that Mother Applegate would have breakfast waiting for me, and already the hash would be sizzling in the pan and doughnuts bubbling in their iron kettle.

So, "Get along, Whitefoot," said I to the roan. "There'll be State's doin's for us at Mother Applegate's."

I rode past the church, the Sundance Theater, the dramshop, Boone's grocery, and on past Black Jack Bannock's notorious Dia-

mond Spring Saloon where the bar was inlaid with silver dollars. I signal this latter out for your attention, Reader, because Black Jack himself looms large in these pages. But I had no faintest premonition of that fact as I rode by his establishment that fine April morning. There was a Mexican boy opening the doors for the business of the day, and within an hour or two Black Jack himself would be dealing the cards out of faro boxes, and his keen-edged voice would be exhorting: "Step right up, gentlemen, and place yer bets! The game's made and the ball's a-rolling!"

Here the trappers would lose in a few mad hours all the fat profits from a year of hunting in the wilderness. They'd be stripped of everything but their buckskins and their rifles, in debt for the very traps their livelihood depended upon; but with a laugh and a curse they'd swing up onto their ponies and turn toward the West once more.

Independence was a town that never slept. It swarmed with traders, emigrants, gamblers, swaggering rivermen and *voyageurs* from the country to the north; blue-clad dragoons from Fort Leavenworth. Indians of the friendly tribes moved silently through the streets like painted shadows. Sky pilots, as ministers were called, preached a scorching hell for the wicked and fought the gamblers for a grip on men's souls. Here were men who lived dangerously and died in violence, their scalps pouring out a red offering to a thirsty land.

At the end of the street a sign swung out before the doorway of a frame house:

SHOO FLY RESTAURANT
Mother Applegate, *Proprietor*

Here Mother Applegate, famous along the frontier for her "corn doin's and chicken fixin's," carried on a thriving trade. Next to the cabin in the hills it was the only home that I had, and everything about the place was heartwarming — from the checkered tablecloths to the stuffed partridge on the mantel. And Mother Applegate, too, bless her hearty soul! As I hitched Whitefoot to the rack, I could see the woman through the window, bustling about among the tables in her shiny black bombazine.

I turned away to mount the steps, then stopped — listening, alert in every sense, for no reason that I could fathom. My ear caught the thunder of galloping hoofs. Familiar enough sound, the good Lord knows. Perhaps it was some shadowy premonition of events soon to close in upon me, which kept me standing there, tense, expectant.

A man was tearing down the road at full gallop. He pulled up with a flourish that brought his black stallion to its haunches, forefeet pawing the air, in front of Mother Applegate's door. The man who swung out of saddle and threw the reins over the rack with the easy grace of long habit, was a young man, overtall, lean of rib, dressed in the fringed buckskins of the trapper. His eyes blazed from under his beaver with the untamed spirit of the wilderness.

"Hola, son!" he hailed me. "Is breakfast past?"

A man pulled up with a flourish.

"No – sir."

"Fine! Then you'll join me?" He flung an arm across my shoulders and together we mounted the steps.

I knew in this instant that here was the most extraordinary man I had ever seen. I could not guess the part that he was to play in my future.

CHAPTER II

I Meet Pierre Leroux

MOTHER APPLEGATE looked up expectantly as we entered. "Lor' have mercy, if it ain't Pierre Leroux! Pierre, you three-horned devil, how are you?"

The man reached her at a bound, gripped her by both shoulders, and planted a kiss first on one cheek, then the other.

"Mother!" he boomed. "How fine to see you again. Years pass slowly when I'm away from you!"

"Lor', there you go," the woman chuckled, backing off and looking him over with dancing eyes. "You may be an American, Pierre, but them French ancestors of yours knew what to say to please a woman, and kind o' looks like they'd passed the knack on to you. I see you know Johnny Starbuck already — but then, you know everybody in the world I reckon. Set down, set down." And she shouted toward the kitchen, "Hash up and come a-runnin'!"

My strange companion and I dropped into chairs beside the table while the good woman whisked plates in front of us, asking a dozen questions to the minute.

"Where you been these last two years, Pierre Leroux? Up to no good, I'll warrant."

"You malign me, Mother," the man protested, handing her his

rifle. "I've been to Washington and dined with President Polk. I've been——"

"There, there... I might-a knowed you'd have some slippery answer ready. Been in jail, most likely."

She stood his rifle in a corner – one of the new English weapons, double-barreled and heavy-stocked. As I tried to count the brass nailheads hammered into its butt, I remembered that the famous Kit Carson never notched his gun to keep toll of slain enemies, but hammered in a brass nail as occasion demanded. Leroux's eyes followed mine.

"Yep, seven of 'em!"

"There are three notches in my own gun," I bragged.

The man's eyes widened. "Come, come, son – not three at your tender years? "

"It was my father's," I explained. "Notches and all. "

"Let's see your rifle, son. "

I handed it over, full of pride in its fineness. The man scrutinized it closely. "Hmmm. . . ." he observed. "A fine piece, and properly made, too. A bit on the light side for buffalo, perhaps. But it's had plenty to say in its time, I'll wager, and it'll say it again. How did your father come by it?"

"He made it, sir."

Dark eyebrows lifted as he ran his hands over the smooth maple stock. "The old Kentucky flintlock," he mused, almost to himself. "As American as Andrew Jackson himself. Did it ever occur to you, Starbuck," he exclaimed, his face lighting, "that the history of this country has been written with the ax and the rifle?" His eye ran along the shining octagonal barrel. Four feet long, that barrel, with a knife blade of silver for its front sight. I saw his eyes light with pleasure, and I found myself wishing that my father could know this stranger who felt such admiration for a flintlock now that the new percussion caps had begun to spell the doom of the older rifle.

Mother Applegate wiped off two cups with her apron and set them down before us. "What brings you here this season, Pierre Leroux?" she queried.

The man looked up at her with quizzical eyes. "You haven't

heard?" he demanded in mock surprise. "Well – it's like this. . . . I'm to guide Black Jack Bannock and his wagon train to Santa Fe."

"Black Jack Bannock!" the woman and I exclaimed simultaneously.

"Right you are."

"But he's no trader," I ventured. "He's —"

"He's a good-for-nothing gambler! " the woman snapped me up. "Taking money out of honest men's pockets in that saloon of his. He'd skin a flea for the hide and tallow!"

"I won't dispute that," Leroux agreed. "But the gambling business must be falling off, for Bannock seems overcome with the desire to trade with the Mexicans. And I'm to guide – one hundred dollars a month and found. I'm broke, Mother, as always. Besides, the grass'll soon be up, and the buffalo'll be moving north, and my feet itch to go."

"Yes," the woman nodded wisely, "you were always one o' those that has to see over the top o' the next hill. Otherwise you'd still be in your father's banking house in St. Louis instead o' bein' —"

"The black sheep of the family," the man finished for her. "But it seems I'd rather run buffalo than add bank figures, Mother."

"But," the woman persisted, "they're sayin' here that war with Mexico waits but the drop of a hat. And where'll you Yankee traders be in Santy Fee if there's a war? In the calaboose or swingin' from the limb of a tree – that's where!" With which dark prediction she bustled off toward the kitchen.

"It's rumored, sir," I put in, "that Colonel Kearny has left Fort Leavenworth for the Mexican border with three thousand dragoons."

The man shot me a quick look while one corner of his mouth quirked. "There are two hundred Santa Fe wagons along the river now, rarin' to go," he observed laconically. "Men with wives and children. Doesn't sound as if they're scared of war with Mexico."

I laughed. "Where's the American, sir," I wanted to know, "who doesn't believe that his army can trim the world? If there's war with Mexico, *of course* we'll win! That's settled. And the first settlers and traders will have the pickings."

"Hmmm — you're a smart lad, Jonathan Starbuck. And there's breeding in your speech. Where are you from?"

"From Madison County, Kentucky, sir."

"Boone's country, eh? What are you doing in Independence?"

"My father brought me out here when I was nine years old," I answered. "My mother had died that winter and—" I checked myself. Here was I telling this stranger things that I had never mentioned to anyone except Lanky Lewis and Mother Applegate. My father had always declared that a man who kept his own counsel was never sorry for it.

But there was something about Pierre Leroux to draw a confidence. You sensed a quality about him like the temper of a fine rifle. As he lounged there across the table with such an easy grace, his eyes blazing out from under heavy, black-arched eyebrows, black hair spilling violently to his shoulders, trapper fashion, he seemed a living embodiment of the prairies, some intangible wildness caught and made animate in his person.

"And what do you do for a living?" he asked.

"I'm learning the saddler's trade at Roybal's."

"Is that what you want to do, be a saddler?" There was surprise, even a hint of scorn in the question.

"No," I answered. "No!"

Be a saddler — when a thousand wagons were camped out along the river; when the streets swarmed with trappers and rang with men's shouts; be a saddler when the Santa Fe Trail lead away and away from the Missouri's west bank and sang its song of danger in my ears, and every nerve and sinew answered to its call!

"No!" I cried again. "That's not what I want to do!"

"Starbuck," Pierre spoke quietly, and his eyes held mine with level magnetism. "Get out of this trumpery town. It's no place for a strapping lad like you. Tell Sabino Roybal and his saddle shop to go to the devil. Hit the trail. Once you jump off the west bank of the Missouri, you're in country fresh-hewn from the hand of God. Nothing else like it in creation. Out there a man's his own master and beholden to none. A hard life? You can wager it is! The cowards never start, and the weak die along the way."

His voice caught me up in its spell and I leaned forward, my breath coming quicker.

"I'll show you how to trap beaver," the man rushed on, "and how to run the buffalo. I'll show you how to kill a grizzly bear. Ho! *There's* an adversary worthy a man's metal." He leaped to his feet, swung toward the corner, and snatched up his rifle, aiming it at an imaginary animal. "You've got to get 'em between the eyes or behind the ear," he flung over his shoulder. "They can keep coming with a bullet through the heart. And if you're caught with an empty gun after inflicting a wound that's not mortal — well, say your prayers. Remember, never fire in a hurry. The bear'll always stop, rise on his hind legs, and make ready for a sideswipe with his forepaws. That's your chance, boy. His head's extended and the ball won't glance. Aim between the eyes and fire!"

The trigger clicked. BANG! went the rifle. The stuffed partridge on the mantel was blown to fragments. Wood splintered. Feathers flew. My eardrums rang with the explosion. The door slammed open.

"Land o' Goshen!" shrieked Mother Applegate. "'Who's shot! What in tarnation — Look at that mess! Pierre, you redskin, you a'most made me drop this platter o' hash."

MOTHER APPLEGATE

"If you had, I'd have shot you," the man promised. "I was just showing this lad how to kill a grizzly."

"Jose," the woman snapped at a scared-looking Mexican boy who had followed with a coffeepot, "fetch in a dustpan, and brisk about it or I'll take the broom to you. These dratted greasers," she complained, "you have to put a rattlesnake under 'em to get 'em to move. And then they'd rather get bit than get up. And I'm a mind to take the broom to you, too, Leroux," she threatened darkly as she set about sweeping up the mess.

Pierre and I fell upon the hash as if neither of us had broken fast for a week, and we spoke never one word till the platter was licked clean and the second cups of coffee were cooling in their crockery mugs.

Pierre lifted his mug and sniffed at the contents, relishing the fragrance. "I presume," he observed with a sly twinkle in his eye, "that you are both acquainted with Tallyrand's recipe for good coffee?" The man knew full well, of course, that neither Mother Applegate nor I could have told if Tallyrand were trader, trapper, or statesman.

"Humph!" the woman sniffed suspiciously. "What is it?"

Pierre grinned. " 'Good coffee,' said Tallyrand, 'should be black as night; hot as fire; pure as an angel; and sweet as love!' " He raised his cup in fine salute. "Tallyrand would have complimented you, Madame Applegate."

The woman gulped and I laughed in spite of myself. There was such an unconscious elegance in the manners of this Pierre Leroux, that bore no relationship to his shining buckskins, the broad belt with a Colt's revolving pistol, the powderhorn and bullet mold hung across his chest. He had been to Washington to see the President, he had said. Well — he would have been as much at home in the White House sitting down to break his fast with President Polk, as he would surely have been out on the wide prairie, roasting a buffalo steak over a camp fire. He relished this audience of two and made the most of it.

"April is all but over," he boomed, "and any day now we'll be off! Down the trail to Santa Fe. Good-by, civilization!" One hand

signed a large farewell while his voice rang forth in gathering volume. "We'll know Diamond Spring and Cottonwood Creek; we'll take that damnable ford of the Little Arkansas at a rush – then on to Cimarron Crossing, and into that desert! *Jornada del Muerto*, the Spaniards call it: the Journey of Death. And never was a stretch of land better named. Sixty miles without a drop of water!" His knuckles showed white while his voice rushed on like an unopposable tide... "Maybe the Comanche'll lift our hair. Maybe the Pawnee'll stampede our stock. There'll be mirages to lure us on, visions of water tantalizing us, mocking us there in the desert, till our black tongues swell in our throats and we'll fall by the wayside and leave the coyotes to harry our bones. But if we make it – we'll top the rise of a hill some fine morning and there at our feet we'll see Santa Fe. She'll be shining in the sun – all gold and copper and silver, too. And we'll yell and yip and fire our rifles into the air. The more pious will thank God. The rest of us will get drunk."

Mother Applegate was breathless. And I – I was hanging upon every word, longing to ask a thousand questions about rivers and Indians and buffalo; swept by an all but irresistible desire to leap upon my pony's back, swing my rife to the pommel, and head for the westering sun.

The woman rallied herself and straightened her apron. "Them can go that's a mind to," she snapped, "but them dratted deserts warn't made for humans."

"A-ha!" Pierre laughed and pinched her round cheek. " 'Full many a flower is born to blush unseen, and waste its sweetness on the desert air.' "

"Look a-here," Mother Applegate scolded, slapping at his hand, "don't you go filling this boy's head full o' nonsense. All this clatter about adventure – nothin' very romantic in dyin' o' thirst or gettin' your scalp trimmed by a godless redskin."

"Mother," Pierre came back at her grandly, "life is filled with hazard. No man who's half a man should slink at home when danger and adventure ride the horizon!"

"Now you stop that nonsense, Pierre Leroux!" exploded the

exasperated woman. "Just because *you've* flaunted every danger in tarnation since the day you was born. Johnny hasn't got no sensible person in this jumping-off place 'cept me to give him a word of sound talk. And what's more, his father has bound him out to learn a trade. He's goin' to grow up a decent, law-abidin' citizen — and the good Lord knows we need 'em a-plenty. There's enough of you — you fly-by-nights, as it is."

Mother Applegate was perspiring with indignation and her eyes snapped sparks. Pierre flung back his head and laughed, laughed till the rafters rang and tears coursed down his tanned cheeks.

"All right, Mother, I'll be good," he promised. Then leaning swiftly across the table he clapped me on the shoulder. "Stick to your trade, Johnny boy," he admonished solemnly. "Forget all this rubbish I've been talking about Comanches and grizzlies. And some day maybe, when you're ninety or a hundred, you'll be an excellent — er — saddle maker." He sprang to his feet while glasses and dishes rattled to the movement.

"Hola! I must be off!" came his shout. "Good-by, Starbuck. Be diligent. Be sober. And you, Mother — may your shadow never grow less!"

Then he seized his rifle and swung it to his shoulder, and with roweling spurs and a laugh still lingering in our ears, he was gone.

Mother Applegate and I stood there for a moment hearing the diminishing thunder of the stallion's hoofs.

"Well!" exclaimed the woman, breaking the spell. "Well, if he don't beat all! Guide for the Santa Fe caravan, eh? Hmmm... he's a deep 'un. I wonder — I wonder—"

CHAPTER III

OLD CHIEF THROWER

THERE was a pile of wood to be chopped for Mother Applegate, cows to be milked, and a dozen-odd chores to be done
about the place. So it was late afternoon before I bade her good-
by and turned my back on the Shoo Fly. As I rode through the
town, out and up into the hills, the sun was dropping low on the
western horizon and blue shadows crept like slowly lengthening
fingers up the eastward slopes.

At the end of the muddy road that led to the cabin in the clearing, I could see Lanky's Indian pony hitched to a fence rail, and I
knew that the old trapper had survived his meeting of the morning with Joe Meeker and had come out to our cabin, as he often
did of a Sunday night, to fry sausages and make flapjacks. My
father was sitting in front of the door, white-headed, motionless,
wide of shoulder. On warm days he sat there for hours at a time,
with his rifle across his knees, or perhaps with some weighty volume propped up before him.

So straight and tall he looked as he sat there, that it was hard
to believe his legs were paralyzed, and that when he wanted to
move from one place to another, he must drag himself by the force
of his great arms, as a child. The accident had happened when first
we had come to Independence; the very day, in fact, we had fin-

ished building the cabin: the tree that fell across his body, pinning him to earth. He had never walked again. During these six years his hair had turned white and sometimes his great frame sagged, as a tree might droop, deprived of its rightful sustenance.

As I rode across the stumpy clearing, I knew without being told that he had been cleaning his rifle – Old Chief Thrower, as he called it. Men named their rifles in token of some eventful moment in their lives: "Old Knock-him-stiff," "Old Greaser." Daniel Boone had made this particular rifle and given it to my grandfather. It weighed eleven pounds and had a barrel forty inches from lock plate to muzzle, a length which made for most accurate sighting. In its pips beneath the barrel was the ramrod; and the patch box was a recess covered by a silver lid in the right side of the stock. I had never been allowed to shoot Old Chief Thrower, scarcely even to handle it, having to content myself with the lesser piece which my father had given me some years back.

The ascendancy of the Mountain Man over the Kentucky hunter had given gunsmiths an opportunity which they were quick to realize. Down in St. Louis, the shop of Hawkins & Company had risen to wide fame. The Hawkins rifle became as good as sterling in this wild country, the very name itself signifying perfection. When men talked about "a regular Hawkins hoss," they spoke of an animal of superlative points. But my father disdained the newfangled contraptions – percussion caps, double-barreled pieces, and such – and clung to his beloved flintlock. Though six years had passed since he had put his rifle to actual use, not a day went by in which the ritual of its cleaning was neglected. He was forever shining the octagonal barrel to a high polish, swabbing out the gleaming bore with bear's grease, and rubbing the stock with tallow till it glowed with the full warmth of its curly maple.

"How, Pop!" I hailed him.

Sometimes when I spoke to him, he did not hear, but this time his eyes looked toward me with a smile in their depths, and he answered, "How, Son."

"Giving Old Chief Thrower his overhauling, I see."

My home — a cabin in the clearing.

"A man never knows when his rifle may be needed," came his answer. "It must be ready."

I skinned off Whitefoot's bridle, slung the saddle across the top rail of the fence, and turned her loose to graze. From within the cabin Lanky's thin voice issued, raised in song, and I smelled sizzling sausages and heard the rattle of the griddle. At that moment the old trapper appeared in the doorway with a steaming plate in hand.

"Come an' git it!" he barked and hobbled over to an up-ended box which served for a table. Balancing his own plate on his good knee, he gave vent to his favorite bit of philosophy: "Why any man who's ever tasted buffler kin be content to chaw on hog is more'n this coon kin see." A whole sausage cake disappeared into his cavernous mouth almost before the sentence ended.

I grabbed a flapjack, wrapped it around a sausage, and took a mouthful. "I've never tasted buffler, as you know," said I, "but it can't be much better than this fodder."

"Humph!" he snorted in scorn. "It's right hard to believe that they's some folks in this world as ain't never seen an Injun scalped. Eff that's the way a man's stick floats, I reckon he cain't help it. But he jest cain't spit even with a Mountain Man, any ways you fix it." He aimed a stream of tobacco juice at Archimedes, the cat, who sidestepped it neatly to sit in the doorway and wash his paws with lofty disdain.

My father drank his coffee and smiled. He made no reply to Lanky's garrulity. But the old trapper and his talk seemed to bring him out of himself to an awareness that was absent most of the time these days.

"Yes, sir," Lanky was going on, "how any man who's ever used his saddle fer a pillow kin put up with the settlements is more'n this coon kin see. Less'n he *has* ter, that is! Fer a man who's lived a life like mine—" He shook his head sadly. "'D I ever tell you 'bout the time that Cheyenne got me cornered on that rocky ledge up to the Platte?" He paused hopefully, trusting that we would forget having heard the story some hundred times.

"No, Lank," I obliged. "What happened, anyway?"

Lanky chuckled at the recollection of that moment and aimed another stream at Archimedes. "Waal, sir, that pesky redskin had me in as ticklish a preedicament as you'd want to be in. Thar I was, high an' dry on thet one-way ledge. Couldn't go back, 'cause I knew they was a dozen Cheyennes behind me; an' eff I went forward, thar was thet coot a-layin' fer me. I couldn't climb up the danged cliff 'cause they wasn't a toehold big enough fer a goat. An' eff I jumped over, thar warn't nothin' to stop me fer a mile or so."

He rolled the hopeless situation over with vast delight, looking expectantly from one to the other of us. It was my father who spoke up this time to demand, "Well, Lanky – what happened?"

Lanky bit off another chunk of tobacco and dropped his eyes. "Thet Injun killt me!" he answered.

"Did you ever hear of a Mountain Man named Pierre Leroux?" I demanded, to stall off further reminiscences.

"Yep," came the old trapper's ready answer. "The black sheep o' the St. Louis Leroux's. Rich as Croesus they was, too. But Pierre, he must a-been a throwback, 'cause he runs away from the fancy school whar they'd put him an' takes to the Trail when he warn't

more'n knee-high to a beaver pup. He was brought up on store clothes and yaller buttons, and eddicated proper, but he took to buckskins like an Injun takes to ha'r. I heerd it said that he went back home fer some more book larnin' after a time; but it didn't 'pear to harm him none. Ain't seen him around goin' on a couple of year now. Heerd tell he'd been rubbed out by the Sioux."

"He's in town now," I volunteered. "He's going to guide Black Jack Bannock's train to Santa Fe."

The old trapper whistled in amazement. "What-all's got into Black Jack?" he queried. "Ain't he makin' beaver enough in thet saloon of his, takin' the shirts right off pore unsuspectin' Mountain Men?"

"Whatever Bannock's up to, you can wager it's no good," my father put in, unexpectedly.

"An' *that's* so! He's the horns o' the Devil himself, as shore as my rifle's got hindsights and shoots center."

He dismissed the subject with his fiddle, tucking it under his chin and rasping out a few preliminary notes. It was dark by now, and frog voices and tree toads were tuning it up, too. Lanky's thin music somehow merged with this elemental chorus and became a part of it. He had a knack with the fiddle, had Lanky, and could set your feet tapping with his rhythms. He launched into the "Arkansas Traveller," that quick-reel tune with a backwoods story talked to it while played. It seemed to have sprung out of the soil itself, sweeping the frontier like a prairie fire. Sometimes as Lanky played and "sang," I joined in on the responses; and to give you some idea of how it must have sounded, picture us sitting there on the doorstep of the cabin in the falling dusk; old Lanky sawing away and taking up the tale thus:

Lanky: "Hello, Stranger!"
Johnny: "Hello, yourself!"
Lanky: "Kin you give me a night's lodging?"
Johnny: "No room, Stranger."

"Cain't you make room?"

"Nope! Mought rain."

"What eff it does rain?"

"Thar's only one dry spot in the house an' me an' Sal sleeps on that!"

"Why don't you put a new roof on your house?"

"When it's dry, I don't want a roof. When it's wet, I cain't."

And so on, and so on, throughout endless complications concerning the poor traveler who asked but a night's lodging.

Night had closed in on us by now, and fireflies sparked and dimmed in the darkness. A whippoorwill reiterated its insistent note and a hoot owl sounded its mournful call. I found myself thinking of Pierre Leroux, seeing the pictures that he brought to mind — Indian raids and wagons corralled, and the soft whir of arrows speeding to their marks. . . .

"Guess I'll be dustin' along," the old trapper announced. And without further ceremony, he tucked his fiddle under his arm and hopped off into the darkness like a one-legged bird. We could hear him talking to Hawk Eye as if she were a human being, after the manner of men who live much alone with their animals: "Git yore ole fleece along thar, do ee hyar now? Night's on us, ole hoss, an' it's time fer settlement folks like us to be in our own diggin's."

My father and I sat there for some time in silence, listening to the night sounds. Down in the lower lands along the river, camp fires of the caravans stabbed the darkness. Perhaps we each knew what the other was thinking, and I rose abruptly and entered the cabin and made a great commotion of starting the fire. Then I helped him indoors, got him into his chair by the fire, and hung Old Chief Thrower on the pegs above the mantel. Archimedes moved out of the corner and arched his back against my father's knee. I lighted the square buffalo-tallow candles, and shadows leaped to life about the room.

"What book tonight, Pop?"

"King Lear, Son."

It was his favorite. I reached up on the shelf for the weighty, dog-eared volume of *Shakespeare's Complete Works* and placed it on his knees. From long habit his fingers turned to the proper page.

As a boy, my father had longed to become a scholar, to feel at ease in foreign tongues, to probe the romance that was history, to nourish his mind with the wisdom of wise books. Working all day with the ax or the plow, helping to clear a foothold in the wilderness, yet at night had he stolen hours for reading so that by the time he was sixteen he had mastered enough book learning to teach the district school. But the schoolmaster's desk was not for him. Books at best seemed but substitutes for living, and the blood in his veins coursed too swiftly for him to savor second-hand experience. Besides, he was a Starbuck, and the urge to look upon new horizons gave him no rest. So it was that when my mother died, and he loaded a few possessions into a farm wagon, he stuck books into every chink and crevice, books over which I was later to pore through many a long night. You'd have said that a man who had been a school-teacher would have taught his son to read. He didn't. He taught me to shoot straight and to tell the truth. I taught myself to read: a jumble of things — history, mathematics, philosophy — all manner of subjects mixed up and befuddled in my youthful mind.

The only playmate of my own age that I had ever had was Timothy Cooper. The Coopers had come to Independence the year after my father and me, and had settled not far from us. But the following spring found them joining up with a wagon train for Santa Fe. They were never heard from again. Rumors reached us that the whole train had been wiped out by the Comanches, but we never knew the truth. It was lonely after Tim went west, and there were only horses and dogs for playmates. But when I was thirteen, my father apprenticed me to Sabino Roybal for a period of three years. There was no time then to be lonely, for the domineering Mexican saw to it that my nose was kept to the grindstone.

Tonight I seemed possessed of a vague restlessness that would not let me settle to anything. I searched the bookshelf for some volume that might match my mood, or take me out of it. How strange a collection those books would have seemed to anyone stumbling upon that cabin in the clearing! Defoe was there, and Addison and Steele, and Tobias Smollett; *Gulliver's Travels*, and that altogether crazy masterpiece, *Tristram Shandy*. Strong meat for small fry, but by the time I was fourteen, there were few of them into whose pages I hadn't dipped.

I took down the *Odyssey* and tried to lose myself in its colorful pages. But pictures vastly more exciting than the mythical wanderings of Ulysses came between the printed page and my eyes — stampeding buffalo, tens of thousands strong, rolling in wild thunder across the plains; the high whoop of the Pawnee attack; the wagons corralled; the shrill scream of a horse mortally wounded.... I kept seeing Pierre Leroux with his mocking eyes, his knowledge of the wide world and his Mountain Man air; his black stallion with the silver-mounted trappings. And the man's voice still ringing in my ears: "Get out of this trumpery town! Hit the Trail! Once you jump off the west bank of the Missouri, you're in country fresh-hewn from the hand of God."

I flung down the book, rose to my feet, and closed the door to shut out the night air — or the vision. Then I grabbed up a pair of moccasins that I had been working over of nights and threw myself into the job. I *would* shut my mind to those pictures of the Trail! My fingers tensed about the buckhorn handle of the worn awl.

I stole a glance at my father as I worked. How straight and still he sat. His eyes were lifted from the printed page, looking into the fire, seeing images perhaps whose like haunted me. Easy enough for Pierre Leroux to say, "Hit the Trail," but what would have become of this crippled giant of a man? Roybal paid me three dollars a week, and I picked up a bit extra with my moccasins. No vast sum, but one ample for our small needs. In that moment I seemed to see my father with new eyes — a gaunt giant, grown old before his time, an untidy wreck of a man, existing in this rude shack littered with ragged books and stray cats and a general clutter of whatnot. Yet as he sat there staring into the fire, holding his book

with the fine hands that not even the roughest work had mis-
shaped, there hovered about him something of the eager aspira-
tions of youth. And I wanted to cry out against the monstrous
injustice that had brought such a man, like some splendid eagle,
to earth. I knew that his longing to leave this frontier was as great
as my own; that his spirit thirsted for the rivers of the great plains,
for the sight of the shining Rockies locked within the silence of
ten thousand years. But while he stayed, then I must stay, too.

"Son!"

His voice broke my thought. There was insistence in the way
he spoke, and I looked up in surprise.

"What is it, Pop?"

"Come here, Son — over here where I can look at you."

I stood before him looking down. He sat straighter till his eyes
were not so much below the level of my own as he looked me
over.

"The runt of the litter," he said, with his old smile, just as he
had said it for years, with all the pride of his six-feet-four. And I
laughed, happy in the rediscovered communion with this man
whose retreat within himself had come to make him seem almost
a stranger.

"Son," he said again, and he might have been thinking aloud,
"because I sit here day after day, maybe you think I've grown out
of touch with what's happening. Well — I haven't. I know that the
West is out there, still waiting to be conquered! I'll never see it
now. But you will. That thought warms me. You want to go, don't
you?"

"No, Pop, I—"

He smiled and his fingers tightened on my arms, and the firelight glistened on his white mane. "You wouldn't be a Starbuck if
you didn't. You'll be going one of these fine days. Before — long."

"But, Pop, I tell you—"

"It'll change, Johnny. You'll see the buffalo grass plowed under
and wheat growing. Men and their families, more and more of 'em
every day, heading for the West, just as I saw 'em come into
Kentucky when I was a lad. You'll see — some fine day all the land

west of the Missouri will be one land: one nation reaching from sea to sea!"

His eyes were alight with all man's living memory of morning, youth, and high adventure. With a gesture he swept away the sovereignty of the Spanish from the Rio Grande to the Pacific, the occupation of the British in Oregon, the impregnability of a continent teeming with savage tribes and wild beasts.

"You'll see!" he reiterated. "You'll look back and, remember that your pop spoke the truth. Men like Lanky Lewis and Joe Meeker are the earth's salt. They have a part to play, too: they'll be the guides for the men who build. But guides they'll remain till they die. I want more than that for you!"

He reached upward and gripped me by both shoulders, half rising in his chair. And as long as I live, I'll remember the awful solemnity of his words. They were a charge, and an obligation.

"Ride your pony West with the Mountain Men," his voice rushed on. "Trap your beaver and run your buffalo. But that's only part of it! I want you to grow with this great country through all its changes. Learn to know it like the back of your hand, so that when they need men to point the way, you'll be ready. But *grow* with it!" His voice dropped and for a second he seemed to sag. Then he straightened and said, "Hand me Old Chief Thrower."

In a daze I walked over to the mantel and reached to lift the precious rifle from its pegs. I placed it in my father's hands. He looked at it for a moment, his fine fingers caressing the stock.

"Old Chief Thrower," he muttered. Then he looked up, his eyes ablaze. "Dan'l Boone made this rifle with his own two hands. He gave it to my father. My father gave it to me, just before he died. Now I'm giving it to you. Take Old Chief Thrower! He doesn't belong here any more than you do. And — and take good care of him."

He thrust the rifle into my cold hands.

"Take him!" he cried again, and the tone was a command.

I couldn't speak. Reverently I moved my hands over the smooth stock — this rifle that I had always known, had seen my father work over, cherish. . . . I lifted it to my shoulder, ran my eye

along the gleaming barrel. My father watched me, his eyes shining.

"You mean — it's mine?" I stammered.

He nodded.

Suddenly the cabin was too small to hold me. The walls of it closed in upon me and I had to remember that at fifteen you're too old to cry. I stumbled across the room, flung open the door, and stepped out into the darkness. The night pressed down upon me like a hand. Overhead, the Milky Way threw its dusty arch across the heavens: Indian sky-dust stirred up by the passage of some starry herd. Whitefoot trotted up, nickering softly, and sank her velvety muzzle against my shoulder.

Down in the valley, fires blazed upward: camp fires of the westward caravans. Like beacons, warning.... Beckoning....

CHAPTER IV

"THE GRASS IS UP!"

THE GRASS is up! The grass is up!
The cry swept its magic through the town and over the encampments like a prairie fire, wind driven. Men shouted it, sang it, yes — even whispered it with awe. Boys whistled it, dogs barked it; women called it from neighbor to neighbor. It was the bugle cry sounding the beginning of their great adventure. "The grass is up!" Now there was fodder for the stock on the westward journey across prairie and plain; sustenance for horse and ox and mule. It was the cry that set the shifting population of Independence half wild with excitement.

During the night large parties of the Oregon emigrants had pulled out. There were a hundred wagons now, rumbling through the town. These were the homemakers, going West with all their household possessions; taking with them plow and church and school. Builders of empire.

I sat on Whitefoot by the corner of Courthouse Square, watching the teams pull their wagons down the muddy street; oxen plodding, patient, stolid; mules, yet to be broken, protesting against yoke and harness. The ox and the Missouri mule — mud, river, quicksand, desert, and burning sun, all would be alike to them. The history of America would have been different but for these creatures. Men were riding their ponies beside the wagons, half delirious with joy, shouting, calling to one another and to the bystanders; some firing rifle shots into the air in excess of high spirit. There were others more serious, silent, with some sense of the significance of this undertaking, its hazards and its doubtful rewards. Dogs leaped about and barked. Chickens clucked in swaying crates. Babies squalled.

These people... I looked after them with envy in my heart and a dry feeling in my throat. Young faces, old faces, middle-aged, and babes — each stamped with some imprint of this great undertaking. They were not John Smith and Tom Green and Timothy Brown — they were America marching. Men with a continent to conquer; children with a continent for a playground. The bloodstream of America flowing westward. Perhaps some of them were beset by doubts, by terrors of the unknown perils whispered about the Trail ahead; women who clutched their babes closer to their breasts, and men, new to all this, whose knuckles tightened on the stocks of their rifles. But they were swinging true to their heritage, as the needle of a compass swings true to north. Had this not been so, these people would still be plowing their Illinois fields or trying to wring a living from Connecticut's rocky hills.

I looked for Pierre Leroux, and knew a feeling of relief when I couldn't find him. The Santa Fe wagons, I guessed, had not yet pulled out. They would be the traders; men I who would be coming back, if they were lucky, rich with specie and silver. Their families could wait at home for them; no women in their caravans, except perhaps the wife of some rich trader.

"Good-by! Good-by!" I shouted.

Even Whitefoot trembled with the excitement of it. The last wagon rumbled out of sight around Courthouse Square, and then I turned away, struggling to shake off the weight that lay upon me. Sabino Roybal and his saddle shop — I'd be late if I didn't hurry. I urged Whitefoot into a canter down the muddy street. Before a one-story frame building I hitched her to the rack. Sabino Roybal's. I cast one backward glance over my shoulder — I could still hear the shouts of the drivers; the crack of the bull whips. Then squaring my shoulders, I entered the shop.

"So! The fine gentleman is late again!"

Sabino Roybal's voice flicked me like a lash. It was the tone that never failed to stir hair on the back of my neck and set my blood

a-boil. I looked up at the clock. Two minutes after six — yes, I was late by two minutes.

The Mexican turned to the man standing beside him and laughed with heavy sarcasm. "This young saddle maker," he sneered, "should, perhaps, have been a banker, *no es verdad?* Such a profession would have been more congenial to one of his leisurely habits."

The two men laughed together at this sally, and anger seethed in me like tar bubbling in a cauldron. I slumped sullenly on the stool in front of the workbench, hot about the ears; and my hands, as I picked up the bone handled awl, were cold as ice. I could have strangled Sabino Roybal with pleasure and with small loss to the community. The Mexican never lost an opportunity to humiliate me, and preferably before an audience. Not often did a greaser have a chance to lord it over a gringo. Roybal relished the opportunity to the full.

For two years I had been working in his shop — two years of petty insults and tyrannies. I still writhed inwardly at his gibes, and the year of my apprenticeship still to be served seemed long indeed.

The room was low-ceilinged and the floor was the earth itself — a long, dark room except for the area at the front, lighted by two windows which gave upon the street. Here my workbench was placed, and here I plied my awl, my cutting knife, and my hammer. I picked up a strip of buffalo hide and set to work — saw that my Green River knife must be sharpened on the stone. But perhaps for the benefit of those who don't know what a Green River knife is, I had better explain: it has a broad seven-inch blade, single-edged, and is the Mountain Man's inseparable companion. It serves him for skinning, scalping, whittling and eating — weapon and implement rolled into one. High on the blade is stamped the sign mark G. R. — George Rex, bespeaking its English origin. But to the Mountain Man, "G. R." meant Green River — that summer rendezvous dear to all trappers' hearts. The term had entered the Mountain Man's vocabulary, and when, in the heat of battle, the cry could be heard, "Give 'em Green River, boys!" it meant a war to the bloody hilt.

The workbench was piled high with the work of the day — sweat leathers to be cut, saddle strings and *apishamores* (saddle blankets of buffalo calfskin). There was a sheath for a skinning knife to be fashioned from sole leather — enough work, in truth, to keep me bent over the bench for the next twelve hours to come. But as my hands flew with the awl, my ears caught bits of the conversation which Sabino Roybal was carrying on with his visitor. They were talking about guns. Nothing unusual in that. Guns were as familiar a topic in Independence as was horseflesh. But they were talking about a job lot of five thousand guns. That *was* unusual.

The two men had dropped their voices till only isolated words of their conversation struck my ear. One of the words was *Armijo*. Armijo, I knew, was the Governor of New Mexico. Another word was "war." Of course war with Mexico was upon most men's lips these days. But men didn't whisper about it.

I glanced up to steal a look at Roybal's companion. I saw a tall man, heavy-set, with a hard, reckless face and ice-blue eyes set close together. He was leaning indolently against the wall with arms crossed, and instead of the crude buckskin of the trapper or the coarse linsey of the ordinary citizen, he was dressed in black broadcloth, with a broad-brimmed hat of fine beaver. His right hand held a Mexican cigar, and I saw that the third and fourth fingers of that hand were missing. Then I knew him. Black Jack Bannock, owner of the Diamond Spring Saloon; the man who was outfitting a caravan to trade with the New Mexicans; the man who was employing Pierre Leroux to guide his caravan across the *Jornada del Muerto*.

Sabino Roybal, turning suddenly, saw me glancing up from my work and grated: "*Dios!* Will you please to keep your gringo nose out of the affairs of others?"

So malevolent was his look, that I felt an involuntary shudder. Then he led Black Jack into the back room and I could hear only the low hum of their voices through the closed door. That they were up to no good was a certainty. Roybal was a scoundrel whom no man in his right mind would have trusted. And Black Jack had ruined many an unsuspecting trapper. But — it was none of my affair.

Through the window as I worked, I was conscious of the life swarming and bustling by outside: Indians jogging past on their painted ponies; the smart Concord coaches of the claret-coated dandies in silk hats — merchants, these, and bankers, far removed from the sweating roustabouts and mule skinners who swaggered down the streets of the town.

A pair of horses pulled up with a flourish at the door of the shop and two stalwart figures swung to the ground. I saw Joe Meeker and his spotted Indian pony; and, with quickening interest, the black stallion with silver-mounted harness of Pierre Leroux.... The men entered the shop with the flourish of a minor tornado, their moccasined feet stamping on the hard earth floor, the long fringes of their buckskins dangling with every movement.

"How, there, young lad," Pierre grinned, and flung an *apishamore* down on the workbench before me. "Let's see a sample of your skill! See — here where she's ripped. Reinforce it with braided buckskin...." His lean fingers seized upon a piece of leather to show me what he wanted done.

Joe Meeker unbuckled a worn leather sheath from his belt and laid it down. "Make me a new case to fit this knife, young 'un," he barked, "an' see that you git the notch cut right so's the knife'll slip out easy-like. Ever see a knife like thet before, Leroux?" he demanded, holding up for inspection a skinning knife whose blade was no less than ten inches. It was of beautifully tempered steel, needle-pointed and honed to razor-sharpness. Leroux accorded it the expected admiration. Then Meeker turned back to me. "I'll leave this knife here fer ye to cut yer leather by, young 'un; an' see that nothin' happens to it, or I'll take it out o' yer hide. Thet knife," he continued, "has saved my Life more'n oncet. Last time was out to Pawnee Rock — thet time when the Comanches cut off the Cooper's wagon from the rest o' the train and butchered Cooper and his wife an' made off with the kid."

Pierre whistled through his teeth. "I didn't know you were in that brush, Joe," he exclaimed.

"Was so!" came the emphatic answer. "Say, young 'un, whar's Roybal?"

"In the back room," I answered. "But, about the Coopers — I knew Tim Cooper!"

Meeker interrupted me with a brusque gesture, pointing to Sabino Roybal's bull whip, hanging by its wooden pegs on the farther wall.

"Wagh!" he exclaimed. "An ole he-whip, thet one, an' no mistake. I've heerd tell thet Roybal's right smart with it, too. Took a man's head half off his shoulders with it once, down to the Pecos. Would ha' been all right if the man hadn't been a friend o' Armijo's! Thet's the reason Roybal's here in Independence, they do say. New Mexico got too hot even fer him."

I'd never heard this version of Roybal's presence in our midst, but I did know that the Mexican was said to possess devilish skill with the bull whip. An evil-looking affair it was, with its stock as thick as a man's wrist, and its twenty- foot lash of braided rawhide, tipped with glistening nailhead.

"'That kind of weapon would appeal to a man of Roybal's stripe," observed Leroux. "Knives or pistols would be too clean for him."

The door of the back room creaked and swung on its hinges. The three of us turned about. Sabino Roybal emerged, followed by Black Jack Bannock. "Speak of the Devil," Pierre murmured under his breath. Joe Meeker's eyes went stony and his mouth snapped shut like the sides of a wolf trap.

"Ah — *señores!*" The Mexican moved forward, spreading his hands with unction. "What can I do for you gentlemen?"

Meeker vouchsafed no answer and turned his back abruptly. Leroux explained with a gesture, pointing to the *apishamore* and to the skinning knife which must have a new sheath.

Roybal swung toward me, his eyes snapping. "See that you do it properly," he warned. "A poor workman, this boy," he went on to apologize to his customers. "But " een Independence all good men go West. Eet is only the worthless who—" He made a futile gesture with his fat hands, and I controlled an impulse to smash him in the face.

Pierre grinned at my discomfiture, but it was a grin which said, "Buck up, lad! Don't let this greaser get under your skin."

Roybal introduced his companion with a Latin flourish, almost bending double with the effort. "Do you two *señores* know *Señor* Bannock?"

Meeker grunted shortly while Leroux laughed outright. "I have that pleasure," he acknowledged. "I am in the *Señor's* employ."

Roybal drew in his breath with a hiss of amazement. "I do not understand, *Señor* Leroux," he said slowly, eyes narrowing with suspicion.

"Then perhaps Bannock will enlighten you," the Mountain Man responded easily, moving toward the door. "I'll pick up that *apishamore* this afternoon, before we break camp, Starbuck," he called across the room to me.

"You're rolling out today?" The words were out before I could stop them, and I was conscious of Roybal's ill-suppressed exclamation of anger.

So they were breaking camp. I had known, of course, that any day now they'd be on their way, but I felt my heart sink as the door banged upon the two buckskin-clad figures.

Roybal turned upon Black Jack with an explosive shout. "What does he talk about, that Leroux?" he demanded hotly. "How does he mean — he is in your employ?"

Bannock looked down from his height with surprise dilating his cold eyes. "It means," he came back querulously, "that if I'm to cross the *Jornada* on the Dry Route, I've got to have a guide. I'm no plainsman, Roybal. Leroux's said to be the best in the country."

"I could have found you a guide," the Mexican snapped angrily. "What for you did not tell me?"

"Say, listen here, Sabino," the other cried with rising voice, "I'm running my end of this show — savvy? They told me Leroux's the best man to be had. Knows the Cimarron route like the back of his hand."

"*They* told you!" the Mexican snapped. "Who have told you?"

He seemed to have forgotten my presence; caution cast to the winds of his anger.

"I've heard it everywhere since I've been in Independence. Say — what's the matter with Leroux, anyhow?"

"The matter with him?" the Mexican mocked sarcastically. "Nothing, *amigo*, except that he has just returned from Washington, and it is said——" He halted abruptly, conscious of my presence once more, and threw a baleful look at me. "Get on with your work!" he shouted, making as if to strike a blow. Then he gripped Black Jack by the arm and drew him toward the back room.

The door slammed behind them with a vicious bang, and I heard their voices rise from time to time as anger got the better of the two men. They were speaking Spanish now, but I had picked up a good bit of that language in Independence and so I was able to understand the few words which detached themselves from the hum and struck my ear. Roybal's voice saying... "*El Presidente* Polk..." Then a short laugh from Black Jack Bannock as he answered, "What I want's a guide, savvy? Once in sight of Santa Fe——" The pause was significant, and I determined that when Pierre Leroux returned, I would warn him of what I had overheard.

The two men in the back room were up to some dirty work; no

doubt about that. Something concerning the war with Mexico and Armijo. What part Black Jack Bannock could be playing, I had no idea. Nor did I see that it was in Sabino Roybal's power to do damage to anyone in Independence. Months later I was to marvel at my own stupidity. But that was to be long hence, when all the facts were clear.

Bannock strode out of the back room at last, black coat tails swinging angrily. I saw him unhitch his horse and climb into his smart dearborn — heard the whip crack over his animal's ears. I looked out through the window after the disappearing vehicle, puzzled, wondering. . . .

Then I felt a sudden chill of apprehension; some nameless force compelling me to turn around; a sinister presence there in that room with me. No sound broke the silence. I held my eyes upon my work by pure force of will, although the hair prickled on my neck and gooseflesh raised the surface of my skin. Sabino Roybal. . . . I *would* not turn!

The silence was broken now by the quick, low rhythm of a man's breathing. Sweat broke out on my forehead. Suddenly I could stand it no longer. I swung about on the bench, taut as a string about to snap.

Roybal was standing against the wall, just under the bullwhip. A strange glitter in his eyes; fat fingers closing and opening spasmodically. He spoke — almost a whisper. It chilled me to the marrow.

"So . . . spying . . . sneaking!"

"I was not!" I answered hotly, flinging down Joe Meeker's knife. I was filled with a sort of cold fury for this monster now. My hands were trembling.

"So! Answer me with your impertinence, will you?" The man's voice rose on a note of anger. He took a step toward me. "But what could one expect from the son of a half-cracked—"

He got no further. I leaped to my feet, quivering in every nerve. "By God!" I cried, fighting for control, "you'll not talk about my father! You're not fit to feed his pigs!"

"*Dios!*" the Mexican shouted, going yellow. "Miserable gringo — I'll teach you!" He half turned and reached upward for his bull whip. One hand closed upon the stock. I watched, my eyes upon that hand, fascinated, unable to move. That hand... it seemed not a thing of flesh and blood. It seemed... I fell back against the workbench. My fingers closed about the handle of a knife – Joe Meeker's. The whip was in Roybal's hands. One blow from that nail-tipped lash and I'd be blinded, killed.... Then, without conscious volition, I did it. The knife flashed an arc through the air... A dull thud... A scream of pain.

The knife pinned Sabino Roybal's hand, hilt-deep, to the wall.

Then I laughed aloud with new-found confidence. I reached for my own knife, not so long or fierce as Joe's, but terrible enough. I held it tantalizingly as the Mexican, stammering with rage and pain, strove to pull the embedded blade from his hand.

"This is a good knife, too, *señor,*" I suggested, "and your neck would make a fat target."

The man's face drained. "Stop!" he screamed, fright leaping in his eyes and sagging his body. "Get out of here! Never show your pale face here again!"

"It will be a pleasure," I promised, and stooped to gather up my tools.

The man had succeeded in pulling free the knife. Blood flowed copiously from his hand and he strove to staunch its flow.

"That knife, *señor,* belongs to Joe Meeker," I grinned. "Drop it on the floor and stand back!"

For a second he hesitated. I still held my own blade ready for action and the flash of it caught the Mexican's eye. "I'm a good shot, *señor,*" I suggested shortly.

With a curse, Roybal dropped the knife and moved back several paces. "Take it!" he ground out, "and get out of here!"

Once outside the door, I unhitched Whitefoot and swung up into the saddle filled with high elation. I couldn't breathe deeply enough of the pure air of freedom. Free! After two years of tyranny. *Free!*

But as I rode out of the town and approached the cabin in the clearing, I sobered somewhat. Free – yes. But where were the few dollars to come from that would assure food for my father and

A strange glitter shone in Roybal's eyes.

me? The thought didn't weigh upon me for long, for I was confident of being able to find something else to do.

Crossing the ridge that overlooked the banks of the river, I glanced back at the wagon camps, many of them standing empty now. With reluctance I drew near the cabin. Somehow I hated to tell my father what had taken place in the saddle shop. Knowing his deep feeling about a word given in bond, he might feel that I had been unduly hasty. I swung slowly out of saddle and turned Whitefoot loose. Then I climbed the steps and opened the door. Archimedes, with plaintive purr, rubbed against me. My father was sitting in his chair by the window, a book spread open on his lap. He stared at me, a question in his eyes. "Pop," I said in a low voice, hesitant. "I'm through at Roybal's. He's fired me. I'm — not to go back."

He made no answer.

"Pop," I said again. Then stopped. "*Pop!*"

My father was dead.

CHAPTER V

WEST WITH THE SUN

WAAL, here's whar I'll be leavin' ye, lad." Lanky Lewis tried to speak casually but the effort turned his voice gruff and he cleared his throat with a rasp.

We were riding down the muddy path along the ridge of high bluffs that bordered the Missouri. Lanky was forking my roan, Whitefoot, and I was riding Hawk Eye. There was a buffalo robe rolled up behind me, a small coffeepot swinging from my cantle, and the barrel of Old Chief Thrower shining across the saddle horn. I wore a suit of new buckskins, soft as a glove, fringed along the seams in trapper fashion, and a coonskin cap with dangling tail. Oh, I was all slicked up, you can believe, inordinately proud of my Mountain Man finery; yet humble about it withal. Scared of it, perhaps; for it stood for much.

"You ain't got a right to that thar outfit, young 'un," Lanky said, after I had traded for it at Owen & Aull's store. "An' it's up to you to earn the right. Mebby so you'll be a real live Mountain Man some day, eff that's the way yer stick floats. Anyways – the plains'll bring it out eff it's in ye. An' eff it ain't——"

I knew that he was right. It *was* up to me to prove my right to it. And to Old Chief Thrower, too. We reined in where a path turned sharply to the left. For a moment neither of us spoke.

"Take good keer of old Hawk Eye an' she'll take keer of you," Lanky said shortly and reached over to give the animal a swat on her flank. There was more to the gruff act than met the eye. The old trapper was parting from his horse — the horse that had run buffalo with him and shared his dangers on the plains.

"But, Lanky," I protested, once again, "I don't want to take Hawk Eye. Whitefoot'll do for me."

"Snap yer trap!" the old man barked. "Ye don't think thet Kaintucky hoss of yourn would ever git ye 'cross the plains, do ye? She'd fall into the fust prairie-dog hole she come to, and bust her cussed neck and yourn, too."

"She's a grand animal!" I came back at him in warm defense, for Whitefoot had carried me for four years, and my affection for her went deep.

"She'll do all right," he admitted, "fer white man's kentry. But ole Hawk Eye's a buffler hoss, don't fergit that. Mebby so she's gittin' along some in years, but thar's plenty o' spark to her yit. She was reared on the plains an' she kin smell Injun like a beaver kin smell bait; better'n a dozen watchdogs. An' she knows you, else don't think I'd be givin' her to you; an' don't think she'd let anybody else fork her, nuther. She's an ornery piece when she's a-mind to it. But when yo're up on her, you knows yo're up on a hoss."

I leaned forward and rubbed the Indian pony's neck. "I'll take good care of her, Lanky," I promised. "And — and you take care of Whitefoot — till I come back."

Hawk Eye arched her neck against the bit and blew impatiently through her nostrils, one forefoot pawing at the muddy trail. She was headed West and she knew it. I could feel the tenseness of her, the eager quiver of her muscles awaiting the touch of my heel and the lift of my bridle hand.

I looked at Lanky as he sat there, grim and tense, giving me my last instructions; and I remembered suddenly all the years I'd known him; the Pawnee bow he'd made for me, and the patience with which he had taught me to shoot it. And I remembered above all what he'd done these last three days since my father died. I'd carry West with me the picture of the old trapper as he had stood propped on his one leg, beside my father's open grave, watching the rude box that he had helped to build lowered beneath the ground. There were tears, unashamed and manly, running down the grooves in his old face as the sky pilot intoned: "'In my Father's house are many mansions... If it were not so, I would have told you...'"

And Lanky it was who had said, almost as he turned away from the grave, "Yer Pop gave ye Old Chief Thrower to take West. I'm givin' ye Hawk Eye."

That was all. He was giving his best. And young though I was, I knew that I would range the world across and not know another man so fine. Harsh and austere as the plains that bred him, but straight as a Comanche arrow and as true as steel.

"You'd orter make Blue Camp, come noon," he was saying. "That'd be twenty mile, as I recollect. Then ye should push on to Black Jack Point come night. But take it easy, lad. Ye got a long ride ahead o' ye to Santy Fee, an' a hoss is only flesh and blood. Black Jack Point's about four mile beyond the Oregon Trail junction. An' come mornin', ye'd orter catch up with Leroux's Santy Fee outfit. They couldn't have got much farther than The Narrows — not with the weight they was pullin'."

"I wish you were coming too, Lanky," I burst out in spite of myself.

He looked down at the stump of his left leg, silent for a moment. "Thar's no place for an ole coot like me out thar," he returned grimly. "But I've had it, lad! A hull lifetime of it. An' now it's yore turn. Better git goin'," he finished gruffly. "Good luck to ye, young 'un. An' remember — thar's only one law on the plains, an' that is every man's a law unto himself. Don't never take no orders from no man. An' when ye reach the Injun kentry, bear in mind thet ye got a thick head o' ha'r, an' don't be gittin' keerless with it."

I wrung his hand, unable to speak one word. And then I swung

Hawk Eye's head toward the West and prodded her ribs. She sprang ahead, alert and eager. Before the woods closed in on us, I looked back — there was old Lanky at the trail's fork, a lonely figure, gaunt and bent. He straightened and made a salute with one long arm. I waved in answer, then turned my head with forward resolution and urged Hawk Eye into a canter. Somewhere beyond the curve of the earth waited all the things that I'd dreamed of — buffalo, Indians, strange peoples in a strange land; the Spanish settlements of the Rio Grande. . . . But my heart was heavy with a sudden sense of loss.

It was impossible, however, to be long depressed in this world through which I was moving. As the muddy banks of the Missouri fell behind and I turned into the sun-dappled shadow of a deep woods, I felt my spirits surge upward. Woodpeckers were rattling their long tattoo against the tree trunks, like a roll of drums triumphant, and in the deeper shadows orioles flamed and darted like banners of a marching army. Black squirrels chirked and scolded at me as I rode down upon their stronghold, and a sudden hum in the air bespoke a flight of pigeons winging upward in their escape. There came a crash in the underbrush as a startled deer bounded away, flaunting his white tail and whistling in alarm.

"Hawk Eye," said I, "we're headed for your old stamping grounds, you and I. Don't play out on me, old hoss! Get into your stride and we'll quit for noon when the sun's at its zenith."

The Comanche pony gave a long-drawn sigh, as if she understood every word that I uttered, and she broke into a fox trot, her nose keen-pointed toward the West. Straight as a drawn line she headed toward the distant horizon. Mile after mile . . . the fox trot shifting imperceptibly into a pace — the pace that was known as the "trapper's rack", easy and rapid, eating up the miles.

The Santa Fe caravan of Black Jack Bannock had started three days ahead of me. Naturally I could travel faster than the heavily loaded wagons, and I expected to overtake them at The Narrows, a ridge separating the Kansas and Osage waters, some sixty-five miles distant. I figured that I should meet up with them by the next noon, with good luck and not losing my way. What sort of reception I would have from Black Jack himself I could not hazard. Perhaps he'd refuse to let me join the train, since I had no money to pay for my keep. Also, being a friend of Sabino Roybal's, he had doubtless heard the story of my fight with that gentleman. But I would work for my coffee and beans. I had my own pony and my rifle; and one more rifle was not to be sneezed at in country where every Indian tribe was known to be upon the warpath. And when I should reach Santa Fe — well, that could take care of itself when the time came. It was enough now to be heading West, riding out to meet whatever lay beyond the wide-curving earth. Besides, I felt that even if I proved unable to persuade Black Jack to take me on with his outfit, Pierre Leroux would put in a word for me. Hadn't the man urged me to get out of Independence? "I'll show you how to trap the beaver and how to run the buffalo," he had promised. And he had meant it.

I relaxed in the saddle — gave myself up to the swift movement of the Indian pony. Now we were entering the country of the half-civilized Shawnoes: Indian farmers who lived in log houses and cultivated the land. Indians hitched to a plow: the civilizing touch of the white man! Some day, thought I aloud, they'll be hitching the buffalo to a plow, but I hope I'll not live to see it. The Shawanoe farms straggled over the fertile countryside, fenced in with rail to keep the wandering cattle out of the young corn. I saw tender shoots thrusting up in the oozy soil; young corn growing green; wild apple blossoms; the branches of the swamp-maple bright with clusters of red flowers; blackbirds flying above the fences. Under the brown last year's grass, new grass was struggling upward, spattered with a myriad wildflowers. I heard the song of the lark spiraling in upward flight, while hawks soared and wheeled high in the immaculate sky.

Then suddenly, topping a rise, I beheld the prairie — grass growing high as Hawk Eye's belly, silver-rippling in the wind. As far as the eye could reach, those undulating swells stretched away and away; a limitless ocean too wide for man's small eye to measure. A land that rose and dipped, its monotony relieved by trees clus-

tered like oases about some spring, or following the course of a stream through some fertile hollow. And always green — an endless circle of which we were the moving center. Hawk Eye, having fallen into her natural pace, held it, mile after mile, while I relaxed in the saddle and shouted the "Arkansas Traveller" for sheer joy in being alive and being here with my horse and my rifle. We splashed through streams and clambered up steep banks — topping the next green rise, then on to the next and the next; into the country of the Sacs, the Kansas, and the Osages; friendly savages these. Nothing to be feared from them. But today this land was empty of all human life. Only Hawk Eye and I, and the sky arching blue overhead, and larks springing upward from my pony's hoofs.

The beds of the streams were deeply indented into the soil and their banks almost vertical, but all of them could be forded without difficulty. The country of thickets and forests lay far behind us now, and the only trees to be seen were along the margins of the streams, mighty hedges for mighty fields; hedges of oak and walnut; of buckeye and sycamore; American elm and pignut hickory. Farther on, I knew, all these would disappear, to give way to the cottonwood. Then, in the Great Desert, the cottonwood would vanish as well, and no shade would be offered to the parched traveler and his horse.

We passed Blue Camp, a favorite nooning spot for the caravans, and saw signs of their recent passage. But so fresh was Hawk Eye that I decided to push on to Lone Elm Tree before nooning-it.

Hawk Eye lifted her head suddenly, sniffed, and thrust her ears forward. In the distance I made out a dark speck, unaccountable in that limitless land of green, and I knew a quickening of pulse. "She kin smell an Injun like a beaver kin smell bait," old Lanky had claimed for his Comanche pony. Indians? Nonsense — or if they were, only friendly ones. Hawk Eye paced ahead, her gait undiminished. Soon the dark speck had resolved itself into the outlines of a wagon drawn by two plodding oxen. They were coming toward me. A figure seemed to be trudging beside the wagon.

Close range proved that the man was an Indian, probably an Osage.

"How, friend," I hailed him, reining in my pony alongside him.

"How," came his noncommittal answer. His black eyes, restless and vital, took in my horse, my rifle, myself.

"Where you from?" I asked.

"The Narrows," came his answer. He pointed to his wagon full of empty water casks. "Me go out with Santa Fe wagons with water. Come back now."

"The Santa Fe caravan!" I exclaimed excitedly. "Then they *are* at The Narrows?"

He nodded. "Cattle, she stampede by wolves," he volunteered. "Roundup, she tak' much time. Where you go, boy?"

"I'm joining up with Bannock's outfit," I answered, not without pride. "You savvy Black Jack Bannock?"

"Me savvy. No good kind!" The Indian moved close up to Hawk Eye and his black eyes bored into my own. "You got whisky?" he demanded arrogantly, with a hint of threat in his tones.

I shifted Old Chief Thrower across the pommel. "No got," I answered shortly.

The man's eye rested on the barrel of the rifle and his voice changed to a whine. "Big man, me," he begged. "Love American heap. Love whisky heap. White man good. Whisky good. No give Black Warrior whisky? Make Black Warrior strong. Fight him bad Indian no love white man. Kill him!"

"Sorry. Only got tobacco." I proffered a plug which the man fell upon greedily. "How far's the next water hole beyond Lone Elm Tree?" I demanded.

He rolled the tobacco over in his cheek with relish before answering. "Black Jack Point. You stay there tonight. No can make The Narrows before sun."

We parted company the best of friends, I elated at the news that Bannock's outfit was no farther along on its journey. Now I would surely catch up with it by tomorrow's noon. Old Lanky had figured well.

The sun was all but directly overhead when at last I raised Lone Elm Tree. The heat was dry and I was thirsty, and I knew that my horse must be needing water soon, too. A beautiful spot was Lone Elm Tree as we rode down upon it — a single tall tree offering grateful shade, with a stream running clear over a gravelly base and

deep enough to invite me to a swim. While Hawk Eye sank her muzzle into the water and relished its coolness in long-sustaining draughts, I pulled off my buckskins and dove into the stream. As I walked back to my outfit, I kept a wary eye open for rattlers, for all during the morning we had stirred them up in our passage and heard their warning signals about us. But now there was no sign of snake or other unpleasant thing; and while Hawk Eye ate her fill of the fresh grass, I sat on a rock to dry off in the sun, and chewed some of my supply of salt meat. After which, as I made ready to resume my journey, I raised Old Chief Thrower, drew forth the ramrod and worm and oiled its bore for the hundredth time.

Then I swung up into the saddle once more. The Trail was broad and well-defined at this point, the deep ruts of countless wagons having cut their scars ineradicably in the soft soil of the prairie. Some eight miles beyond Lone Elm Tree, I made out a signpost standing upright, ludicrous to see in that broad and spacious land — absurd reminder of a puny civilization that dared to encroach upon this overpowering vastness. As I drew nearer, I observed that a trail forked off to the right of the signpost and crude letters painted on the board spelled the inscription: ROAD TO OREGON. The gaunt ribs of an ox half devoured by wolves lay beside the road, and a turkey buzzard rose from the feast with wide-flapping wings. Already the weak had begun to fall by the way — weeded out by the harsh law of survival. It was the Santa Fe route that I wanted. So straight ahead we went, Hawk Eye and I, toward the sinking sun. Not many miles beyond the Oregon Trail Junction, I should find Black Jack Point, and there I would pass the night.

The far-flung quietude of the closing day lay its spell upon me. The hush that stole over the earth was almost palpable. Waterfowl moved in dark formation across the sky. The ocean of grasses rippled in long parallels to the touch of the dying wind. The whole aspect of the earth changed and grew somber with approaching night.

The forms of dwarfish oaks appeared in the distance, and I knew from Lanky's description that Black Jack Point must lie in their midst. I was glad, for I was weary with all the excitement of the day. Forty-seven miles we had come from Independence and

I, Jonathan Starbuck

I knew that the Comanche pony would be glad of a respite, too, for it was long since she had had such a workout.

I swung to the ground in the midst of a clump of trees, unsaddled, and spread my buffalo robe. Then I gathered some dried grass and twisted it into a nest, ignited it with flint and steel, threw on some oak chips, and soon had a fire blazing. When the sun had disappeared over the earth's curve, it left no afterglow in the coppery sky to tell its passage. Dark closed in suddenly, blacking out everything beyond the small circle of my fire. All at once the night seemed to possess some hostile power that would overwhelm me if it could. I was swept by a terrible sense of aloneness there on the solitary prairie and I busied myself with my small tasks, scarce daring to look about me lest the forces of darkness take some actual shape which I must meet.

Hawk Eye was picketed close at hand and I sat down by the fire waiting for the coffee to boil. I found myself thinking of old Lanky Lewis as I sat there — he'd be feeding Whitefoot by this time, making flapjacks perhaps, and lighting the buffalo-tallow candles in the cabin. And Mother Applegate — she'd be closing the SHOO FLY for the night and mixing the dough for the next day's bread, setting it to rise in the brick oven in the chimney. I had stopped to say good-by to her that morning at daybreak, and found her waiting for me.

"I knew ye'd be headin' West as soon as I heard your father had passed on," she declared. "An' here's something I found for ye to take with ye."

She handed me a book. I glanced at the title and read: INDISPENSABLE ASSISTANT: Being a Treatise on the Home Treatment of All Known Ailments.

I laughed and gave her a mighty hug. She kissed me and pushed me toward the door, smiling, tears on her cheeks.

Now I reached into the saddlebag and extracted the book — turned over its pages and leaned close to examine them by the light of the flickering camp fire. And I couldn't help but laugh as I read the INDISPENSABLE ASSISTANT. Here's a sample of its contents:

Good remedy for fits: Take of tincture of foxglove ten drops at a time, twice a day; and increase one drop as long as the stomach will bear it.

Another, to cure rattlesnake bites:

Chew and swallow alum, the size of a hickory nut; put on thoro-wort leaves and wet them with water. If person is very sick, black, or purple, let him drink a little of the juice, if he can.

While still a third prescription read:

For windy stomach: Chew saffron leaves and swallow the spittle.

It was hard to reconcile a life on the Great Plains with Painter's Colic, or Liver Complaint, or Inward Ulcers, or any of the multifarious ailments prescribed for in this treatise, but my heart warmed anew to Mother Applegate. I remembered all her kindnesses, standing like milestones in the recollection of my lonely childhood. I scarce recalled my own mother, so young was I when she died. But somehow in the years on the Missouri frontier, the generous form of Mother Applegate had merged into the shadowy outlines of the mother I had lost. They must have been alike, these two women.

I threw more chips on the fire and settled back to drink my coffee. Frogs and whippoorwills were tuning up by the stream. Suddenly I heard the long-drawn howl of a wolf; eerie sound, not so far away. A sound that struck the entrails, rather than the ear, and I shivered with the sudden chill in the air and drew closer to the fire.

The edge of the moon was cutting the horizon, throwing its radiance over the wide earth. I thought of Pierre Leroux — vital, challenging, carrying with him the very breath of this country. I thought of my father as he had been that last night in the cabin — the solemnity of his words: "I want you to grow with this country, son, through all its changes."

And as I rolled over in my buffalo robe and sleep claimed my tired body, I knew the smell of this clean earth in my nostrils; heard the wind above it singing in my ears; and saw the stars climbing the tall sky.

CHAPTER VI

PIERRE TAKES A HAND

"THAR'S a likely-lookin' young cub wants to talk to ye, Cap'n Bannock."

Black Jack Bannock straightened up from the wagon tongue and looked around. His close-set eyes raked me with a glance. Not a pleasant look, penetrating and cruel. I had been riding since daybreak and I swung out of saddle and stood beside Hawk Eye.

"Where you from?" he demanded tersely.

"Independence, sir."

"What have you followed me out hyar for?" His eyes were narrow with suspicion.

"I want to join up with your outfit and go to Santa Fe, sir."

"Humph! Got the money to pay fer yer keep?"

"No. But I can work."

The man laughed shortly. "Work, eh?" he jeered. "We've got hands enough to do that, and I don't want any more mouths to feed, less'n they can pay for the privilege." He turned away, dismissing me with abrupt dispatch.

For a moment I could scarce believe my ears. Here was I on the threshold of the great West, having ridden one hundred miles since yesterday to join up with this outfit, only to be told that there was no place for me. I looked desperately around at the circle of men's faces: some looked interested, some amused, some twisted with derision. Hard faces most of them, stamped with every degree of brutality. Then I saw Pierre Leroux. He was leaning against the frame of a Conestoga, arms crossed easily on his chest. His eyes surveyed me with an enigmatic expression that I could not fathom. I had the feeling that he was waiting to see how I would handle this situation; that, in some obscure sense, it was to be a test of my mettle.

I swung about and faced Black Jack once more, compelling his attention with my voice. "Look here, Mister Bannock——"

The man turned on me, his mouth twisting. "*Cap'n* Bannock," he corrected. "Well – what are you standing there for? I thought I told you——"

"You did," I answered stubbornly, looking back at him eye for eye and standing my ground. "It's no charity I'm asking for, Cap'n Bannock. I can do more than herd cattle and make myself useful around camp!"

"That so? What else can you do?" At the scorn in his tone I felt my ears go hot.

I raised Old Chief Thrower and patted the stock with confidence. "I'll stake my shooting against any man's in this-here outfit," I said quietly, controlling my inward excitement as best I might.

A chorus of guffaws greeted this.

"Modest lad, ain't he?"

"Thinks he kin spit even with Mountain Men. Ho! Ho!"

Their jeers stung me to anger and I fought for control.

"Cap'n Bannock," I went on stubbornly, "with the Pawnees raiding the Trail, a good shot isn't to be sneezed at!"

There was truth to that, I knew, and any wagon master would be a fool to pass up a good hand with a rifle for the sake of the few beans and the flour that might be consumed on the route. Black Jack shifted his weight and appraised me for a moment, uncertainly. He was used to men who backed down before his displeasure, and perhaps the fact that I'd talked up to him did the trick.

"All right," he agreed after a second. "Let's see what you can do with that antiquated piece of yours, Dan'l Boone! If yo're the shot you say you are, you'll have to be pretty good. And in that case, my smart lad, mebbe we can talk business?" He turned about and pointed a long arm. "See that cottonwood over yonder?"

The tree was a good seventy-five yards distant.

"Yes, sir."

"See that limb stretching out farther than all the others, on the north side?"

"Yes, sir."

"And see that twig, barren of leaves, out on the very end?"

"I do."

"Well — just figger that that twig is an Injun's eye. Let's see what you kin do to it!"

It was a shot that would have been more than average under any circumstances. And now there was much at stake. Why — my whole future hinged upon this moment! Could I do it? My hands were trembling as they gripped Old Chief Thrower. I threw a swift glance at Pierre Leroux. His eyes still held that noncommittal look. Yes, I must prove myself to Black Jack Bannock — and to Pierre as well.

I steadied myself by an effort of will. Then I loaded Old Chief Thrower, and never had I done it more carefully, shaking the exact amount of French powder into the conical measure that hung beneath the powderhorn; then I centered precisely the linen patch beneath the ball and drove the missile home without undue pressure, and with fingers that still trembled a bit, shook the fine grains of priming powder into the pan. Then I closed down the frizzen and lifted the barrel of the rifle to the mark. The front sight came to rest upon the twig indicated by Black Jack and settled slowly into the notch of the hindsight.

I pressed the trigger. There came a futile click.

The rifle, for the first time in my remembrance, had missed fire! A guffaw went up from the crowd.

"Ho! Ho! Thar's a shot fer ye!"

"Yes, sir-ee! Nicked thet Injun right in the eye!"

"Thar's yer fust scalp, lad! Well done!"

I boiled with humiliation. Black Jack turned away with a laugh. I saw everything collapse about me. Filled with anger, I shouted: "By thunder! I *will* show you!" All nervousness had vanished. Men leaned forward, keen with interest. There was something electric in the air, perhaps born of my own extremity. Swiftly I took sight and pressed the trigger.

The rifle barked. The twig snapped off clean as a whistle. Up went a cheer from the men, the same men who had jeered but a second since. It was a good shot, and I felt an uprush of pride.

"There's another twig under that one," I suggested, not without swagger, I'm afraid. "Does anyone want to try it?" I offered the rifle around the circle. But no one did.

Black Jack grunted. "I reckon you win the hand, young 'un. Guess we'll have to make room for you in this outfit. But don't think you won't have to work for your keep!"

Filled with elation, I turned about and started to unsaddle Hawk Eye. I had just loosened the cinch when the man's voice cracked like a whip. "Wait!"

I looked up in surprise.

Black Jack took a step toward me, his eyes narrowing. "I've been trying to remember where I first saw you," he said quietly. "In Sabino Roybal's, wasn't it?"

"Yes – sir," I faltered.

"What are you doing out here then?" His voice was as hard as flint now and he was watching me closely.

He hadn't heard then. "Roybal kicked me out," I answered. "Said he – said he didn't want me any longer."

"Why not?"

I hesitated. If I told the truth—

"What difference does it make?" It was Pierre Leroux speaking up for the first time. "I have an idea the kid was a rotten saddle maker. But he's a first-class shot, Bannock, and you'd do well to take him along." Then he turned to me. "*Habla español?*" he demanded.

"*Si, Señor.*"

Leroux grinned triumphantly. "You can't afford to pass up a

good shot or a man who can speak Spanish, either, Bannock," he said with insistence. "He'll be useful on the Trail, and in Santa Fe as well. Besides, this cub looks to me as if he might have some strips of good tough leather in him, and any outfit is the stronger for such."

I felt my heart grow warm to this man, for I had done all that I could.

"Oh – all right." Bannock turned away, dismissing me from his mind.

The rest of the men went about their business as well, and once again I set about unsaddling Hawk Eye.

Pierre came up to me. Under cover of filling his pipe, he spoke in a low voice. "Good lad!" he said. "I'm glad to see you took my advice and hit the trail. This is a tough outfit you're with, son. *How* tough you've no idea – yet. But if you stick it out, mebbe so you'll be a real, live Mountain Man!" He laughed, then turned away and left me to myself.

The wagons were scattered about through the camp at The Narrows, and cattle grazed loosely over the countryside under the desultory eye of the "cavvyard." There was no need as yet for vigilance. Time a-plenty for that when we should reach the Indian country. At night, however, I felt sure, a loose guard would be stationed—for even peaceful Osages were known to steal a horse under cover of darkness if they thought they could get away with it unscathed. Probably that would be my job – herding cattle and riding in the dust at the rear of the caravan. And, I doubted not, there would be plenty of other chores to occupy every waking moment.

I turned Hawk Eye loose to graze and slung my saddle over the wagon tongue where I saw Pierre Leroux's saddle. It was the first time that I had seen it at close hand and my eye was caught by the beauty of it. I knew something about leather after two years in Sabino Roybal's, but seldom had I seen such a handsome piece of saddle work as this. The neck of the pommel was thin and gracefully curved; the cantle high-rising; there was a smooth-slipping cinch that made it possible for the rider to tighten his saddle even when traveling at top speed; great leather stirrup housings, whose weight made for easy recovery of the stirrup if lost in combat; silver *concha* decorations, beautifully wrought, shining resplendently in the sun. These Mountain Men lavished on their mounts and trappings all the luxury that they rigorously denied their own persons.

There was a fifty-foot lariat, or *reata*, of plaited rawhide that had been dressed until it was as soft as a lady's glove; light of weight but steel-strong, looped around the saddle horn. An effective weapon in the hands of an expert and I had small doubt that Pierre Leroux was a past master in its use.

"Here, you! Star gazin', are ye?" A harsh voice broke in on my speculations. "Git busy and earn yer keep!" I looked up to see a thick-set man, about my own height, glaring at me from under black brows.

I grew hot with sudden anger, for I've never been able to stomach that tone from any man, and out here on the plains it seemed to strike with even greater offense than it might have back in Independence.

"I'm not taking any orders from you as I know of," I answered shortly.

"O-ho! Top-lofty, ain't you?" the man returned. "Well, I'm the boss cook, an' Cap'n Bannock says as how ye're workin' fer me. So I guess you'll take orders when I give 'em!"

Now, Reader, I ask your indulgence. I have never been able to take orders — or to give them. Every man his own master, Lanky had said. It was a belief that I had been brought up on. And therein lay the reason why, many years later when I scouted for General Crook on the border, I could never shake off the conviction that I was as good as any general, and that the lowest mess boy was as good as I. Not the proper temper to make a soldier, you will agree.

And so at this man's arrogant tone, my blood began to boil, and I controlled myself with diffculty, But — this was no time to get into trouble with Black Jack and his outfit. So I swallowed my pride as best I might, and answered meekly: "What do you want?"

"Kin you cook?" the other demanded with belligerence.

"I'm no fancy expert," I returned, "but I can boil beans and fry meat and make coffee."

"What the devil do ye think we want on the plains? Punkin pies?"

The sarcasm of the man was maddening. I found out later that he was Jake Bailey, one of those swaggering bullies who lorded it over anyone smaller than he physically, or over anyone else who appeared impressed with his bluster. I was to find out, also, that Black Jack accorded him a special indulgence; the two of them being somewhat of the same stripe, covering up the innate cowardice in their natures with an outward show of noise.

I sensed even in that moment that there would be trouble ahead in plenty between the boss cook and Jonathan Starbuck. It should be explained that cooking in the plains country is no simple affair. For after the timber country has been left behind, fuel is scarcer than down on an egg; and dust and sand have an exas-

perating way of getting into the coffee and beans; and the winds
that sweep across the wide spaces make cook fires so irregular and
fitful as to try a saint's endurance.   Baking bread, for instance,
without charring it becomes something of an achievement. The
bread that I cooked that first noon in Black Jack's service was
burned top and bottom and hard as a board. The men accepted
this good-naturedly enough, all except Jake Bailey.

"Listen, snipe," he threw at me. "You burn one more batch of
bread on me, and s'help me, I'll split yer tough skull open!"

Now, I have no apology for what happened. Perhaps I was flus-
tered and overwrought by the many things which I had had to
meet. Anyway, this was too much for me.

"You mean you'll *try* to!" I answered hotly.

"What's that?" Bailey advanced a step toward me, his bullet
head thrust forward on his thick neck at a bellicose angle.

"You heard me!"

We faced each other, eyes flashing. It was a show-down. We took
one another's measure as we stood there, and to him I must have
seemed an easy victory. He was no taller than I, but some fifty
pounds heavier. But if he'd been a foot taller, I'd have faced him
down.

"Cocky young rooster, ain't ye?" he sneered. "I'll clip your spurs
fer ye!"

I leaped upon him and we struck the ground with a thud. Over
and under we rolled, dust choking us, cries and grunts tearing our
throats. Dimly I knew that the men had gathered around us, urging us on.

"Split his head open, Bailey!"

"Give 'im Green River, Jake!"

Bailey twisted in my grasp — reached to his belt for his pistol.
I fought for a grip on his wrist. He would kill me if he could, that
I knew. No rules of decency in frontier fighting. Anything went.
Kicking. Clawing. Biting. Eye-gouging. Men fought as animals
fought, with one aim: to cripple — to kill. The best man won.

My fingers found his wrist as we twisted and sweat there in the
dust, then closed upon it. Not for nothing had I lived a boyhood
in the open. My lack of weight gave me a greater agility. I twisted

the man's arm up his back till one ounce more of pressure would have snapped the bone. His eyes started in his head. He let out a howl of pain.

"Had enough?" I panted.

Again he cursed me.

I increased the pressure with a vicious twist hooked to the end of it.

A choking cry wrung from him: "Stop! Stop!" he howled. "Bannock! Bannock!"

A hand seized me suddenly by the scruff and pulled me, fighting, to my feet. I whirled about, furious at the interference, to face Black Jack Bannock.

"So! You're making trouble as soon as you join up, eh?" he grated.

"I didn't start it," I protested hotly. "You don't expect me to stand by and let another man kill me, do you?"

"Don't talk up to me like that, you whelp!" Black Jack exploded.

"You're not my master!" I shouted, beside myself by now. Everything swam before me in a haze — Santa Fe — everything forgotten except these two bullies, one of whom had tried to kill me, and the other who was now berating me for having defended myself.

Pistol and knife had fallen from my belt during the struggle. I was unarmed. Black Jack was gripping his rawhide quirt. "I've a mind to thrash you within an inch of your life," he ground out.

"Try it, and by God, I'll kill you!" I flashed back, heedless of the rash words that tumbled from my lips.

The man raised his arm to strike. There came a whir through the air. A sound like a whiplash. I must have closed my eyes with some instinct of self-preservation. Then I heard a shout, and looked up. Pierre's lariat, expertly thrown, pinned Black Jack's arms to his sides.

"I wouldn't do that if I were you, Bannock," Leroux was saying quietly.

There was a second of intense silence. No man spoke. Black Jack, white to the lips, cried, "Take this cursed rope off me!" He was helpless, powerless, and he knew it.

"Certainly — when you've cooled off a bit," Pierre answered.

We faced each other, eyes flashing.

"Damn you, Leroux! Don't you know I'm the captain of this outfit?"

"And I'm the scout, old man," the other responded easily. "If you want to map your own route across the Cimarron, I'll pull out now and head for Independence."

He paused with significance. There was fifty feet of space between these men, and an antagonism as deep as a canyon. Not another man in the wagon train, we all knew, could have guided this party across the desert wastes that lay beyond Cimarron Crossing. If Pierre Leroux withdrew, it would mean a delay of days, perhaps two weeks, before Bannock could replace him with another reliable guide. And time was precious to Black Jack; there was no doubt about that. Pierre held the trump card, and bitter as the pill was to swallow, the wagon captain could take his medicine and relish it.

"All right," the defeated man muttered at last, with full sense of being discredited before his men. "Take this cursed thing off me, I tell you! And you—" he snarled, turning toward me, "you git saddled and head for Independence, if you know what's good for you! "

"If he goes, Bannock, I go," Pierre answered, and his voice was quiet.

Black Jack whirled. "Say — what's this anyhow?" he demanded, his eyes narrowing dangerously. "A conspiracy?"

I held my breath. One wrong word from Leroux, and I knew that I'd be sent packing back to the frontier, and all my hopes would go glimmering.

"Listen, Bannock." Pierre's level voice cut the silence. "This cub has ridden a hundred miles to join up with an outfit going to Santa Fe. He's passed the rifle test you set for him — a test you couldn't have passed yourself. And then he stood up for his rights when that coyote of yours threatened to kill him. Give the kid a deal from the top of the deck — if it's in you!"

"Aye!" assented a voice from one of the bystanders. "Give the lad a square deal, Bannock! He fought fair."

Black Jack hesitated, torn with doubt, furious at his humiliation.

"All right, then," he ground out at last, sullenly. "But if there's any more trouble out of you—" And the look he threw in my direction was not one to warm the heart.

And when, later, I saw him in earnest confab with Jake Bailey, I knew that I had made two enemies who would leave no stone unturned to see me eat humble pie. As I took my way down to the stream to think over these sudden developments in the camp, I was joined within a moment by Pierre Leroux.

He was smoking a Mexican cigar, blew out a ring of smoke, and smiled with mockery in his eye. "Well, young 'un, your first day on the plains hasn't been exactly uneventful!"

I felt sheepish now, and wondered if, possibly, I couldn't have avoided some of this if I had held my temper. But the man brushed aside my speculations with a brusque gesture.

"Listen, Starbuck," he hurried on in a low voice, "I told you this was a tough outfit you'd nosed into. Tough a-plenty. Now listen, and remember what I'm going to tell you: keep out of trouble as much as you can in the future. I've a notion I may be needing your help before we reach Santa Fe. Sleep with your eyes open, and your ears, too, and report to me anything suspicious that you hear!"

"You mean—"

"I'll explain when there's not so many big ears flapping around," he answered shortly. "There's more to this trip to the Rio Grande than meets the eye, lad. Black Jack's as slippery a weasel as ever wiggled out of a rabbit hole. All I can tell you now is this — he's headed into the rabbit hole. And it's up to us, to you and me, to see that he doesn't snake out of it."

With which cryptic remark, he swung back toward the bustling wagon camp.

CHAPTER VII

Council Grove

THREE days later we rode down upon Council Grove in ragged formation, ill-assembled and green at trail work. The unbroken stock was rendering the life of the cavvyard one of misery indeed, and never did a spot look so altogether welcome as did Council Grove, with its cool shade and its river flashing in the sun.

Scattered throughout the beautiful valley were the camps of the Oregon and Santa Fe emigrants. Here were the very people I had seen leaving Independence but a few days before — the people I had watched with such high envy for their good luck. And now here was I in their midst. Men were felling trees, tarring wheel hubs, cutting spare axles, repairing harness against the rough going ahead. They straightened up from their labors to greet us with hails and shouts — friends of the Trail calling to one another, passing jokes and gibes with much good humor.

Washing fluttered from every bush, drying in the crisp air. Greenhorns were using up their ammunition at target practice, popping away at squirrels and blackbirds. I saw children playing games about the camp fires, mothers caring for their babes, daughters washing linen to snowy whiteness, while the men cut hickory for extra gunsticks and laid in a supply of timber for all emergencies. For once Council Grove should be left behind, there would be no more hardwood for many a long mile. Here was every

type of wagon imaginable — from the splendid Conestogas of Pittsburgh make, down to old top-buggies and rude farm wagons.

We went into camp at one end of the grove, Bannock's wagons
holding apart from the others and keeping to themselves, a fact
which should have sounded a warning in our ears if we hadn't been
too occupied with the pressure of more obvious things. Already
there was repair work for us to do, and I was sure that it would be
a full forty-eight hours before we should again be on our way.

By noon we found that the Oregon wagons were preparing to
organize, beginning their electioneering for a wagon captain, map-
ping out a plan of march. Their numbers had swelled until now
they were some three or four hundred strong. The Santa Fe train
appeared to number some two hundred wagons. They, too, were
talking about electing a captain and laying plans for organization.
No one knew whether Black Jack Bannock would throw in his lot
with them or take his own train through.

Bannock's twelve wagons were the finest that could be pur-
chased at that time — long-geared Conestogas flaring upward from
the bottom, sixteen feet long, with a six-foot depth of hold, and a
capacity of from 5,000 to 16,000 pounds. That they were well filled
with merchandise was obvious to anyone who saw the yokes of
oxen, eight strong, straining at their yokes.

The average person knows something of the hazards that faced
the wagon trains, the dangers and ill luck that could overtake a
handful of men in hostile country. But I wonder how many know
the actual cost involved in the equipment of such an undertaking?
For example — the common Missouri wagon cost $200 each; mules
$100 each; harness could be figured at $100 to a team; water kegs
and sundries $25.00. Such wagons demanded eight or ten mules
to pull them, so that the initial cost was in the neighborhood of
$1,200 per wagon. Add another two dozen oxen or mules for emer-
gencies, a wagon master at a fee of $100 a month, a driver for every
wagon at $25, with additional herders (the "cavvyard"), and you
can readily see that the equipment of a train reached a high figure
before it was even under way with its merchandise.

Bear in mind that these wagons of which I speak were the average. The mighty Conestogas, or Pittsburgh "schooners," cost frequently in the neighborhood of $800 to $1,500 each, and the kind of mules necessary to haul these, $500 to $1,000 a pair. So it was small wonder that the merchants who financed these risky ventures would demand high profits from their investment.

Some of the Oregon and Santa Fe wagons had been camped in Council Grove for a week or more and were chafing at the bit to be off. Men who had come from the States east of the Missouri, having already traveled some thousand miles, were eager to have Oregon's additional two-thousand-mile jaunt behind them. But they knew that safety lay in numbers and in organization. Few

Indian war parties would dare to attack a large, well-organized train. But the very principles of organization and system were still to be absorbed by this free-thinking and independent lot of men, where the law, "each man for himself," was part of the basic warp of their natures. Every man wanted to be the first to see the Rio Grande or Oregon, and no man relished the dust from his neighbor's team in his nostrils. So lots must be drawn for proper place in the lines of march.

The blast of a bugle announced that the electioneeringfor a captain was to begin. The Oregon men congregated at one end of the grove. The Santa Fe group met in another. Party spirit ran high and the balloting was carried on with gusto. In the Oregon camp it was especially loud and vociferous, due to their greater numbers.

In the Santa Fe group there were two men of position to be looked upon as potential captain: Black Jack Bannock and Ephraim

Webster. Webster had made numerous successful trips across the plains. He was a man who made no extravagant bid for personal popularity; his record could speak for him. He alone seemed to understand the thanklessness of the task of captain, for he knew only too well how nominal was the power among men who looked upon a command as something that could be obeyed if they saw fit, or disregarded if they so chose. Black Jack seemed to be second choice by common consent. He was known to all men by his reputed wealth, while his swaggering manner was of the sort that could be relied upon to impress and attract followers of a certain nature. Thus the more lawless element seemed drawn to Bannock. But the greater portion of the train was made up of soberer citizens, and these leaned toward Ephraim Webster.

You should understand that this year of 1846 was one of unsettlement on the plains and border. New Mexico was inflamed against the annexation of Texas, and, for all we knew, war might already have broken out between the United States and Mexico. We were beyond the reach of news by now, and we wouldn't know the status of affairs until we tried to enter Santa Fe. There was no doubt in any man's mind that war was an insistent probability. Moreover, the plains Indians were stirred up to furious revolt against the great numbers of white men who were crossing the lands of their fathers, slaying the buffalo in countless thousands. It was rumored that the New Mexican governor, Armijo, had bribed the border Comanches to challenge the arrival of every American caravan. Thus it can be seen that there was plenty of excitement in store for the traveler of 1846.

And so a choice of proper man for captain became a decision of great import for the safety of all.

The meeting was called to order. Ephraim Webster arose to state his convictions as to the proper way of organizing the work of the Trail. It proved to be a conservative plan and the one used by practically all previous Santa Fe caravans.

"I propose," he boomed, "that we march in columns of four. At night, or when corralling in face of Indian attack, the two outside columns will close in together at the front, the other two angling outward, wagon tongue overlapping tail gate. Then you've got a

hollow square, men, into which you can drive your stock every night after grazing. You men yourselves can pitch camp and build your fires outside the corral, except in case of danger, when the enclosure presents a fine fortress."

As he went on to amplify the details of this well-precedented plan, Black Jack Bannock stood on the outskirts of the crowd, watching which way the wind of favor would shift. Perhaps his vanity inspired the hope that he might be elected captain of the train. Possibly he had more devious plans of his own. In any case, he stood on the sidelines now with a sneer twisting his lips as he listened to the comments of the men and to the exposition so fairly set forth by Ephraim Webster.

"Well – there's my plan, men," Webster wound up. "You can take it or leave it. The Santa Fe traders have found it good enough for fifteen years past, and it's always worked. If any of you's got a better idea or the experience to back it up, step forward and say so. Or if there's any of you that wants to pull out now and tackle the Trail by yourselves, say so now, or hold your peace!"

This was a democratic congress, and there were men in it who resented such high-handed dictatorship. It went against their free-moving natures. One of such was Jedediah Aiken. Aiken was a middle-aged farmer from Vermont, making the long trip to Santa Fe in two rude farm wagons with his wife and three sons. He was going out not as a trader, but as a settler, confident that Kearny's army would seize New Mexico and annex it to the United States. And he "cal'lated" that he was going to be right on the spot to lay claim to the richest piece of farm land in the lush valley of the Rio Grande.

Aiken leaped to his feet now, his hickory face red with indignation. "I don't hold with all this folderol!" he shouted. "I ain't j'ined up fer the Army, as I know of. When a man cain't stop his own wagons and build his own fires whenever he's a-mind to, it's time to call a halt, *I* say!"

We looked at his lean, rangy figure with quickened interest, stirred in spite of ourselves by this dissenting voice.

"Aye!" echoed from half a dozen throats. "That's the proper spirit for a man!"

Aiken's wife moved timidly to her husband's side. "But, Jed——"
she protested in a small voice, laying a restraining hand on his arm.

The man shook it off.

Webster rose to full height. "Are you plumb daft, Aiken?" he
shot back at the farmer. "Ain't you ever heard of Injun country?"

Aiken snorted. "Injuns!" he scoffed derisively. "My pop plugged
the critters full o' holes when I was a boy; and my grandpop afore
him. I cal'late what they could do, *I* kin!"

"But, Jed——" his wife protested again, faintly this time, "you'd
better heed——" She was a pale woman who moved through this
rough land with the nervous reluctance of a small bird. You felt
that she longed for New England's pocket landscapes, its miniature fields. Not for her this vast and terrifying wilderness.

"I'm not fer delayin' any further!" the farmer reiterated stubbornly, and called to his oldest son: "Harness up, Hank! We're
pullin' out right now. Guess we kin handle ourselves without any
help from Missoury!"

"Listen to the danged Yankee!" scoffed a round of voices.

But Aiken and his sons heeded not, and set about harnessing
the four horses that were to pull the wagons across half a continent. Some of the women in the other wagons commiserated with
the man's tearful wife. Pierre Leroux, taking part in affairs for the
first time, tried to dissuade the Vermont farmer from an action that
seemed the height of stubborn folly. But the man was adamant
and there was no moving him.

"We'll fetch Diamond Spring come night," he promised, leaping
to the seat of the wagon and flourishing his whip at us. "An' we'll
be settled in Santy Fee afore you chicken-livered greenhorns make
up yer minds to pull out o' Council Grove!"

His hickory face cracked into a grin of derision. Mrs. Aiken,
beside her husband on the high seat, sat with strained face, looking neither to right nor left, her hands twisting the blue gingham
of her dress. Hank Aiken drove the second wagon, while the other
two boys rode each his own horse. They didn't share their father's
optimism, and there was no jollity in the gestures with which they
waved us their final salutes. We did not know that we would never
see them again in this life; but perhaps some premonition of the

disaster which was to overtake them communicated itself to us all. A silence lay upon us as we watched the little company pull out of the Grove and climb the western slope — small and insignificant under the wide sky.

Then the pressure of our own business claimed our attention once again. Black Jack Bannock stepped dramatically up on a stump and all eyes swung toward him.

"There's *some* wisdom to what Mr. Webster has to say, men," he acknowledged, and his tone was in itself an insult. "Any fool knows that there's got to be some sort of regular system to an outfit of this size. But what I want to know before I throw in my lot with the rest of you is this — what route are you taking?"

"Bent's Fort route, of course!" Webster snapped back at him.

"I thought so," Bannock replied insolently. "Well — I'm not. I'm taking the Dry Route across the Cimarron Desert. It clips three or four days off the Bent's Fort Trail, Webster. And with a bunch of men on high wages and eating their fool heads off, time means money."

"To take the Dry Route this year is walking plumb into trouble," Webster retaliated hotly, "and everybody knows it, Bannock. The Comanches—"

Bannock made a sound of contempt. "What are rifles for, Mister Webster?" he queried, "to pop squirrels with? The Comanches and the Kiowas between them haven't got an up-to-date firearm — a lot of rusty *escopetas,* and such like."

"All right," the other grudged, "but they can do a powerful lot of damage with 'em when they're two or three thousand strong."

Black Jack chose to disregard that. "One other little point," came his insistent voice. "Where is Kearny?"

"Kearny?" echoed Webster. "What's that got to do with it?"

"Just this — it's rumored that he's camped outside of Bent's Fort, waiting for war to be declared so's he can march on Santa Fe. If you take the Bent's Fort route, you'll certainly be turned back by our good Colonel, and it'll be slim pickings waiting around in the desert till his dragoons win a war and give their august permission to the traders to enter Santa Fe!"

This was obviously a thought that hadn't occurred to any man present except Black Jack, and the murmur of voices rose steadily in debate.

"All right, men!" Webster shouted above the babel, "We'll have to chance that!"

Bannock laughed loudly. "Play safe if you want to, Mister Webster, but I'm taking my wagons across the Cimarron, and any man who's got guts enough can join up with me. The rest of you can go to hell — by way of Bent's Fort."

Ephraim Webster blanched with anger and it seemed for a moment that he would surely spring upon Black Jack. But that individual sauntered leisurely back to his wagons, leaving the company in furious debate behind him. Everyone knew that the Bent's Fort route over Raton Pass *was* longer; and delay might mean the loss of thousands of dollars, since the first traders to enter Santa Fe would skim off the cream of the trade. But it was the safer route — no doubt about that. As for being held up by Kearny's army — well, they'd have to run that risk. Thus the men were torn between the desire for larger profits and the greater danger in getting them. Bannock, it was known to all, had never crossed the plains, whereas Webster was a seasoned traveler. But Black Jack had had the forethought to hire Pierre Leroux, who was an acknowledged veteran of the Trail despite his comparative youth. Anyway, Bannock's declaration brought an end to the voting almost as it began. He was taking his own train by way of the *Jornada* whether or no. Any man who wanted to come with him could do so. The rest could go to the devil.

Ultimately the entire group, with the exception of eight men, sided with Webster. These eight attached themselves to Bannock's train, bringing it up to twenty wagons and some forty-five men. Of these eight independent traders, only two had ever crossed the plains before: Sandy Smith, a trapper who, in his old age, was taking a fling at trading; and Zenas Kent, another old plainsman. These two had known each other of yore and had a vast distrust of this Bannock outfit. They joined it only for the greater speed they would make by the Cimarron route. They knew Leroux, too,

and trusted his judgment, but for the rest of us they had nothing but scorn.

"Dang it all," Sandy muttered within my hearing, "eff it warn't fer them Comanches bein' stirred up by the greasers an' out fer ha'r, me an' Zenas would take our wagons across by ourselves. This is the likeliest bunch o' green scalps ever I see. Pawnee meat, else why was Injuns made, I'm askin'?"

The other newcomers were all past middle years, rivermen from the Missouri who had decided to look around inland, had borrowed money to buy wagons and take out a stock on shares. Hard men these, and quickly adaptable to the new life of the prairie. The men who were driving Bannock's own wagons were for the most part lawless roustabouts that he had picked up in Independence. With a goodly sprinkling of Mexicans for the cavvyard — there you have us.

"We'll pull out first thing in the morning, Leroux," Black Jack ordered. "Have every man ready."

There was a note of peremptory command in his voice, and I saw Leroux's eyes narrow dangerously at the tone.

"Am I the captain of this outfit as well as the scout, Bannock?" he asked quietly.

Black Jack modified his tone. "You understand this sort of thing better than I do, Leroux," he amended. "Take charge of it." And he disappeared into his private wagon.

Pierre's face relaxed and broke into a grin. "I reckon *Captain* Bannock's going to learn a lot before he hits the Rio Grande, son," he chuckled. "Yes, sir, plenty."

But perhaps Bannock was smarter than we realized. In passing on to Leroux the business of organizing the caravan, he passed on a sense of antagonism as well. Leroux, the men muttered — who was he to lay command upon men free to do as they chose? He wasn't the captain, but here he was issuing orders in a tone that expected and exacted obedience.

So, at the very outset, a feeling was bred that was to persist through many days to come.

CHAPTER VIII

THE FATE OF THE COOPERS

AN EARLY start Black Jack had ordered. Scarce had dawn lighted the east the following morning but we were hitching up. The loose stock had been rounded up and sorted out, unbroken animals balking and kicking against unaccustomed yoke and harness. It was a pandemonium of braying mules, lowing oxen, and plunging horses.

Men rushed about looking for articles lost, lent, or stolen, doing last-minute chores that should have been done the day before. Sandy Smith and Zenas Kent, old hands that they were, had everything where they could find it: extra picket staked, and firewood stored into every available chink against the woodless plains ahead; water casks filled to keep them swelling and proof against leakage. But these things the greenhorns would have to learn by hard experience. They turned deaf ears to suggestion and order alike.

"Catch up! Catch up!" came from the captain's quarters.

It was a cry that as to become well familiar during the days ahead. Now the drivers swore vociferously at their unruly animals. There was a bedlam of jangling chains, rattling yokes and harness,

rushing figures. Each man tried to best his fellows in speed — a sort of game in which the first man to cry, "All's set!" could preen himself with overweening pride.

The cry cam at last. Instantly, a dozen voices took it up, like echoes: "All's set! All's set!"

"Stretch out!" came the next command from the captain.

Whereupon followed an unbelievable clamor of grinding wheels, cracking whips, and shouting drivers.

"Fall in!" Bannock sang out as he pranced about on a beautiful chestnut gelding, enjoying himself with relish now that Leroux had accomplished the thankless task of organizing the train. Forthwith the wagons lumbered onto line upon the long slope. The wagon drivers fought to get their teams into the positions agreed upon, the noses of the leading team animals close to the tail gates of the wagon ahead. Two columns, clumsy and unaccustomed, stretched up the western slope of the valley toward the high plateau at its top.

Men sang and laughed and joked — called gibes and rude jokes to the watching Bent's fort caravan under Ephraim Webster's guidance. For myself — my heart beat high. We were leaving the last jumping-off place, the final security. Every mile now would take us straight into the heart of the buffalo and Indian country, nearer and nearer to the valley of the Rio Grande.

The wide track stretched ahead from the sunrise, deeply marked into the earth; the ineradicable scars of countless wagons. We were off! With our backs to the sunrise and our faces set toward the Unknown, we labored up the westward slope. And from far off in the unseen draws and swells, there came a vast stirring — the wind riding forth to greet us. The grass of the wide plain shimmered to every passing breeze. It grew so high as to sweep our knees as we rode. In the distance we could make out antelope moving through it. Often, with the timid curiosity of their kind, they'd pause to give us a tremulous scrutiny from their black eyes. Their white throats, as delicate as snow, were just visible through the rank grasses. Wolves loped and skulked on the outskirts, furtive yet bold.

I knew each member of this company now, even though I had

been in their midst but a few days — knew them as well as I had known the inhabitants of Independence. How unreal that old life of mine appeared in the presence of this reality. Like a dream, it was. Or perhaps that was the reality and this was the dream, so fantastic did it seem that I should be here, riding my pony toward the West.

How quickly men revealed the different facets of their natures under the pressure of this new life. Sandy Smith and Zenas Kent; the Mexican muleskinners; the redoubtable Bailey who watched me as a cat watches the proverbial mouse. Pierre Leroux dominated this assemblage with the gift and instinct of a born leader, which fact, doubtless, contributed to Bannock's growing antagonism toward him.

My mess duties were soon limited to the noon meal, for which I was duly grateful, having small stomach for association with Bailey. It was the pressure of the *cavvyard* which brought this about. The word *cavvyard* is a plains corruption of the Spanish caballada, meaning "one who tends the spare riding horses." Actually it included keeping an eye upon all the loose stock, mules and oxen. The Mexicans who made up this cavvyard were a wretched lot, with one exception: that was Manuel, a youth of my own age; good-tempered, riding the Trail with a guitar slung across his back and a song on his lips most of the time. He had great admiration for Old Chief Thrower, (boasting only an ancient matchlock of his own) and his joy was boundless when I let him use it to bring down a black-tailed deer one afternoon.

We traveled in two columns of ten wagons each, a pretty sight stretched out over the plain. At the rear of the procession the cavvyard drew up in the dust. Two riders called *point men,* of which I was one and Manuel the other, rode out and well back from the lead animals. We would ride forward and close in whenever necessary to direct the course of the herd. The main body of the loose stock straggled along behind their leaders under the careless eye of the shiftless Mexicans. I began to amplify my knowledge of the Spanish language by practicing on my companions, a practice which was to stand me in good stead.

Bannock's twelve wagons were drawn each by a yoke of eight oxen. The rest of the wagons were pulled by mules. Thus there were ninety-six oxen and sixty-four mules in actual use. There were, moreover, some fifty oxen to spare in case of accident, and another twenty-five mules to serve the same purpose. With thirty-odd horses it brought our total stock up to some two hundred sixty head. All of these animals, with the exception of the horses, were green at trail work, which meant constant vigilance on the part of the cavvyard — herding and guarding the working stock at night, and keeping the spare animals in formation at the end of the train while in action. This, coupled with the job of helping Bailey at the noon mess, left me with little spare time on my hands, as you can imagine.

Perhaps a word would not be out of place here concerning the respective merits of the ox and the mule in plains work. The mule had come, in recent years, to be held the superior; for the ox, despite his ability to pull a greater load, was apt to fall off in strength as he moved into the short-grass country. He was, in addition, tender in the feet — a weakness which often forced the teamster to the extremity of shoeing his animals with moccasins of raw buffalo hide, whereas the mule could cross the continent without being shod at all. Perhaps one of the major points in favor of the ox was the fact that the Indian had no use for him and seldom tried to steal him. But this superiority of one animal over the

other was ultimately a matter of personal preference. The fact remained in this instance that the great weight of Black Jack's wagons demanded the pulling power of oxen. It so happened that the remaining eight wagons of the train were drawn by mules. Thus I was enabled to become familiar with the oddities and vagaries of these two exasperating animals.

Even before Indian country should be reached, it was necessary to keep them under close guard, for green animals were frequently homesick and when the notion seized them, they would make off at top speed in the direction of the lost frontier. Or perhaps an ox would take sudden fright at the bark of a dog or the smell of a wild animal, and in swift panic would stampede the whole herd. Nothing could stop the headlong flight of a herd of frightened oxen. If we were taken unawares, it meant a ride of miles before they could be recovered, with the resulting loss of much time.

Our riding horses were fairly well broken to camp life and gave us little trouble. But Pierre Leroux had noticed several who seemed disposed to wander on day herd, and these leaders he instructed me to put a side hobble on. At night, until Indian country, they were free to graze and rounded up easily in the morning. This freedom kept them in good condition and flesh.

Pierre always kept Black Knight, his magnificent stallion, on picket during the night, and often took the herd himself as it left the bed ground at first flush of dawn. He must have slept with both ears and at least one eye open, for there seemed no least activity in the camp which escaped his attention. During those first days at trail work, I should have made a sorry mess of things if Pierre hadn't given me a hand. I had, as the saying goes, been born with horse sweat in the seat of my pants, but riding herd in open plains country was strange to my experience.

That first night out of Council Grove, filled with anxiety to make good on this, my first night with the stock, I was vastly relieved to see Pierre riding toward me to help bed down the cattle for the night.

"There's a trick to it," he explained, "that you'll get onto soon enough, son. Never let the critters know they're under restraint. Let 'em think they're doing everything of their own free will and you won't have any trouble. But you've got to keep your eye skinned to do it! Once this herd is trail-broke, they'll be as easy to handle as a parcel of sheep, at least in this part of the country. Always be sure they're well watered and full of grass when you bed 'em down, for hunger and thirst are responsible for more stampedes than all the Indians on the plains."

So it was that that night Manuel and I saw to it that the stock was well watered and fed, and they all seemed willing enough to bed down without trouble. The night guard must ride in a circle outside the sleeping cattle, and by riding in opposite directions, it was impossible for an animal to escape from the herd without being seen. Sometimes we sang as we rode, and the sleeping animals quickly became accustomed to the familiar sound of our voices and slept secure in the knowledge that there was no threat of prowling enemies at hand.

A pretty sight it was to see the cattle sleeping by the moon, the ghostly light glistening on their horns, the shadows black and full of mystery, and to hear Manuel's young voice lifted in the "Wagoner's Song":

> Chico! Moro! Zaino
> Vamos pingo por favor.
> Que pa, subir el repecho,
> No falta mas que un tirón.

> Chico! Moro! Zaino!
> Come gallop, and away!
> Red as sunset on the sierra
> Are the lips I'll kiss today!

"Pierre," I said, voicing a thought that had been uppermost in my mind for several days, "Joe Meeker started to tell about the Coopers the other day – that day in Roybal's. He didn't finish. Do you know what happened?"

"Yes," Pierre answered. "He told me the story. But Sandy Smith can tell it better than I can – for he claims he was there with Meeker and saw the whole thing. Ho-o-o, Sandy!" he called.

Sandy Smith's gaunt form took shape in the darkness as he rode toward us, his pony falling into leisurely stride with ours as we circled the sleeping cattle.

"Sandy," Pierre went on, "Starbuck here used to know the Coopers back in Independence. Tell him what happened to them. You saw the whole thing, didn't you?"

"Did so!" came Sandy's emphatic answer. The end of his pipe glowed in the darkness as he took a deep draw on it, and the momentary glow touched his roughhewn features. Sandy must have been as old as Lanky Lewis and Joe Meeker, and certain it was that a lifetime spent in the wilderness had set its stamp upon him also, some essence distilled from silence and danger and hardship that bound all those who shared such a life into closest kinship and set them apart forever from other men.

"I used to play with Tim Cooper," I ventured. "We never heard what became of him."

Sandy grunted. "Five or six years back, it must be by now," he mused. Me and Jim Eustace and Joe Meeker had been trappin' up to Powder River. We'd been thar goin' on two year, and had a pile o' beaver and mink and otter. And we concluded we'd better git 'em down to the Arkansas that spring 'cause they was wuth a considerable amount. We reached the river 'bout mid-June. Come out near Pawnee Fork. We was all afoot and drivin' our mules with the skins packed onto 'em, with one mule carryin' our blankets and possibles. We went into camp 'bout sundown, as I reckollect – hobbled the mules and was jest about to roast us a young antelope steak when—" He paused and took another draw on his pipe.

I could hardly contain my impatience. Sensing my curiosity, Leroux put in: "Go on, Sandy! Don't hang us up like that, man."

"Wa-al," the old trapper's voice resumed its leisurely tale, unperturbed by interruption and impatience alike, "we hadn't no more'n begun to eat when I noticed them mules was gittin' powerful oneasylike, and mine in pertickler was settin' up a snort. 'Boys,' sez I to Jim and Joe, 'thet means jest one thing!' 'What's that?' sez they, jest as eff they didn't know. 'Injuns,' I sez. 'Thet critter o' mine kin smell brown skin as fer as an eagle kin see.' Wa-al, my mule had started up the others by that time, and they was kickin' at their hobbles and squealin' like to have every Injun on the plains down on us in no time. So we picks up our rifles, cautiouslike, and crawls over to the top of the ledge. A grand lookout we had, too. You could see in all directions fer miles, and we seen somethin' all right, But it ain't Injuns."

"What was it?" I cried.

"A wagon train," he answered with slow deliberation. "Fifteen or so wagons pulled by oxen and traveling powerful slow in the sandhills by the river. We found out later it was jest some private enterprise headin' fer Santy Fee without a real good plainsman amongst the hull lot. And still not a plaguey Injun in sight an' them mules of ourn kickin' up the dust. 'Hyar's wet powder and no fire to dry it,' sez I; and I tell you fer once I nigh lost faith in thet long-earred critter o' mine. But not fer long! In less'n a second they was all the Injuns you'd want to see! Dozens of 'em, coming out o' the sandhills like prairie dogs, howlin' like devils. They rode down upon that train screechin' to high heaven, and tryin' to stampede the stock so's they could set the men afoot and finish 'em off easier. Comanches they was, and eff they's anything *wuss* packin' moccasins, may I never set trap again!" He stuffed his pipe and fought the wind for a light.

It was all I could do to hold back from interrupting.

"Wa-al, sir," the old trapper went on at last, "me and Jim and Joe, we hobbled our mules tighter and we grabs our rifles and down to the river we goes on the run, to lend a hand to that dumb wagon train. And jest as we reached the head o' the train, we see that the Injuns had cut off the last wagon. The red devils was circlin' 'round and 'round that lone wagon, yippin' like to bust yore ears. We saw a white man standin' with his back to the oxen, aimin'

his rifle and skeered to fire his single shot. In five seconds he was
as full of arrers as a porkypine's full o' quills. When he fell to the
ground, the arrers was so thick they propped him up. Then we saw
a woman. She jumped off the seat with a little boy — the kid could-
n't have been more'n nine or ten. They started runnin' fer the rest
o' the train as fast their legs would carry 'em, and half a dozen
Injuns ridin' at 'em on their ponies, yellin' like to freeze yer blood.
Wa-al — we saw one red devil lean from his pony's neck and fair
split the woman's head in two with a hatchet. Then another Injun
grabs hold of the boy (fightin' like a badger he was, too), and
swings the cub to his horse's back. The next second the hull pack
o' Comanches was disappearin' over the sandhills, takin' the kid
with 'em."

"What — what happened then?" the words tumbled from my lips.

"Don't interrupt, young 'un," the old trapper reproached. "I'm
comin' to that. Me and Joe, we borrers a couple of the train's
fastest horses and puts out after them brown skins. But they guv
us the slip. Trailed 'em fer two days, too. Nobody's ever saw hide
nor hair o' that Cooper young 'un since. Colonel Bent tried to
trade with old Bald Head, the Comanche chief, to git the kid back.
But they swore they'd killed him. Said he cried too much. An'
probably they did, too. But, sometimes I wonder—"

It seemed only yesterday that I had played with Tim Cooper,
played at being pursued by Indians! I could see him still, tearing
over the rough settlement roads on his pony, his hair as yellow as
corn silk in the sun. Who would have thought that those childish
games of ours would have materialized into stern reality? Tim
Cooper abducted by Comanches, unable to escape. Killed by
them, perhaps, because "he cried too much." Or, it was barely possible, growing up among them, taking a man's place in the tribe.
Such things had precedent enough in this savage country.
Everyone knew the story of the Hobbs boy and Jean Baptiste, who
had been overtaken by the Comanches when hunting buffalo. It
had happened some fifteen years back. The two boys were held
captive by the tribe for several years, hunting with them and
becoming great favorites with the Comanches; Hobbs finally

being given the daughter of Old Wolf in marriage. After several years they were ransomed by Colonel Bent, and they became Indian fighters second to none, due to the knowledge they had gained of Indian strategy during their years of bondage.

I couldn't get the thought of Tim Cooper out of my mind. He had been but a year older than I. I wondered if some merciless fate had been dealt out to him, or if he had, like Hobbs and Jean Baptiste, been spared.

Lost in these speculations, I continued my leisurely rounds on Hawk Eye. The cattle slept undisturbed. Pierre's dark shadow moved slowly at my side, and I felt my heart kindle with gratitude for this man's companionship. Black Knight was blowing softly through his nostrils. Overhead the stars leaned close and the soft wind fanned my cheek.

"The only life for a man, eh, Starbuck." Pierre was saying, and it was a statement, not a question. "I suppose," he went on, almost as if he were thinking aloud, "in the end we'll die wolf meat, and people who follow our trail west fifty years hence will wonder where that creek or camp site got its name. Leroux Creek, maybe. Or Starbuck Camp, for all we know. But at least it's better than dying in a bed, like a settlement squaw. An arrow in your hump ribs is as good a way as any and better than most!" And he rapped out the ashes of his pipe upon his thumbnail, Indian fashion.

"Yep," chuckled Sandy softly, "and eff we only knew it, the arrow's probably feathered a'ready!"

But these gloomy predictions had naught to do with me. Food, a horse to ride, the sky for a roof, and tomorrow for another adventure — what more could the heart of youth demand? As the moon waned and I dozed in my saddle, Manuel's soft voice came to my ears:

> Chico! Moro! Zaino!
> Vamos pingo por favor.
> Que pa, subir el repecho,
> No falta mas que un tirón.

Something far back in my blood caught in my veins; and whenever in later years I was to hear the "Wagoner's Song," I could see again the whole scene taking shape before my eyes: this lonely camp on the wide prairie, dotted with the dark circle of the wagons, the soft flow of the stream reflecting the starry sky, and the camp fires leaping upward while the herd slept undisturbed.

Chico! Moro! Zaino!
Vamos pingo por favor....

CHAPTER IX

Manuel Disappears

DAY AFTER long day the wagon train plodded westward, magnetized bodies of men and animals drawn, it seemed, by the setting sun. Two columns patiently plodding throughout the day; a circle of canvas tops, pale and ghostly in the night. We moved through a world fresh with a pristine newness, as if the dust of creation had settled. The air was of soaring buoyancy, so clear that all scale of distance was confused. Sometimes we were all but overpowered with a sense of human smallness. Something of the mightiness of this untamed land entered our little souls — some awareness of its timeless swing, its majesty, and its cruelty.

As we moved on toward Indian country, the nature of the land changed imperceptibly, the lush richness of the prairie country becoming daily more somber, more subtly forbidding. Men ironed out their grudges and shelved their differences and hung a little closer together for the common good. Even the realization of Bailey's hatred of me receded into the background of my consciousness. There had been no further overt conflict between the cook and me, for I had done my best to keep out of trouble; and my duties in the cavvyard left me little time to cross Bailey's trail. But I knew that his hatred lay as dormant as gunpowder, awaiting the proper spark to touch it off. And (possibly I imagined it) I had

begun to believe that Bannock was watching me with growing suspicion. Had he come to suspect that there might be some connection between my presence here in his outfit, and the day that I had overheard his conversation with Roybal?

The feeling that there was much more to this caravan than met the open eye, as Leroux declared, had grown to a conviction of large proportions. What lay behind it all, I could not fathom; but one day a half-forgotten sentence that had lain fallow in my memory returned: the sentence heard that day in the saddle shop — Bannock saying, "What I want's a guide, savvy? Once in sight of Santa Fe..." I remembered now, with a shadow of apprehension, the break in that unfinished sentence. Pierre must be warned at first opportunity.

Leroux was scouting at the head of the train on Black Knight, searching out obstructions in the trail, examining the banks of streams that were to be crossed, probing for possible quicksands. He rode back along the column to hearten us on. The stream ahead, he said, was steeper banked than usual, and some of the men must go forward with axes and shovels and mattocks to cut down the banks and thus make the descent easier for the heavily loaded wagons. He picked his men — and men were always willing to ride ahead of the plodding wagons no matter how grueling the task that awaited them. For they grew tired of the days' long monotony and looked forward with eagerness to any excitement. They still resented the almost military exactitude, the orderly formation which Pierre Leroux tried to establish and maintain on the Trail. Frequently the outriders, casting discretion to the winds, ranged far and wide in search of game, popping off their rifles at every jackrabbit and rattlesnake that met their eye, with a fine disregard for powder and ball as well as for the safety of the caravan. Leroux said that it usually took at least one good Indian scare to bring home to them a sense of ever-present danger and the necessity for vigilance.

The rear guard, composed mostly of Mexicans, had a disconcerting habit of pulling ahead whenever game was sighted, and soon could be found even in the forefront of the captain and the scout. Thus Manuel and I were frequently left sole members of the

cavvyard, and how we would have kept the stock from stampeding in face of an Indian surprise, I hate to think.

The Indian's favorite hour of attack was said to be just before
dawn. But another was as the caravan broke camp, either in the
early morning or after nooning it, when the confusion of the
unformed train rendered it vulnerable to quick attack, and a hasty
corral was often all but impossible. The Indian also understood
this propensity of the greenhorn for dashing about after game,
leaving the wagons unprotected. There were many occasions in
the bloody annals of the plains when the red man had taken grim
advantage of this weakness.

Pierre tried his best to hammer into the men the necessity for
proper flanking; the need for outriders to scout out every rise and
draw that might conceal hidden horsemen. But there was much
grumbling and discontent over what was termed "army tactics."

The tracks of Jedediah Aiken's two wagons lay plain before us
as, day by day, we advanced. We noticed that the farmer was traveling slower now, for the distance between the ashes of his camp
fires grew shorter. His horses were growing weary, that was certain, and I felt sure that if Jedediah Aiken and his family ever won
through to the Rio Grande, it would be on foot.

"Danged fool!" Sandy Smith muttered, scanning the Vermont
farmer's trail as we rode along, "eff him and his family don't end
wolf meat, then why was Injuns born, I'm askin'?"

The old trapper and his crony, Zenas Kent, found continuous
food for mirth in the antics of the tenderfeet of the outfit — partic-
ularly when it came to packing mules. A few of the rivermen had
been slow to catch on to prairie ways, being thick enough of head
to believe that they knew it all. Such men never disposed to take
advice or seek counsel were in perpetual hot water. Their pack animals balked over the ill-distributed loads, either refusing outright to
carry them, or else letting fly with their hindquarters and taking
to their heels, scattering the contents of the packs over the plains.
The trouble was, of course, that the rivermen, in choosing their
pack animals, passed up any mule that showed marks of crupper,
girth, and *aparejo;* picking instead the sleek, smooth-coated animal

of nattier appearance. They were ignorant of the fact that a veteran pack mule is chosen by the very signs which they scorned.

For a while Pierre let them flounder in their bullheaded ignorance. Then he took hold — picked out the likeliest mule of the outfit, tied her to the rear wagon of the right column, and fastened a bell about her neck. It would take her several days to learn that this was to be her position under all circumstances; but, once learning it, she would hold that place in the train in spite of hell or high water.

The other pack animals, hearing the tinkle of the bell, thrust forward their ears with quickened interest and trotted docilely into line after the bell mare. And it is an amazing fact, but a true one, that the pack mules gave no further trouble after that. A ludicrous sight it was to see the satisfaction with which the bell mare enjoyed her favored position, and the unquestioning alertness with which the other animals trotted after her.

Thus we left the miles behind. Diamond Spring. Lost Spring. Cottonwood Creek. Turkey Creek. Now we were 217 miles out from Independence, bearing down upon the Little Arkansas. There we knew that we could expect trouble, for the ill fame of that damnable ford had spread throughout the frontier country.

We were destined to have trouble there, right enough, but not entirely with the ford. Though the name Little Arkansas suggests a certain importance, we found it but a small creek with a current some five or six yards in width. However, the steepness of its banks and its treacherous bed made crossing with heavy wagons a dangerous hazard. Pierre and his men had gone ahead to cut down the banks and to lay cross layers of willow and long grass with coverings of earth to ease the passage of the wagons and prevent miring down. But in spite of their precautions, the depth of the stream and its swift current remained formidable indeed. It was the first ford in which we had encountered serious difficulty, and every man responded to the excitement of the moment.

The river had to be taken at a rush if we were to be successful. The wagons could not be allowed to settle for an instant in midstream. The first thing that we noticed when we reached the banks of the creek were the marks of Jedediah Aiken's passage cutting deep into the mud. Somehow the Vermont farmer and his little train had floundered across. And something about those twin canyons of mud, telling their mute tale of struggle and victory, stirred our hearts to admiration for the man, foolhardy though he may have been. Judging by the sign, the Aikens couldn't be more than twenty-four hours ahead of us now.

Pierre Leroux and Black Jack were in heated dispute over the crossing. Black Jack was in favor of camping on the near bank for the night, arguing that in the morning the depth and speed of the current might have slackened. Pierre pointed out that, on the other hand, if it should rain during the night, the stream would be all but impassable and cause a delay of a day or more. Besides, the teams never pull as well in the morning in "cold collars," and it is the part of wisdom to cross a stream at the end of a day for that reason, if for no other. At length Black Jack gave in, but with poor grace. We would cross. His face was as dark as a thundercloud as he mounted his gelding, and woe unto the man who should incur his displeasure. He and Pierre spurred their mounts into the water with a shout, the depth of it compelling the animals to swim as they made for the opposite bank. We stood on the near bank, watching, waiting orders. The teamsters held themselves in readiness, some of them unhitching their animals to double up the teams, each wagon in line, set to take the stream at a rush.

Sandy Smith was picked to drive the first wagon across with his eight mules.

"All's set!"

Yipping like a Comanche, turning the air blue with his cries, Sandy got the mules under way. Down the steep bank they plunged, half wading, half swimming, slithering in the mud and struggling for a foothold on the treacherous bottom. The whiplash licked viciously at their ears. Leroux and Bannock waited tensely on the opposite bank, bawling orders at the top of their lungs. The rest of us watched nervously, awaiting our turn. The heavy wagon paused for a second, seemed to settle.... Our hearts sank. Then lurching wildly, it was hauled across. Braying in protest, hoofs sliding in the mud, the heaving animals were half dragged up the opposite slope to safety.

Wagon after wagon made the ford without serious mishap — the stream one wild chaos of plunging animals and shouting drivers. Men leaped into the water to haul at settling wheel rims, the water churned up about their bodies in a foam of mud.

The long afternoon was drawing to a close before two thirds of the wagons were across. In country where the Indian loomed already an existent menace, it would never do to split up a wagon train. When one wagon crosses, all must cross. I watched with thumping heart, knowing that when the last team should be safely over, it would be the part of the cavvyard to drive across the unruly loose stock. Bannock's mood of black fury had abated not one whit, and I had no desire to run athwart it with any clumsiness of mine.

At length all the teams but one were safely across. This was one of Black Jack's heavily loaded Conestogas. The oxen, balky and nervous, took the water at top speed. Then, to our consternation, some instinct for deviltry prompted them to stop in midstream. The wagon settled swiftly in the quicksands. The driver lashed at them with his whip, shouted himself hoarse, cursed, implored, in vain. Bannock, on the opposite bank, was fairly livid with fury. Water was pouring over the side of the wagon into his precious merchandise. He hurled orders and threats across the stream. The wagon settled — leaned over on its side.

Manuel, the young Mexican boy, sprang from his horse and plunged into the water to help. With a furious oath, Black Jack urged his horse into the stream. Manuel had gripped the spokes of a wheel, trying his utmost to move the wagon onward in vain.

"You clumsy fool!" Black Jack shouted at him. "Pull! Pull!"

Manuel strained till the muscles knotted in his arms and the veins stood out on his forehead. Then, raising his rawhide quirt, Bannock lashed at the boy's face with savage ferocity. The hiss of that lash would have stopped your heart. With a scream of agony, Manuel threw up his hands across his eyes. Blood spouted through his fingers.

"Gawd!" muttered Zenas Kent. "He's blinded!"

I felt sick with impotent rage at the brutality of the act.

"Damn you, Bannock!" Pierre shouted, white to the lips. "You'd kill your own mother to get your wagons across!"

Some instinct, stronger than I, lifted Old Chief Thrower in my hands. Zenas Kent knocked up the muzzle with an oath that brought me to my senses.

"Every man to his own battles!" he rapped out.

"But—" I protested furiously.

"Shut up!" he rumbled. "Thar's enough fer us to do. Into the stream, lad — we've got to set that danged wagon aright."

Into the stream we all plunged, poor Manuel forgotten in the uproar that followed. Another yoke of eight oxen was hitched to the one that was mired down. Hauling, heaving, straining at the hubs, beating the frantic animals, pulling, groaning, sweating, cursing — at last! Up — up and over the bank went the wagon. Men sank to the ground panting with exhaustion.

But weary though we were, there was still the loose stock to be herded across. Yelling at the top of our lungs, we got them going on the run. They took the steep decline at full gallop. We followed them as far as midstream, shouting like demons. On the opposite bank drivers were waiting to haul them up and herd them to the bedding ground. When the mules were all but half across, one of them turned and headed for the bank whence it had come. Despite all our efforts the ornery critter gained the bank and stood there, feet planted, teeth bared, ears laid back as it brayed its anger. Gingerly I grabbed the rope about its neck and pulled — to no purpose. Sandy came to my assistance with the force of his great muscle and the added weight of his accomplished profanity. Without result.

Pierre urged Black Knight into the stream and swam to our aid. "There's no time to pamper a mule," he cried as he clambered up the bank. "Blindfold him!"

This done, we backed the animal to the stream's edge. Pierre took a hitch around the critter's forelegs and threw him. Then we hog-tied him and rolled him into the water and hauled him ignominiously to the farther shore.

Already cook fires were leaping upward, beans and coffee a-

boil for weary men. Night had fallen and stars were a-glitter in the serene sky. The guards were moving into position. The rest of us, soaked to the skin and altogether exhausted, huddled about the fires, wolfing down our evening meal. Pierre appeared suddenly in our midst, his eyes black as twin coals in a white face.

"Where's Manuel?" he queried.

Manuel — we had forgotten him. We looked blankly from one face to another.

"Where is he, men?" Pierre reiterated with impatience, "He'll be needing attention."

But though we took the count of the camp and scouted along the banks of the creek, the Mexican boy was nowhere to be found. It was discovered that a horse was missing.... Manuel had stolen a mount and disappeared, swallowed up in the engulfing darkness.

It was here by the Little Arkansas that the range of the buffalo had its eastern limits. Buffalo country meant Indian country — hunting parties which could be transformed into war parties in one shake of a mule's tail. It was a bloody strip of land from here to Coon Creek, for the Pawnee claimed sovereignty of this territory, and when the mood was upon him or the hunting was poor, would challenge all encroachers, red or white. This sovereignty was forever being disputed by warriors from the south, the west, and the north: Kiowas, Comanches, Arapahoes, and Cheyennes; even the far-ranging Apaches and Utes, the Blackfeet and the Sioux. All these met from time to time in this land which the Pawnee claimed as the land of his fathers, and the earth was stained with the blood of the vanquished.

Because of this, small parties of Indians were seldom encountered; or, if seen, were but scouts or vanguard of larger numbers. The Pawnees were reputed to have a trick of their own: by dark of night small groups would roam on foot to steal the horses of the careless traveler. For the horse was the Indian's wealth and the joy of his life, and he would go to any length to add to his string. With savage cunning the Pawnees had mastered the trick of creeping up on a herd of draft animals under the very noses of the guards, and sending the stock headlong in stampede. Many an unhappy trader had thus been set afoot and forced to pack on his back all that he could carry as he made tracks for safety.

As yet, however, we had seen neither Indian nor buffalo, and Sandy and Zenas were grumbling. Beans and bacon were getting low. There was much discontent in the ranks. Men fought at the drop of a hat. As Zenas put it, "We need some juicy hump steak to set things aright. Men don't pick a fight on a full stomach." So it was that the discovery of buffalo grass was hailed with delight, for the buffalo themselves could not be far off now. Their trails, some twenty feet wide, crisscrossed the surface of the plain, graven indelibly into the hard earth by countless thousands of hoofs in the yearly migrations.

The luxuriant grasses of the country behind us were giving way more and more to the short, curly buffalo grass.

"Yere's proper fodder fer the stock!" Sandy exulted, pointing it out to me.

And so it seemed. The animals found more of real nourishment, strangely enough, in this sparse-looking herbage than they had in the richer grass we had left behind.

At last scouts brought back word that threw the whole train into excitement and freshened the pace of the weary animals.

"The Arkansas! The Arkansas!"

The cry rippled down the length of the columns like wind through a field. Few of us could resist riding ahead of a glimpse of the great river. There it lay before us, dotted with green islets, fresh to the eye in those endless wastes of sand. Four or five hundred yards wide, perhaps, shallow and fordable at many points, white with alkali and glittering in the sun. The low banks were barren save for occasional scrub, inconceivably desolate, yet not without a certain solemn majesty of their own. As far as the eye could see, the sandhills rolled away, like waves of some strange inland sea, gleaming yellow in the burnished glare. So gradual was the rise of the plains floor to the river's rim, that an unknowing traveler might almost have stumbled into it unaware. Here was the boundary line between the United States and Texas, according to Texas claims. In point of fact, however, the opposite bank still marked Mexican soil, the arm of Texas being not yet long enough to reach and hold it.

The northern bank was practically void of timber, but ragged patches of cottonwood were visible to the south, protected from prairie fires by the river to the north, as well as by the great sand-hills themselves, upon which the terrible fires must die of starvation. On our right the land stretched away into limitless swells, while on our left the river twisted sluggishly on its course, pale-gleaming over its treacherous bottom.

Stubbornly, we rolled up the river in a rough parallel, over ground of flintlike hardness. We pushed ahead until nightfall and gave our weary stock no rest until we were safely on the farther side of Walnut Creek. Not far from the mouth of the creek we came upon a little valley bordered in timber and rich with fine grass. We watered the stock before corralling them for the night, and went into camp happy in the knowledge that we would stay here while, on the morrow, scouts would ride ahead searching for buffalo. We were oblivious to the fact that this was the greatest danger spot on the Trail to date. Here, at the eastern edge of the great buffalo range, we could look for Indians at any moment.

That night the fires blazed high. Buffalo chip fires, short-lived, that leaped upward with constant replenishment. Men's spirits soared with the promise of buffalo and no threat of danger seemed to lay a silencing hand upon them. They sang and laughed and joked as they stuffed down their supper. The first night guard moved into position, and the rest of us, awaiting our own turn, dragged out our pipes and made ourselves comfortable about the camp fires, content in the belief that tomorrow we would feast high on hump steak and marrow and drippings. Within the circle of corralled wagons, the stock slept undisturbed. Out beyond our fires, beyond the vigilant guards, in that mysterious outer darkness — who knew what lay in wait? Who cared?

My turn at guard duty would be from midnight till dawn. I rolled up in my buffalo robe beside the fire, my saddle pillowing my head, my rifle to hand. Zenas Kent and Sandy Smith lay half recumbent on the ground, pulling at their pipes, recalling, as they always did when together, incidents from the past. Somewhere the Mexicans were singing softly; haunting, half-savage songs that quivered along the nerves; and I thought of Manuel and wondered where he was, and how he fared. I missed the sound of his young voice singing the rollicking Wagoner's Song, with its "Chico! Moro! Zaino...." Would he, I wondered, win through to Santa Fe alone?

Pierre Leroux emerged from the shadows and threw himself down on the ground to rest. He didn't speak, but his eyes flashed a friendly greeting. As he lay there leaning back against the wheel of a Conestoga, his eyes looking off into space, the firelight picking his fine head out of the darkness, I wondered for the thousandth time at the potency of the spell that could draw and hold such a man to such a life. Other men moved to join the circle about our fire. The pipes and the companionship loosened their tongues, and they spoke of things that lay hidden in their minds and hearts.

As long as I lived, I was to remember those nights on the Great Plains, with the hard-living, hard-fighting, hard-dying men who sat about the fires. Blood and thirst and hunger made up their span. But they laughed at it, enjoyed it, survived it. There were men here who had been set afoot by the Injuns in waterless wastes; men who had been robbed of their peltries after a year's trapping in the wilderness; men who had been all but scalped, and who would carry to the grave arrowheads embedded under their hump ribs. They bragged of their rifles, their horses, their packs, and their squaws, in due order of value. And I listened to it all and never tired of it. It seemed that all my childhood I had dreamed of some day finding such a life as this, and now that I had found it, it seemed to me that all I had dreamed was but a hollow counterfeit of this reality. It was just as I had always known it would be, and yet I came upon it with a sense of discovery and wonder.

Sandy and Zenas, by right of seniority and experience, usually controlled the conversation, shifting it into whatever channels suited their moods. Sandy, who fancied himself something of a heartbreaker in many an Indian village, spoke out of his checkered past:

"No squaw kin beat a Nez Percé fer a handy lodge keeper," said he.

"An' *that's* so," Zenas acknowledged. "But jest the same it takes a Ute fer tannin' skins."

"Aye, Zenas — and a Cheyenne fer stirrin' up trouble. Never seed their like. When I was married to the datter of old Spoiled Meat, thar warn't a day went by that I didn't have to give her a lodgepolin'. Couldn't seem to knock no sense into her. Finally I traded her in fer a good Hawkins two-shoot gun, and next I thought I'd try me a Crow. But if they's anythin' packin' moccasins that's cusseder than a Crow, I ain't heerd tell of hit!"

"Less'n it's a 'Rapaho," Zenas threw back. "But fer dry moccasins and handy lodge-keeper you cain't beat a Nez Percé, an' eff that ain't so, may I never draw bead ag'in!"

Half sleeping, half awake, I settled my head more comfortably on my saddle, listening to the monotonous drone of voices, watching the sparks leap skyward, smelling the smell of this warm earth.

"What ever come of Old Bill Williams, Zenas?" Sandy was asking, reaching down for a coal to light his pipe.

"Bill Williams? Oh — he was rubbed out by the Blackfeet on the Little Ojibway last year. Dangest liar as ever drew breath, he war, as shore as my rifle's got hindsights and shoots center."

"An' *that's* so, scalp my old hide!" chuckled Sandy. "I reckollect the time he'd been trappin' two year or more up to the headwaters o' the Platte. He gits back to Independence with a pile o' beaver, an' decides to settle down like a white man an' trap himself a white squaw what owns a house thar. She invites him to feed paunch one Sunday, see? an' she says to him, 'O, Mister Williams, it must be wonnerful to be such a travelyer!'

" 'Travelyer, ma'am?' says Bill. 'Dang me, I ain't no travelyer. I'm a trapper. Wagh!'

"'But a trapper's a travelyer, too,' says she. 'An' what sights you must o' seen in yore travels, Mister Williams.

"'Sights, ma'am,' says he. 'Scalp me, I've seen sights you'd never dream on Have you ever heerd tell of the Putrified Forest, ma'am!'

"'Mercy on us, Mister Williams! Whatever is that?' she says.

"'Wa-al, ma'am, I'll tell ye: I'd been lost oncet up to the Black Hills and was down to eatin' my moccasins and chawin' the tail o' my mule — half froze fer food and none in sight. When all on a sudden, we crosses a divide, and s'help me! right afore my eyes is the purtiest little green valley ever you see. Thar was birds a-singin' and a brook a-flowin', despite it was mid-January and snow all over the rest o' the world. I throws my cap in the air and the mule kicks up her feet and frisks her tail. An' I picks up Old Silver Heels and takes a shot at one o' them warblin' birds. Knocks its danged head right off, but still it goes on singin'! When I picks the critter up, s'help me, it's made o' stone! Wa-al, ma'am, I was sorter put out at that. So I ups with my ax and lets fly at a handy tree. The blinking blade turns over its edge like it was made o' butter. That tree was stone, too. My ole mule, meantime, was tryin' to gnaw at the cussed grass; and dang me eff the grass warn't stone. You could break it off like pipestems. What was it, you ask, ma'am? Putrefactions — that's what it was. I was in the Putrified Forest.'

"'Putrified, Mister Williams?' says Bill's squaw. 'Mercy me! How it must o' smelled!'

"'Smelled, ma'am?' says Bill. 'Smelled you say? Would a skunk stink eff he was made o' stone?'"

I had heard this old plains story in a hundred variations, as had all others present; but Sandy told it as if it had happened the day before, with a wealth of pantomime that tickled our ribs with laughter.

The talk shifted into other channels. They spoke of a land that lay beyond the snowy heights of the Rockies, a land of tall forests and swift rivers. They spoke of beaver and elk and grizzly; of great buttes lifting from the painted plains; of underground streams and boiling springs. They talked of Lewis and Clark, of Andrew Henry and Zebulon Pike. They had trapped with Kit Carson and Jim

Bridger and "Uncle" Dick Wooton, and made merry with them at the great Green River rendezvous. I had learned many things during the past weeks from these old plainsmen; learned that a saddle could become a pillow and a barricade of nights, with rifle laid above it, ready to the hand; learned to spread my robe where the ground rose highest, and to trench it 'round with my Green River knife. I had learned to keep my rifle dry — a never-ending ritual of grease rag from the patch box, looking to see if moisture had seeped through the lock cover; repriming. . . . I had learned that the best way to extract an embedded arrow was to push it on through the wound and then, having cut off the arrowhead, to yank free the feathered shaft. But above all else, had I learned the trapper's creed: that vigilance, caution, and courage could triumph over most situations; and that, if the cards were stacked against you, you did the best that you possibly could, and in the end you died like a white man .

Now, too, I understood many things about Pierre Leroux. His background, his fine family, his book learning . . . what did these things weigh in the scales against a new camp always just over the rise, a new dawn for a fresh adventure? The fine freedom of this life, the threat of hostile forces which called upon man's unceasing self-reliance, the essential *rightness* of it seemed to me the life about which all men secretly dream; the life toward which they aspire.

Lying there, I became aware of a new sound, not loud nor close at hand, different in some vague way from the accustomed sounds about me. I saw that Pierre had raised up on one elbow, listening. . . .

"Buffalo wolf," he whispered.

The rising note, ghostly and mournful, shivered across the night.

"That's good sign. Buffalo talk! Tomorrow we'll have meat."

As I dozed there, and sleep lay heavy on my eyelids, the moon swung high and the stars looked down, and I knew — Oh! then I knew that I'd never return to Independence to sleep in a bed!

CHAPTER X

BUFFALO AND INJUNS

BUFFALO! Buffalo!"
Scouts rode into camp on the wings of the magic cry. Instantly the little valley of Walnut Creek resounded with shouts and leaped to life and swift activity. The wagon train was plunged into pandemonium. Men sprang from their robes standing, reached automatically for their rifles, threw saddles on their horses. Here was a long-awaited meat at hand. Buffalo! To the older hunters it meant only a renewal of a thrilling sport and the satisfaction of an appetite. But for the greenhorn it was a dream come true.

Hawk Eye knew the word, or perhaps had sensed the presence of the buffalo long since, for she was chafing at the picket rope, trembling with eagerness to be up and off. I flung the saddle across her back, cinched it tight, and grabbed Old Chief Thrower.

Sandy howled with wolfish delight. "Buffler, boys!" he crowed, dancing a fancy caper. "We'll be havin' hump fer supper, else why was buffler made, I'm askin'?"

Pierre, stripped to the waist, swept up at a gallop, a wild figure and as dark as any Indian. He hadn't even paused to saddle Black Knight, but had flung a buffalo hide across the animal's back and cinched it with a band of rawhide, guiding his mount by a jaw rope. He pulled up and threw out an arm toward the end of the valley.

"They're around that elbow!" he shouted. "They'll run up wind and go out by that pass yonder, so look to your priming." His eyes met mine for a minute. "Is Old Chief Thrower ready?" he grinned. "When the rifles begin to pop, then down and into 'em, son, and let's see if you can tell fat cow from pore bull!"

Every man was mounted by now. With weapons a-flourish and yipping at the top of our lungs we went over and across, out through the little valley, charging to harry the buffalo herd.

We topped a rise of land and every nerve leaped in response to the sight. The green floor of the plain was suddenly wiped out by a carpet of brown — a moving carpet of dark bodies. It stretched to the horizon, stunning the eye. Buffalo — thousands, tens of thousands, legions of them. It was a sight to thrill the stoutest heart. For the greenhorn it was touched with terror as well. The herd seemed nervous and restless, shaggy heads lifting, short-visioned eyes trying to pierce the haze of distance. Clouds of dust rose where bulls locked horns in combat. A dull, rumbling bellow struck my ears: the earth thunder of the buffalo horde. Trails cut deep into the soil, crisscrossing in every direction. Wallows pitted the plain in wide circles of white alkali. All my life I had imagined this scene, pictured it, relived it in countless tales of trapper and hunter. Now here I was, riding down into it on my pony with Old Chief Thrower gripped in my cold hands. "Run your buffalo!" my father had said, and how I wished he might have been here to run them with me. Blackbirds were flying about, devouring the flies that were the inseparable companions of the animals.

I saw Pierre and Zenas sweep past in a wide circuit to stalk the buffalo from down wind, and I watched them eagerly as they took full advantage of every hollow, emerging, disappearing again.

Sandy, riding a high, clay-colored mare, shouted above the noise: "They's been redskins worryin' that herd. It's nervous as a settlement squaw. Injuns been after 'em, and not so long ago, nuther."

A vague uneasiness seemed to be running through the herd. The animals were pawing, rumbling, lifting their ponderous bosses, horns flashing in the bright sun. Their shortsighted eyes told them nothing, but their uplifted nostrils sorted the air currents and caught the warning that flashed along the nerves of heredity.

"Dang the wind!" cursed Sandy, "she's shiftin'. See you shoot center, cub, or thar be no meat in pot tonight."

Men were riding everywhere. Then came two sharp rifle reports. Leroux's, maybe, and Kent's. Like a flash the herd swung as a unit. One second they were grazing. The next, pounding in full flight.

"*Ow-owgh!*" sounded the shrill battle cry. "Down and into 'em, boys!"

Every man with brandishing gun and wild-pitched yell poured over the rise and down. The herd fled, torrential, mighty, out toward the opening in the valley's end. Bosses low, tails straight, headlong in flight. Calves leaped and blatted. Bulls bellowed. Men were shouting with victory. Their rifles barked and puffs of smoke mingled with the choking dust. The herd was rocketing at top speed up the draw.

I swung my quirt across Hawk Eye's rump. She stretched out her neck and fairly flew over the rough ground. The air was thick with clouds of dust, blinding, strangling, and within that dense wall buffalo unnumbered fled in wild escape and I was riding into them. Another second and I was in the center of the mass. A terrible din assailed my ears. The air reeled and trembled with noise. The ground shook beneath me. The roar of the bulls, the lowing of the cows, the thunder of a million hoofs.... An instant of panic stabbed at me. Suppose Hawk Eye should stumble in a dog hole? I'd be ground into the plain, pulverized to a powder. The very earth was rocking. It was a world gone mad. Buffalo in front, behind, on both sides of me now. As far as I could see, only heaving bodies, tossing horns.

The ground was bad at best and growing worse; abrupt rises and sudden hollows, unsuspected gullies that could spell annihilation. Wheeling, shoving, shouldering, the herd raced in a flight that was deceptively clumsy but incredibly swift. The green horses showed signs of arrant terror at being urged into that heaving mass of flesh. I thanked old Lanky Lewis from the bottom of my heart for the horse between my knees. Hawk Eye was in her element, no doubt about that.

Almost as if a signal had been given, the herd seemed to break

I was alone with the thundering herd.

into half a dozen groups, scampering off in as many different directions. Some hunters followed one group, some another. I lost sight of my companions in the general confusion and they were soon blotted out by the clouds of dust. Glancing about me, I saw that they had all disappeared from my range of vision and I was alone within the plunging herd.

Now I began to collect myself, trying to distinguish cows from bulls. I picked out a fat cow and urged Hawk Eye abreast of her — lifted Old Chief Thrower and took flying aim. Before I could press the trigger, the cow was suddenly plunging head over heels out of sight. Then next moment the ground seemed to have dropped from beneath me, and I knew a terrible sensation of falling.... Buffalo all around me, pitching into this deep, unseen gully where we had unwittingly been swept. Impossible to stop.... Down, down, ten feet, fifteen, maybe.... Sliding, plunging, Hawk Eye and I were hurled into it as were the buffalo themselves by the pressure behind. We brought up sharply at the bottom. Hawk Eye went down on her knees there in that chaos. I was thrown forward almost over her neck and hooked one knee wildly over the saddle horn to save myself from being pitched headlong. Quick as a flash, the pony was scrambling to her feet and up the opposite bank. It was so steep it seemed that she must fall backward and crush me with her weight and leave my body to the pulverizing hoofs of the herd. For a split second her forefeet clung to the rim, while my heart caught in my throat. Then she was up and over and on — on once more with the rumbling horde.

Buffalo now on all sides of me; ugly-looking, shaggy-maned, matted shreds of hair flying down wind behind them. They were panting heavily, their backs streaked with sweat, tongues lolling loosely from their mouths. From somewhere beyond the enveloping clouds of dust, the shrill cries of the hunters rose above the drumming of the hoofs. At top speed we fled. A large bull on my right turned to gore me, but Hawk Eye was too quick for him. She leaped sideways with a speed that almost unseated me, and on we raced.

There was a fat cow just ahead.... I urged Hawk Eye up to her

side, pulled abreast. The cow sprang at my pony with lowered horns, but once more the little mare dodged the lunge and I fought to hold my saddle. The cow had disappeared. On we thundered, mile after mile, Hawk Eye holding her top speed and showing no signs of weakening.

I picked out another animal and fired again – saw where the bullet entered. A good shot, not too high. Then in trying to reload, I lost sight of my quarry. But I was certain that she was mortally wounded.

I slackened pace gradually, letting the herd sweep past me, and looking for my wounded cow to drop out. On, on they rocketed, leaving me and my pony behind in clouds of dust and sand. A short distance ahead I could make out a solitary buffalo galloping heavily. A cow – wounded. I spurred my pony to her side. The buffalo turned her head, mane bristling, little eyes red with rage. Before I could draw bead, she swung and rushed me. Once again the Comanche pony dodged neatly. Had my mare been anything less than expert, surely I would have been killed, for I seemed to have conducted my first buffalo hunt clumsily indeed.

Now my victim was weakening – bleeding at the mouth. Taking careful sight, I fired once again. The cow sank to her knees, rolled over. Lay still. I leaped to the ground and ran forward. Then, for the first time, I noticed that there was an arrow, deeply driven, embedded in her haunch. Someone else had shot at this buffalo.... *An Indian!* I straightened up suddenly and looked about me. The main body of the herd had vanished from sight. Only a few old bulls were grazing by themselves.

The realization that I was lost swept over me with stunning impact. I was alone with my slain buffalo in the middle of a deserted plain. I had no idea how many miles I had come, or whether I was west, east, south, or north of my starting point. All sense of direction seemed to have left me in the excitement of the chase and its devious twists. A hush, incredibly intensified after the noise of battle, had fallen over the land. Hawk Eye, exhausted from the grilling pace to which I had subjected her, stood with drooping head and heaving sides. Given time, she would doubt-

less have carried me back to camp. But now she was played out, winded. The undulating swells of the plain on every hand offered no familiar landmark for a guide. To my left was a low ledge of yellow sandstone, flat as a wall; nothing else as far as my eye could see except sandhills and scrubby buffalo grass.

I knew a second of panic, then caught hold of myself. I had my horse and my rifle, and here was meat. I set about butchering the animal, clumsily cutting off a slab above the hump. And whether I was more upset by my predicament or by the stupidity which had led me into it, it would be hard to say. The shadows lengthened as the sun dropped, and I tried to figure on what angle the Arkansas would be running, and in which direction I should strike out. But I would have to give Hawk Eye time to get her wind. Perhaps if I waited till after dark, I'd see the camp fires of the wagon train, wherever they might be.

Suddenly I was listening intently. Hawk Eye pricked up her ears. From somewhere beyond the rise I heard hoofbeats on the hard sand. Indians? I swallowed hard as I loaded Old Chief Thrower, trying not to see how my hand shook. Then I set my back to Hawk Eye and stood with the butchered cow at my feet. Before I could stop her, the Comanche pony had lifted her head and neighed sharply. With sudden rage, I struck her across the muzzle.

"You fool!" I cried, "do you want every Indian in the plains down on us?"

I might have known. . . . The figure that rode over the top of the rise was Pierre Leroux. He halted for a second, looking down at me with a faint smile playing on his lips, taking in at a glance my plight, my winded horse, the badly butchered cow,

"I'm not lost!" I threw out quickly, before he could speak.

"No," he answered solemnly as he rode down the slope. "I know you're not lost, son. Just thought I'd drop around to help you pack some of your cow back to camp."

He slid to the ground and his eye was arrested by sight of the arrow still embedded in the cow's flank. He was all serious in an instant and dropped to his knees to examine the feathered shaft. I had forgotten this, too, in my plight. Every Indian tribe makes its arrows differently, and it's by such "sign" that the experienced Mountain Man is able to keep some check on his enemies. An arrow found in the carcass of animal or man is a message to be read by the knowing eye. Pierre butchered out the embedded arrowhead — scrutinized it closely. I saw that it was wrapped with elk sinew.

"Just as I thought," he muttered. "Pawnee... planted this morning, or I can't read sign. I thought that herd was powerful uneasy. Always means Injuns have been at 'em."

"But we haven't seen hide nor track of Injuns," I offered, not feeling too proud of my showing to date.

"True enough," he returned, "but if they haven't seen us, then I've never lifted ha'r, my lad! They've probably decided we'd be richer picking than the buffalo. An Injun's always after ha'r or horses, and buffalo can wait." He straightened up and looked around.

"Then you think—?"

"I've a notion you may be seeing Injuns any time now, Starbuck, my lad!"

Something in his tone made my breath catch and I swung about. There, on top of the low table-land to the west, outlined against the sky, was a figure on horseback. The wind stirred the feathers of a headdress. *Indians!* A moment before, nothing but unbroken expanse of ridge line. I looked at my companion.

"Pierre — do you see?" The scout nodded grimly.

"Saw him a full thirty seconds ago. Where's your eyes, son?"

Another figure had joined the motionless horseman on the ridge, then a third.... I felt my heart thump, but my hands were steady. I had wondered how I would face the first real scare. Now here it was, and it wasn't so bad. In the mounting tension Old Chief Thrower seemed suddenly friendly and close and warm to the hand. With thumb upon gun cock and eyes straining, I waited for Pierre to call the turn.

"I reckon those boys are the answer to the arrow in your cow," he cried. "They've come to collect it, maybe. They'll collect more than that, as sure as my rifle shoots center!"

Behind us came the high

yells of the Indians.

Still the three Indians sat their ponies, sharply outlined against the sky, motionless, the sun glistening on their painted bodies and flashing points of light from their lanceheads.

"That horse of yours is about done in," Pierre muttered. "We'd better make tracks for that rock pile yonder and fight it out if we have to. They're probably only Pawnee scouts for some larger party. Maybe we won't have to fight."

The words had scarce left his lips when the three horsemen leaped to sudden life and action. Down the slope they poured, feathers flying, bodies bent, lashing at their ponies and yelling as they came.

Pierre leaped to Black Knight's back. "It's cache or lose ha'r, lad!" he shouted. "To that pile of rock, and hang on to your rifle for hoss and beaver!"

I sprang into saddle and together we raced for the precarious protection of that ledge of sandstone. Behind us came the high yells of the Indians in pursuit. We gained the rock and leaped to the ground.

"I'll hold 'em off while you hobble the animals," Pierre sang out. "Throw a hobble around their forelegs and look to your priming. We're not gone beaver yet!"

I stooped swiftly to obey, took a turn with the rawhide rope about the forelegs of the two horses — hobbled them tightly together. The Indians, screeching like demons, split and rode to right and left while they were still some two hundred yards from us. My hands trembled now with excitement as I raised Old Chief Thrower.

From the corner of his eye Pierre saw my nervousness and his voice rapped out: "Take it easy, son! Here's your first lesson in Indian fighting. Don't go firing your piece first crack out of the box. Remember you've only got one shot, and an empty gun's no use. You'll never have a chance to reload! Wait till you hear my gun. I've got two shots, remember. There's only three Injuns. So we've an even chance."

The Indians had swung their ponies in a wide circle and now they were dashing back toward us again, arrows whipped to the strings. With wild, high-pitched "Whoooop!" on they came, screeching like to split our eardrums. They had no stomach for facing loaded rifles at close range. They spent their energies in shout and action, in long-range insult and chance arrow. But each time as they wheeled and rode in swiftly toward us, they came a little closer.

Our horses were plunging and pulling at their hobbles, frightened with the din and clamor. But the hobbles held. Pierre threw a sharp word of command at the stallion and it quieted, stood taut and trembling. Pierre remained at ease, lean jaw tight-shut and out-thrust, watching the advance. This time the wild riders moved within range of rifle shot. Pierre whipped his two-shoot to position. I did the same.

Of single impulse the three Indians disappeared to the opposite side of their horses. It was astounding, the speed with which they accomplished the feat. Only the tip of a moccasin showing below their ponies' belly for a target! Closer in they came. Old Chief Thrower trembled in my hands. No use to pretend I wasn't scared. I was.

"Hold your fire!" Pierre warned.

"But——"

"Do as I tell you!" he flashed.

Back and forth the savages swung, closer — closer. . . . The manes and tails of their ponies, braided with bright cloth, streamed on the wind of their passage. In mounting excitement I found myself admiring the superb horsemanship of these savages; caught my breath when I saw them draw an arrow to the head in threat — then withhold it.

Suddenly one Indian, bolder than the others, wheeled like a flash of light and thundered in straight toward me. I saw the glint of his teeth and the white of his eyes. Should I fire? Uncertainty swept me. Should I. . . . His arrow was drawn to the head.

"Hold your fire!" came Pierre's shout.

I braced my feet, willed myself to stillness as the front sight of Old Chief Thrower came into line with that ferocious face. A whining *pinnnng!* The warrior had released his arrow. The shaft splintered against my rifle stock — stung my face with the fragments. At that second Pierre's rifle roared almost in my ear. The

Indian's pony reared, pawed the air, then sprawled at our feet, the red rider rolling in the dust. The horse pulled itself up and scampered over the plain, but the Indian lay where he had fallen, paunch-shot, still.

"*Ow-owgh! Ow-owgh!*" Pierre's high-pitched battle cry rang out above the tumult. As he wheeled to face the charge of the two remaining horsemen, he was all Mountain Man — savage fighting savage, eyes flashing, teeth bared.

Evidently these Indians didn't know the two-shoot gun and thought we'd be easy picking with only one shot left between us. In they raced. I saw their faces wild with heat of battle and lust for blood. Almost upon us. Now! Old Chief Thrower barked. There came a choked-off cry. A rearing horse. A second Indian pitched backward, writhing in the sand.... The third savage wheeled his horse with a motion of the knee — fitted an arrow to the string with deadly intent. Then it was that Pierre fired his second shot. It was his deadly joke.

We saw the Indian stagger, then rally. He dashed in toward his fallen brother. Before we had time to reload, he had swung the wounded man up to his pony's rump. Another second and the two savages were disappearing over the ridge. Only one figure, mute and still, remained to tell of this swift battle.

An arrow had ripped across Pierre's cheek, laying open the flesh to the bone. He dashed the blood from his eyes and bellowed forth his battle cry once again: "*Ow-owgh! Ow-owgh!*" Blood called for blood in the trapper's primitive creed. He was transformed in an instant into a man I had never seen; a lean animal, lion-strong, charged with a lust for revenge. He sprang toward the dead Indian, whipped knife from belt, hooked his fingers into the scalp lock. I caught the flash of steel as it worked and knew a sick feeling in my stomach's pit. Then he was wiping the blade across his thigh, and flung the reeking scalp back upon the body with contempt. I saw him break the bow and snap the arrows one by one, and hurl the pieces upon his enemy.

"Starve on the Ghost Trail!" he spat out. "Hyar's wolf meat, and proper kind!"

I looked on, finding no words. Strange it was to see a man swept at an instant's turn from civilization to savagery. But I knew that except for the grace of God and Pierre Leroux, that scalp might have been my own, dangling tonight from some Pawnee scalp pole.

"Guess we'll leave your buffalo for the wolves, too, Starbuck," the man said presently, quieter by now. "There'll be meat a-plenty in camp tonight, I reckon. But if we don't make tracks, it'll all be gone, if I'm any judge of sign."

Dark was closing in. I unhobbled the horses and we climbed into saddle. As we topped the sandhills, I looked back at the scene of our late battle. Dark forms were closing in. Wolves. . . . I shivered.

We rode on in silence, Pierre lost in his own thoughts. Was he, I wondered, pondering the strangeness of his life and nature? I wanted to ask how many miles I had come in pursuit of my buffalo, but I was not very proud of this day's showing and I held my peace.

The first star was blinking low overhead and the sky above the dark horizon was luminous with promise of an early moon. A faint breeze had sprung up and stirred the damp hair on my forehead. At last, crossing a ridge of sandstone, I saw the distant fires of the caravan and heard the far-off shouts of hungry men gorging themselves after the hunt. "Fools!" Pierre muttered under his breath. "I'll stake my hair the train's wide open to attack! If there's any more Pawnees where those three came from, they'll be around before morning."

His face was grim as we rode into camp, but nothing could dampen the ardor of the wagoners still flushed with the heat of their victorious hunt. Fires flared high. There were countless willing hands to prepare the feast. Hump roast and tenderloin sizzled on the spits. Fleshy ribs baked amid the coals. Intestines, turned inside-out, writhed like snakes on long sticks, while skillets bubbled with marrow and melting fat. Men were cracking marrowbones, guzzling the marrow — "trapper butter" as it was called, yellow and raw and packed with sustenance.

"Hyar's doin's, boys! Let's chaw!" shouted Sandy, dancing with delight. "I'm fair wolfish!" and he buried his teeth into a strip of tenderloin, half cooked, and the blood ran into his beard and dripped off his chin.

Appetites that couldn't wait the slow processes of cooking; men gorged on food half done. Zenas was stuffing down a yard of undercooked *boudins;* other men were dipping warmed liver into gall and relishing it with loud-smacking lips; others pulled half-raw flesh from simmering skillets and cursed the heat that burned their gullets even as they gorged. Faces thick with grease glistened in the firelight. Buckskins and hands reeked of it. The plainsman's orgy — the moment to which he looked forward with keenest anticipation; making him forget for the moment the privations and dangers of his violent life.

I slid wearily out of saddle and joined the feast. The smell of sizzling meat brought me sudden realization of my own hunger. Pierre shoved a pan of marrow and drippings toward me. "Mug on to this, lad!" he cried. "It'll put meat on your ribs, and make you shed water like a beaver!"

As the sharp edge of appetite dulled, the cries and grunts of the voracious men changed imperceptibly to sighs of repletion. They patted their paunches with deep satisfaction; unrolled their buffalo robes, and lay down to sleep for a while. Later they would awake and gorge themselves anew.

And out beyond the circle of the fires, piles of bones glistened in the light and wolves sat waiting in the outer darkness, their eyes like green, unblinking signals in the night.

CHAPTER XI

MESSAGES IN THE SKY

OFF TO the north we saw a range of hills rising gradually from the plain. Higher and more rugged it loomed as it approached the Trail, reaching its climax in an ominous cliff of yellow sandstone. Pawnee Rock — magnified by mirages until it towered out of all proportion to its actual height.

"More blood's been spilled thar than any other spot on the plains," mused Sandy Smith as we drew slowly toward it. "More topknot parties between the Injuns themselves as well as with the whites."

What he said was true. In its sinister way, Pawnee Rock was as notorious along the Santa Fe Trail as were Chimney Rock and Courthouse Rock on the emigrant trail up the Platte. From this eagle's lookout Indian scouts could discern a wagon or pack train many miles away, and the red man's smoke signals would call forth painted warriors to battle long hours before the crawling wagons had reached the neighborhood of the rock itself. You must remember that on the Santa Fe Trail men learned these facts by bitter experience, and news traveled on the wings of the wind. The veriest greenhorn was well aware of what might be looked for in this ill-fated spot.

Two trails passed Pawnee Rock — one north and south; the other east and west. The former was used by the Indians themselves as they pillaged the country of the Kiowas and Comanches, the Pawnees and the Cheyennes. It was crossed by the east-and-west trail of the covered wagons, deep-cut into the plain. Over this country of sand and sun there seemed to hang a tenseness, a portent of things about to happen. A rattlesnake felt it and knew, for he roused from his watchful basking on a rock to glide with warning rattle into shelter. Even the sand cranes grew restless and took to the upper air long before their accustomed hour, screaming down their protest at our intrusion. Heat waves like flickering tongues shimmered high into the air, there to quiver and expire.

As we bore down upon this famous landmark, a feeling of nervous tension began to make itself felt throughout the company. Tempers grew shorter. Men broke into high-pitched laughter for no apparent reason, then stifled it abruptly. Here it was that I saw an extraordinary conflict take place between two men — so strange that I must relate it, for I have never encountered its like before or since.

There was in our company a man named Allison. In some subtle way, even before you knew his story, you sensed that he was marked apart from other men as a white man would have been among savages. It was not that in his outward aspect he was so different; it was, rather, that you felt something strange and secret about him, some terrible experience perhaps, which had marked him apart from his fellows and set its stamp, like a brand, upon him. Allison was small-framed and rather stooped, neither young nor old. His pale eyes, sunken in deep sockets, looked as if they had gazed upon things too terrible for the eyes of man to see. There was a hint of madness in his look, yet he went about his business quietly enough, paying no attention to anyone, and never speaking. In fact, it was his very silence which brought him first to my attention, marking him out in this company of roistering and profane bullwhackers.

After some days I had remarked to Sandy about this silence, and the old trapper cleared up the mystery.

"Good reason why Allison cain't cuss like white folks," he

chuckled. "He was captured by the 'Rees once, up on the Missoury. They cut his tongue out. No one knows how he ever got away from 'em, cause nacherally he cain't talk. An' he cain't write nuther. Ain't much he kin do, I reckon, 'cept handle mules. Seems to have a knack with dumb critters." He chuckled again with all the plainsman's indifference to human suffering.

Locked within a prison of silence, this mute seemed to move through some inner world of his own, and it was a fact that he possessed uncanny skill with the livestock, managing the most exasperating animal without show of force.

Jake Bailey, looking about for someone weaker than himself to torment, had made the mute a target for many a rude gibe ever since we left Council Grove. But if the little man was conscious of it, he gave no outward sign. What precipitated their open conflict, I never knew nor sought to learn. But it happened one day while we were nooning it, in the very shadow of bloody Pawnee Rock – the pent-up tension burst in our midst just like a shot from a cannon.

We heard a roar, scarcely human, rip from Bailey's throat, splintering the hot, charged air.

"You keep away from the bean pot, you skulkin' dummy!" he shouted, livid with rage, "or I'll wring your blasted neck fer you!"

The two men, so opposite in all attributes, faced one another across the camp fire. Bailey's bullet head was thrust forward on his thick neck, his fists clenching and unclenching. He was brave indeed before this slight, haunted ghost of a man who lacked power both of muscle and of speech.

Allison stood there squarely upon both feet, his head thrown back slightly, his haunted eyes steady as he faced his tormentor, while Bailey poured forth a string of foul oaths, deluging the mute with vituperation – ugly words that hissed and darted as a snake's tongue. There was something about that silent wreck of a man as he stood there, something poignant and unconquerable, that gripped us like a hand. Perhaps it was his eyes – so rock-steady and unwavering. They pinned Bailey like lance points. We watched, speechless, tranced with the drama of this strange conflict – watched Bailey as he raised his fists to strike, caught the blow in

mid-air; the sledge-hammer blow that never fell. Something in the rocklike impregnability of the mute seemed to throw off Bailey's attack as a shield might turn aside a spear. Bailey could not meet the steady, unafraid gaze. His own eyes flickered and darted snakelike over the little man's shoulder, never coming to rest upon those twin lance points of courage.

"You skulkin' dummy! " he shouted again. "You—"

The words died in his throat. He mumbled ... made one final attempt to strike a blow. Then his hands fell to his sides. Still mumbling, he turned away. He was beaten. It was an extraordinary experience to see that strange battle won without a blow struck or a word spoken, no weapon of defense but a pair of straight eyes and some unconquerable power of spirit. It was a victory that was to have far-reaching results. Something in Bailey's brutish nature was undermined and put to rout. His bluster took on the note of a whine. Every man despised him; and, it seemed, he was coming to despise himself.

We knew a sort of tense relief when the caravan got into motion once again, and we rode on doggedly, our hands gripping our rifles, sweat running down into our eyes, and dust choking our throats. We scanned the skyline for some hint of shadowy horsemen until our eyeballs ached with the strain.

"Thar's brown skin about," Sandy threw out at random, "else why has beaver got tails, I'm askin'?"

"Aye," Zenas Kent assented. "I see a moccasin track this mornin'."

"Whose sign?" Sandy wanted to know.

"Dunno. Pawnee, mebbe. The devil had planted hoof in the mud, accidental-like, gittin' 'cross the crick."

"Fresh sign?" I asked with quickened interest.

"Mornin'-fresh, I reckon. Thar'll be powder burnt yit, travelin' with this pack o' green scalps!"

"Reckon yo're right," muttered Sandy darkly. "My ha'r feels loose. Was the brown skin afoot or ahoss, Zenas?"

"Afoot," came the reply. "But when an Injun goes out afoot, he's layin' to come back ahoss, or I never lifted ha'r!"

There hadn't always been bad feeling between the Indian and the white man. Before Lewis and Clark's expedition to the Far West, a traveler could cross the plains from the Missouri to Santa Fe or up to the headwaters of the Platte with assurance of food and sanctuary in any Indian village as long as he behaved himself. He was as safe on the prairie as on the streets of Boston. The antagonism between white and red developed slowly on the Trail, but once under way it swept onward until it raged with the fury of a prairie fire. The burden of the blame rests rightly upon the shoulders of the white man. There's no use glossing over that fact.

Perhaps to comprehend this point fully, it is necessary to understand something of the buffalo's economic importance to the Indian; since it was primarily the buffalo which opened the bitter wedge between the two races. The buffalo's hide, tanned and decorated, was used to make the lodges of the Indian. Blankets and covering came from the same source. The beaver, the antelope, the bear, and the wolf each contributed its small share; but these were not a dependable source, while the buffalo in its countless numbers and predictable migrations could always be relied upon. Picket ropes and lariats, harness for the pony travois and dogsled; spoons and rude knives, needles and many a useful implement; horns to decorate headdresses; skulls to make masks for the medicine men – these were but some of the uses to which the buffalo was put.

Most important of all, the animal meant food and sustenance, without which the Indian must perish and die. Buffalo meat was the red man's principal article of diet. Dried, it could be kept indefinitely; mashed into a pulp and mixed with chokeberries or wild plums and packed into *parflêches* (containers of buffalo hide) tight-sealed with suet, it could be kept for years on end, a reliable source of food when all others failed. The marrow was used for medicine, as well as for greasing and oiling rifles. The gall was a tonic. In fact, there was scarcely a point in the entire scheme of Indian living where the buffalo did not play some part, great or small. Is it to be wondered at, then, that the Indian refused to countenance wasteful killing of this all-important animal?

Is it cause for surprise that when the white man began his senseless mass slaughter of the buffalo, the Indian should have looked on first with alarm, then with furious resentment?

Now, in 1846, with the caravans at greatest peak, the Indian felt that the whole white nation must be moving into this time-honored land. To make matters worse, there existed a certain type of white man who felt it an enjoyable and harmless sport to take a pot shot at some friendly redskin. The Indian was not slow to retaliate in kind. Thus a feeling had grown up between the two races which nothing but bloodshed or annihilation could ever hope to wipe out.

Pierre Leroux knew the Indian as well as it was possible for a white man to know him, and he was but too well acquainted with the nervous greenhorn's propensity for shooting at the wrong time and thus turning what might be a peaceable parley into bloody slaughter. For this reason, he hurried the wagon train past the sinister shadow of Pawnee Rock, hoping to make Ash Creek before sundown.

A cry from the head of the train sped back along the nerves of the twin columns, throwing the men into a state of high excitement. From the dark summit of Pawnee Rock a column of ominous smoke was rising.... Straight and tall it lifted in the windless air. As its volume increased, a series of short puffs interrupted its ascent. Indians were writing their messages in the sky.

"Makin' smoke talk!" muttered Sandy. "Tellin' their bloody brothers back in the hills how many horses we got, an' rifles, too. Reckon they're even tellin' 'em the color of our ha'r!"

"I knew they was brown skin t'other side of Ash Crick," Zenas Kent broke in. "I had me a dream last night about a talkin' beaver, and that's shore sign. I disremember what that beaver said, but it was bad medicine, all right. And I says to myself we're about due fer a topknot party, and when I woke up, I was a-shake with a fevery chill."

Pierre came galloping down the length of the columns, shouting orders right and left. "Hurry it up, men! Across the creek and corral! We may be having visitors!"

Whips lashed out. Men shouted. Oxen and mules strained their utmost. We were more experienced now in handling our cumbersome wagons and we moved down the slope and across the stream as speedily as possible. Fortunately, we struck no snags, and no man needed to be urged. When we went into corral on the other side of Ash Creek, it was the most carefully formed fortress we had yet contrived. We found that the wagons of Jedediah Aiken and his family had camped here but a short time before us, for their sign was fresh. One of their horses had died and already the buzzards were harrying the beast's bones. Here also we found the fresher sign of men and many horses: Indians.... The Aikens were being closely followed up the Trail. Pierre's mouth was grim and we avoided one another's eyes, not voicing the thought that struck at our entrails.

This time our corral had been formed not as usual in a sheltered bottom, but on top of a rise where we could overlook the country around us. The afternoon was well along by this time and we let the animals graze under heavy guard until dusk, then they were driven into the enclosure where the wagons, tongue to tail gate, presented a fortress-like wall. Still we had seen no more Indians, but our horses were picketed close to where the men were to sleep — short-line pickets for emergency use.

We ate our supper silently and, while still it was dusk, extinguished our fires. The memory of the speaking smoke lay uppermost in every man's mind, though none would admit it. It was hard to believe that this rolling, open country swarmed with Indians, always just out of sight yet fully aware of our presence, the number of our wagons, our horses, and our men. A train of twenty wagons and forty-five men, no matter how well armed and mounted, would be hard put to defend itself against a large war party. Only by extreme vigilance could we hope to keep our hair.

At first it seemed nothing.... A coyote, perhaps, pausing furtively on the hilltop. Then — there it was! Feathers cutting into the sky. Where a second before there had been but empty space, now there was an Indian on his horse, the last rays of the sun glinting on the bronze of his body and on his painted pony.

"Injuns!" The cry swept through the corral like wild fire. *"Injuns!"*

Where there had been one Indian, a hundred materialized out of the earth itself, three hundred yards away, perhaps, silhouetted against the coppery sky.

"They're 'Rapahoes!" a voice shouted.

"Nope — Pawnees!" Zenas Kent threw out.

And Pawnees they were — as events proved.

"Wa-al, boys," drawled Sandy Smith, "run yore bullets and fill yore horns. Hyar's a topknot party, else why was brown skins made?"

"Hold your fire, men!" shouted Pierre, riding swiftly about the corral. "Any man who takes a shot without my order will answer to me!"

"Give 'em lead and Green River, say I!" growled Sandy. "I'm gittin' fâché, pamperin' redskins thisaway."

"We'll do nothing of the sort," Pierre rapped back at him. "Maybe we can settle this thing without bloodshed."

Black Jack stood beside his wagon, his rifle Tipped in hands which showed white at the knuckles. Bailey hovered nervously at his elbow. "Do you think they mean business, Leroux?" the captain asked in a dry voice. Bailey moistened his lips with his tongue.

"An Indian always means business, of one sort or another," Pierre answered coldly. "They may be open to parley. You and I will go out and meet them, Bannock."

A slow red flushed up about the captain's ears. "Take Smith, or — or Starbuck," he muttered shortly, turning away.

"All right!" Pierre threw him a look of withering contempt. "Come on, Starbuck — and leave that rifle behind!"

I handed Old Chief Thrower to Sandy and brought Hawk Eye into line with Black Knight, filled with excitement. My heart was thumping at my ribs. Hawk Eye was as restless and jumpy as a cat, and fortunately the necessity for controlling her displaced such nervousness as I felt. We paused for a second at the outer edge of the corral. In that second, the motionless line of savages on the ridge quickened to life. They came circling down the hill with superb horsemanship, the sun throwing back a refracted glitter of steel and bronze.

Pierre turned his head to shout, "Keep us covered with your rifles, men, but don't fire unless I give the signal."

Then we rode out through an opening in the corral toward the advancing savages. When the distance between us was a hundred yards, Pierre made the motion to halt, and we sat quietly while the savages yanked their mounts to their haunches, stirring up a mighty dust. Pierre signaled for two of them to ride forward. There was a moment of conference in the enemy ranks, then two chiefs trotted toward us on their paint-bedaubed ponies.

Pierre raised one hand, palm out. I followed suit. The red men raised each a hand in similar gesture, then waited silently, without motion, the sun beating down on their black heads and their horses' heaving sides. The scout and I rode forward and halted within ten paces of the chiefs. Two white men, two Indians, facing each other on their ponies across a distance thirty feet in width and an antipathy as wide as the sky. Behind the two chiefs a hundred lanceheads bristled, and feathers of as many war bonnets stirred in the breeze. Behind Pierre and me, twenty wagons presented a compact circle, while the barrels of forty rifles glistened over wagon tongues and wheel spokes, primed and steady for our defense.

Out of the excitement of the moment one detail struck me: two pair of eyes, black as obsidian, savage and lusterless, gauging my strength, my nerve. I saw them take in Hawk Eye and spark with covetousness. Erect and motionless the savages sat their ponies bareback, naught but a rawhide guide rope hitched about the lower jaw. I saw muscles as smoothly rippling as those of a coiled snake. They were racers stripped for speed and action. They waited for us to speak. And Pierre waited, with a patience matching their own. It was a tense silence, charged with gunpowder, awaiting the spark.

At length one of the Indians broke the silence. He spoke in a mixture of Spanish and Shoshone dialect — that common tongue of the plains country — and amplified his speech with the sweeping gestures of the sign language, so simple for the initiate to read.

I found that I had little difficulty in following the gist of the man's talk. Pierre, of course, was as familiar with it as with his own tongue.

The chief's voice quivered with suppressed anger as he spoke: "The braves of my tribe do not welcome the white man in this country," were his opening words. "This land belongs to the Pawnee, and the buffalo is his meat."

"The white man does not want this land, O Chief," Pierre answered easily. "It is but a place of passage for him. He does not linger. The grass nourishes his horse for a day, and the buffalo are as many as the blades of grass."

"Pawnee land, this!" the Indian reiterated with stubborn insistence. "The Apache dares not enter it nor the Arapaho nor the Kiowa, nor yet the Comanche. Is the white man better than they, that we should welcome him?"

"We have been told by the Apache and the Kiowa "that this land is theirs," Leroux answered imperturbably. "Whom shall we believe, O Chief — the Apache, the Kiowa, or the Pawnee?"

The eyes of the two Indians glittered with swift anger and the chief thumped his bare chest with one hand.

"It is the land of the Pawnee!" he shouted defiantly. "My braves burn with anger at the white man's presence."

"And my men burn with anger because their horses are stolen by the Indian," Pierre came back at him, "and they hold anger against me, their chief, because I will not let them fire upon my friends, the Indians. My heart is with you, O Chief, and there are many presents in my wagons for your braves."

The two dark faces did not soften. The chief answered, "The white man speaks with the tongue and not with the heart. Have you powder and lead and whisky for my braves?"

"I have powder and lead and whisky for the chiefs," the scout replied meaningly. "And paint and beads and cloth for your braves."

The Indians conversed hurriedly in low tones for a minute. Then: "It is well, O White Chief. Send over your presents!"

At Pierre's order I rode back to the corral to carry the word. A keg of whisky was rolled out into the open; a bale of scarlet cloth;

a box of vermilion and beads; a small keg of powder and half a dozen bars of lead.

"Have your braves dismount and come on foot for these gifts," Pierre threw out in a tone which brooked no nonsense.

The transaction was carried out with dispatch. The Indians transferred the gifts to their horses' backs. Then the chief spoke once again.

"Listen, O White Chief," he proclaimed. "Up the river, past The Caches, you will find a large war party of Kiowas. They have many rifles — many as the hairs of a dog's back. My braves are filled with gratitude for the white chief's presents. They will accompany your wagons, and fight for you if need be. The Kiowa is the enemy of the white man, and of the Pawnee as well!"

Pierre protested, but there was nothing for it in the end but to accept. The chief gave the order and his braves fell into a line parallel with our corral; picketed their horses and lighted fires.

"I don't like it," Pierre muttered. "And I've never seen an Injun do just this before. Either he attacks or he stays out of sight — waiting to attack."

Bannock was furious. The sinister escort, camped but a hundred yards from our corral, frayed his nerves, as indeed it did the nerves of us all. It was possible that the chief had spoken the truth — maybe there *was* a large party of Kiowas waiting for us in ambush at The Caches. Suppose they should be joined by the Pawnees.... But there was no help for it.

No man slept that night. Of only one thing could we be certain — the Indians would not attack before dawn.

The night was interminable, but when the sun rose next morning to light this oppressive world, every Indian had disappeared! Only the ashes of their camp fires were left to mark their passage. But somehow their stealthy departure held more of subtle menace than had their presence.

CHAPTER XII

CimARRON CROSSING

ASH CREEK, Pawnee Fork, Little Coon, and Big Coon creeks —
on to the lower crossing of the Arkansas. The grass grew ever
shorter and more sparse, the county more hostile and forbidding
as we plodded along the north bank of the Arkansas toward The
Caches. We went into camp near this famous landmark, wondering if the war party of Kiowas that our late friends, the Pawnees,
had warned us about would be waiting for us. But if they knew
our presence, they gave no sign.

That noon two strangers rode into camp. White men, caked
with dust, lean with hunger. Free trappers they claimed to be,
returning from Santa Fe to Independence. They had crossed by
the Dry Route, and confirmed the alarming word that large bands
of Kiowas and Comanches were on the warpath. The two men had
been despoiled of their packs and had barely managed to escape
with their topknots. The unprecedented dryness of the season,
they declared, rendered the *Jornada* a veritable inferno. Indians
were occupying all the water holes, and sure trouble lay in wait
for any wagon train that ventured to the opposite bank of
Cimarron Crossing.

"You'll be gone beaver," one of the men declared to Pierre
Leroux. "I've known Injuns goin' on thirty year, but I never seen 'em
in the state they's in now. Out fer hide an' ha'r, or this coon don't
know pore bull from fat cow. It's the greasers what's stirrin' 'em
up against the Yankees. Fillin' 'em up with promises and Red Eye!"

"Nonsense!" carne Bannock's angry answer. He was always brave
when no danger threatened. "We're well armed and mounted."

"So be the brown skins," came the trapper's imperturbable reply.

"You'd do well to listen to this man, Bannock," Pierre threw in. "What if the Bent's Fort route *does* take a few days longer? You'll stand to lose more than time if there's all the brown skins on the Trail that this man claims."

Jake Bailey was hovering nervously at Bannock's elbow. He whispered something in an undertone to his captain. Bannock nodded – and changed the direction of the conversation. "What's the feeling in Santa Fe toward Americans?" he demanded with seeming irrelevance.

"Gor', man! Didn't you know?" asked the astounded trapper. "War's on!'"

Bannock paled. "War – declared?" he countered, fingering his belt with nervous hands. Bailey's jaw dropped. "Has – has Kearny entered Santa Fe yet?'"

"Nope!" replied the trader. "Kearny's got 'em guessin'. They don't know whar he is, or whar he figgers to strike fust. Some say he's camped jest above Bent's Fort, waitin' fer the proper moment to ripen."

Pierre stepped forward decisively. "That simplifies everything, Bannock," he asserted. "We'll take the Bent's Fort route. If Kearny *is* there, we'll follow his army into Santa Fe."

Bannock's eyes narrowed and he stiffened. "Oh, no we won't, Leroux," he snapped. "This is my outfit, please remember. I'm not following any army anywhere. I'm taking my wagons into Santa Fe before Kearny gets there!"

"You'll be clapped in jail and your goods confiscated – if you ever reach Santa Fe," Pierre warned.

I caught a meaning look flash between Bannock and Bailey. Black Jack smiled craftily. "I don't think so," he replied softly.

Suddenly, fragments of things, like bits of a Chinese puzzle, began to fall into a unified design in my mind. Remembered scraps of sentences; mysterious conversations between Bailey and his captain which had terminated abruptly at my approach; that scene in Roybal's saddle shop – once again I could hear Bannock's voice saying, "Five thousand guns, Sabino——" I had almost forgotten

how strange that partnership between Bannock and the Mexican saddle maker had seemed. But now it was all as plain as the back of your hand, and I cursed myself for my thick-headedness. *Of course* Bannock wouldn't take the Bent's Fort route and follow Kearny's army into Santa Fe! Of course he wouldn't — for those twelve wagons of his packed five thousand rifles and lead and powder for the Mexican army! Doubtless Governor Armijo was paying Black Jack a king's ransom for this ammunition. An American could have transacted a commission of this sort in the States without rousing suspicion, while a Mexican would have been caught red-handed at the first hint of war. What a fine specimen of American Bannock had proved himself, selling out his country to Manuel Armijo! My heart grew hard with loathing for the man.

I could scarce contain myself. It seemed to me that I couldn't wait to convey my suspicions — nay, my convictions, to Pierre Leroux. True, my theory was built upon a web of small circumstances. But I *knew* that I was right. Bannock was a traitor running ammunition to the enemies of his country. It was late afternoon before I could speak with Pierre without being observed. We were watering the stock, and under cover of the commotion I remarked as casually as I could:

"Pierre, do you know what the merchandise is in Bannock's wagons?" My voice trembled with suppressed excitement.

The scout turned toward me, and his eyes widened. "You *are* slow, young 'un! Rifles — of course!"

I was dashed. "Then you've known all along, ever since we left Independence?"

"I've known a goodly bit, since long before I left Independence."

The horses were sinking their muzzles in the stream, breathing gustily. Men swatted at flies and wiped the sweat from their foreheads. Bannock and his henchman were nowhere to be seen.

Pierre moved close up to me and his voice dropped almost to a whisper. "Listen, Starbuck: I told you once I might need your help. If — if anything should happen to me, there are things that someone else must know. You thought I was joking when I said I'd been to Washington and broken fast with President Polk. But I wasn't.

The President sent for me. An order for five thousand rifles had come to the Government's attention; five thousand to be shipped to Independence to a man who was not a trader; a man with a bad-smelling record: Bannock. The War Department pricked up its ears. I've known this country out here ever since I was your age; my father's a friend of Secretary of War, Mr. Marcy — that's why I was called in. Before I'd been back in Independence a week, a stroke of luck threw me in Bannock's way. He hired me on as scout just what I'd hoped for."

"But where did Roybal come in?'"

"He was the go-between for Armijo. The whole plan was Roybal's. He'd been kicked out of New Mexico and he hoped to get back in the Governor's good graces. Listen, son — there's not another man in this outfit I'd dare to trust with this except you. But there's some things I'm not telling even you, because — well, because it might not be healthy for you to know too much if things go wrong. Before we reach Santa Fe, you and I have got to be running this caravan, and Bailey and Bannock will be trussed up like cooking-fowls. Maybe Armijo won't fight after all. Polk's got a rich American trader named James Magoffin in Santa Fe now. Money talks with Armijo's kind, and maybe Magoffin can buy him off. In any case, we've got to prevent Bannock's taking these wagons into Santa Fe before Kearny gets there with his army, savvy?"

"Yes!" I whispered back, thrilling to the excitement of all this intrigue, and like to burst with pride over the confidence which Pierre was placing in me.

"I don't dare say any more about the Bent's Fort Route," the scout went on, "for Bannock is suspicious enough as it is. If he guessed the whole truth, my life wouldn't be worth a coyote's. So it's the Dry Route across the Cimarron for us, my lad. And maybe the Comanches will take things out of our hands, and those wagons will never reach Santa Fe anyway, with our help or without it."

"I heard Bannock tell Sabino Roybal that all he wanted was a guide across the Cimarron, and that once in sight of Santa Fe—"

"I know. He *does* need a guide, and he plans to shoot me in the back once the need is past. But before that day comes, you and I

are going to see to it that Mister Bannock is in no position to draw bead on anybody. Look sharp! Here comes Bailey!"

We fell into a dissembling chatter about the Trail as Bailey rode his horse to water. It was ludicrous to see the man cock his ears to catch the gist of our talk, and the clumsiness with which he tried to conceal his intention.

On the march again, on toward the fateful Cimarron Crossing. The stock eased as they reached a rounded slope of land beside the wide river. The afternoon had been cloudy with a promise of rain, and now with approaching dusk, a wind stirred up out of somewhere, faint but grateful as it touched our damp bodies. Far ahead through the gathering gloom we could just make out the red glow of a camp fire, and our interest quickened as we prodded our tired stock to further effort. A camp fire – must mean white men.

"Reckon we've caught up with the Aikens at last," muttered Sandy. "Thought their sign was powerful fresh this mornin'. Reckon they had sense enough left to wait fer us at the Crossin'."

But as we drew nearer, Sandy's garrulity ceased while a hush fell over the wagon train. What we had taken for a camp fire was the smoldering embers of two charred wagons, the tongues, grotesquely enough, unburned and pointing across the river toward the *Jornada*. Four dark mounds that once had been horses were scattered about. And over the wagon tongues – our hearts grew chill at the sight – three forms, white and mute. As we stared, the gentle breeze ruffled the feathers of a host of embedded arrows.... A shred of blue gingham flapped idly where it had caught on a bush.

Sandy was right – we had caught up with the Aikens at last. A weight of terrible oppression hung over us. For the first time the ever-lurking peril stalking at our elbows was real. We had known these people, sat with them at their camp fires, eaten of their food. Now they were gone, cut down by a merciless hand. The *Jornada del Muerto* – the Journey of Death... no longer a nebulous trapper's tale. So it had proved for Jedediah Aiken and his family. So it might prove for us all.

We were silent as we went about our preparations for the night. A hush muted every voice. Men set down their trappings on the

hard earth softly, almost as if they feared to disturb the dead whom they had just laid to rest. The sun had disappeared without leaving trace of its passage; no sign of red or gold flushing the western sky, only sullen slate banks heavy-hanging and low over the earth. I thought of Manuel who had disappeared so strangely, Manuel with his guitar and his gay songs. Had he managed to win through or had he, too ... I broke the thought. Unconsciously, I found myself facing out across the ring of corralled wagons toward the south — into the *Jornada.* What lay on the other side of the river for us? Would Pierre be able to work out his plan and seize command of the train before it entered Santa Fe? Or would the Comanches take matters into their own hands?

"Guard duty!" cracked the command

We leaped to our rifles.

The next morning found us still encamped at Cimarron Crossing. Pierre and Zenas Kent had forded the river to scout for Indian sign among the treacherous sandhills on the other side of the Arkansas. The day was hot and sultry, the sky leaden with threat of thunderstorm. Flashes of heat lightning fretted the horizon. The men were frankly nervous and irritable as they went about their camp chores, while the stock was jumpy and hard to manage. Bannock fumed against what he considered an unnecessary delay. There was no doubt that he had been greatly upset by the news that Kearny was lying in wait to march upon Santa Fe. He came stamping up while I was helping Bailey with the noon mess and exploded loudly enough for all to hear.

"Indians!" he scoffed. "I've heard plenty about 'em, but the only ones we've run into were tame enough. Holding us up this way — just to see if there's a few redskins ahead. Of course there's Indians on the Cimarron! What's Leroux think this is — a holiday?"

"Looks to me like he's afeered of Injuns," Bailey jeered. "What are rifles for?"

"That's what Jedediah Aiken said, back in Council Grove," I

reminded him. Fools! Did they want to walk open-eyed into ambush and leave our scalps dangling from some bucks' belts? I checked myself before I could say more.

Pierre rode into camp early that afternoon, covered with dust and worn-looking and weary. Even the mighty Black Knight held his head lower than he usually did. Zenas, too, looked done in, his horse spent.

"Out with those fires!" Pierre commanded.

"What the devil?" protested Bailey. "How're we goin' to cook? This crossin's as safe as a prayer meetin'. Have we got to set here all night on empty bellies?"

"Put those fires out and keep them out!" Pierre thundered, taking a step toward Bailey. The latter retreated hastily and, albeit grumbling and reluctant, began to throw sand on the fires.

"Aren't you being overcautious, Leroux?" Black Jack demanded superciliously. "After all—"

"After all, I know more about this country than you do, Bannock," the scout snapped tersely.

The captain flushed with anger, but he controlled himself and asked, "See anything on the Trail ahead?"

"Plenty."

"What?"

"Smoke."

"Smoke? You mean — a prairie fire?"

"No. Signal fires. Listen, Bannock — in ordinary times I'd say roll out and give 'em what they're looking for. But this isn't an ordinary year. You know that as well as I do. Every tribe is out for blood and scalps. After all — we're only twenty wagons. For the last time — take the Bent's Fort route."

"We've been over that, Leroux," Bannock came back angrily. "You want me to go three hundred miles out of my way, and waste God knows how many days, just because you saw some smoke signals in the desert?"

"That's right!" Pierre shot at him.

"Well — listen to this, Mister Leroux!" Black Jack walked up under Pierre's nose, his eyes flashing dangerously, his jaw set. "I'm

the boss of this outfit; don't forget that. And you're just the scout. If I listened to you, I'd never get to Santa Fe!"

"Just what is the pressing hurry, Bannock?" the scout asked pointedly. He nodded his head toward the wagons: "Merchandise won't spoil. You can sell it in Santa Fe the year round."

Bannock folded his arms across his chest and his lips compressed in a tight line. "That's my business," he ground out. "Once for all — we're taking the Dry Route!"

Pierre shrugged. "All right, my friend. And you're walking straight into a pack of trouble. Maybe more than just trouble. But I reckon you've got it coming to you. We'd better get going then. Catch up! Catch up!" he shouted to the wagoners who had been standing about during the altercation.

The corral sprang into life. As I saddled Hawk Eye, I threw a glance across the river. Mexico ... not different to look upon than this land we had been traversing: just low sandhills bordering a river white with alkali. But beyond those sandhills lay sixty miles of desert between us and the nearest water; every rise sheltering, perhaps, a red horde which would sweep us to destruction.

The Arkansas had to be crossed at a rush, for its bottom was treacherous with quicksands that would suck down wagon or animal if it were allowed to pause for a second. During the next two hours to come, the stream was churned to a foam with oxen and mules struggling under the cracking whips and the curses of the drivers.

At last all the wagons were across and the loose stock as well, and I was free to make the crossing myself. I spurred Hawk Eye into the rushing water. Most horses are good swimmers, but not many of them like it. Hawk Eye was no exception. She behaved toward every stream as if it were her first.

It was the one trick she had which never failed to try my patience. A swimming horse needs all the freedom you can give it. If you're ever called upon to swim the Arkansas, Reader, loosen your cinches and skin off your bridle, and get a good mane hold. More than one rider has drowned himself and his mount by pulling his horse over.

Once on the farther bank, we stretched out over the hills in our customary formation, every man with his rifle primed and ready for instant action. Water casks had been filled, and our own saddle flasks as well, and we must make as much distance before nightfall as possible. Sixty miles stretched ahead without a drop of water for man or animal except what we could carry, and the miles ahead were more important than those we left behind.

On we plodded, straight into the *Jornada del Muerto*. Bannock rode within the canvas-shaded protection of his wagon. Pierre at the head of the column was grim and silent, his dark eyes roving restlessly, searching the horizon. The wagons drew as close together as possible. The men were silent, strained. As the long afternoon wore to a close, a sense of fear, nameless, intangible, made itself felt throughout the company. Men were afraid to meet one another's eyes. Afraid to be afraid.

"Mebbe Leroux was right," they began to mutter in an undertone. "Mebbe we should a-taken the Bent's Fort route."

Black Jack heard, and his face grew white and tense. The wagons creaked on. Wheels rolled. Oxen strained, their tongues lolling from their thirsty mouths. No living thing appeared on that vast and undulating plain. Heat shimmered and danced before our aching eyes, while off to the west, a long low line of gray bluffs grew dark as the afternoon waned.

We went into camp and carried out our accustomed chores in

a tense silence. It was as if some portent of evil closed in upon us driven by a thousand miles of space. Through rents in the low hanging clouds the stars looked down, balefully, as if they knew and watched, and held their breath. The sparse, dry grama grass rustled over the plain to the touch of the dying wind, a sound ominous with some premonition of peril. The long-drawn bay of a wolf shivered across the air, silencing the sharp yelp of the coyotes. What shapes of darkness might be lying ahead, seen only by the unseen? Only the hours as they unrolled would tell.

Dawn of the next day found us already plodding onward, deeper and deeper into the *Jornada*. Ours was a trail that led from emptiness to emptiness, and we were but pygmies moving in procession across a limitless void. As the hours advanced, we found that the horses and cattle were wearing to bad condition. We dared not give them much of our meager supply of water, for no man knew what to expect and every precious drop must be hoarded against the unforseen. There was no faintest stir of breeze. The light had turned to a burnished glare — nothing that lived appeared to our scorched vision. Heat veils shimmered upward in shapes of delirium. The ridge of far-off bluffs to the west lifted suddenly to gigantic proportions magnified by the crazy mirage.

There was only the notion of our horses, the endless miles, heat, thirst. And the wagons creaked and the wheels rolled....

Jornada del Muerto — perhaps no route in the world has been

more marked by deadly ambushes, despite the fact that the plain
is as level as a floor and boasts no growth taller than grama grass.
In the days of some ancient eruption, a flow of lava had covered
the surface of the plain many feet deep; a later disturbance had
broken this crust into vast ledges, some of them running for many
miles in length. Thus were natural ambushes formed, behind
which thousands of Indians could have lurked unseen, ready to
spring forth to do battle. Our trail led through this treacherous
region, sometimes so close to these ledges that no safeguard was
possible at such deadly short range.

By late afternoon we went into bivouac, the grass so meager
that it was scarcely filling for the stock, Black Jack had been riding around the camp, and now he came dashing up on his gelding, gesticulation excitedly, a strained look on his face.

"Leroux! he cried. "There's smoke there to the west!"

"That so? Pierre answered laconically. "What manner of smoke?
A column of it, like – say – a camp fire?"

"No! came Bannock's breathless answer. "A – a series of puffs!"

"Hmmm – I've been seeing those all day. I believe I mentioned
it before, Mister Bannock."

"You think—?"

"Indians, my friend, just over the rise."

A murmur rose from the men's throats, merging into a single
sound, giving articulation to the unease that lay upon their spirits,
We all knew that there were Indians off there to the west, yet we
had shoved the knowledge to the back of our minds, refusing to
nourish the thought.

Pierre threw up his head suddenly, a grim smile cracking his
lips. His arm pointed outward in a swift gesture, and all eyes followed his rigid finger.

"And there, Bannock," he cried, "they are!"

It was Sandy's voice that broke the frozen hush. "Gawd!" he
breathed. "*Injuns!* Millions of 'em!"

CHAPTER XIII

THE ATTACK

A MULTITUDE of feathered horsemen had sprung up out of the earth itself. One second — emptiness. The next, painted bodies and brandishing weapons seen through clouds of brassy dust.

"Comanches!" The terrible word shivered throughout the company.

Pierre shook his head. "Kiowas, I'd say at a guess. Probably the same outfit that massacred the Aiken train back yonder. They've had a taste of blood and they want more!"

Black Jack's face drained of color. Hadn't — hadn't we better double back on our trail?" The words were wrung through his white lips.

"No chance for that, Captain Bannock," Pierre laughed.

"Do — do you really think they mean trouble?" Bannock's voice was thin and scarcely audible.

"You can bet your scalp they do, Bannock," came the scout's reassuring answer. "An Indian always means trouble — when he outnumbers his foe ten to one."

"I — wouldn't it be wiser for us to take a chance and turn back?" the captain stammered.

Suddenly the half-light was alive with racing figures.

"You fool!" Pierre shot at him. "We're in fighting formation now. Once we stretch out in line of march, they can pick us off like prairie dogs. Use your head, man, if you've got one."

"How many would you say there was?" The captain's lips were dry and he moistened them with his tongue. His eyes seemed to have sunken in his head; all his fine arrogance shed like a snake's skin.

"Three hundred, at a guess."

"Against forty-five.

"One white man's good as half a dozen brown skins any day," Pierre answered him. "That is — as long as he keeps his nerve up. Your damned pigheadedness has got us into this mess, Bannock. You've got to see it through. Forty-five men well-armed can do some damage to that pack of savages, only—"

"Only what?"

"We've got to do it fast. We've only water enough for two days, and there's not a bivouac strong enough to hold our stock once the thirst is on them. We've got to work!"

"You — you think they'll attack tonight?"

"No — not before dawn, if I know Injuns."

Dusk swooped down upon the hot earth, like the shadow of a hawk's wing. The sky to the west was as red as spilled blood.

The Indians had vanished over the rim of the ridge as suddenly as they had appeared, and a heavy silence shut in upon us, thick with menace, broken only by the camp sounds as the men lighted fires of buffalo chips and set their dinners a-cooking. It was a meal for which no one had heart, but it was a small chore, familiar and homely, binding us together and holding at bay the outer threat that was all but ready to strike us down.

"Every man look to his rifle," came Pierre's order. "See that you've plenty of powder and bullets. Hang your saddles and blankets and pots and pans over the backs of the stock. Any stray arrows that come over the corral wall find a mark somewhere, and we've got to protect our stock or be set afoot."

Set afoot. . . . Here in the *Jornada*. The thought of it was enough to quake the stoutest heart, and we forced the possibility from our minds. Hawk Eye was restless and jumpy. "Smells Injun," I thought grimly, and flipped her split-ear Comanche sign. "These are your haunts, old hoss," I gibed. "No wonder you're a-tremble!" I hobbled her with a side-line hobble, and tied her close to the wagon tongue as an extra precaution.

By this time it was dark. The last spark from the camp fires had been stamped out. Leroux was everywhere, looking to each man's ammunition; cheering the faltering; laughing with the courageous.

"Spread out under the wagons, men," he ordered. "There's nothing for us to do now but wait. They won't strike before dawn, you can stake your ha'r on that. Reckon I won't have to warn you not to fall asleep."

Nothing could have been farther from any man's mind than sleep, unless it might have been that last sleep from which there is no waking in this world. Aye – the thought of that long sleep closed in upon us now, ringed us about, heavy as the lowering sky.

Thunderclouds were piling up in the southwest, ripped through by flashes of lightning. Thunder rumbled, distant and profoundly disturbing, increasing the tension of our nerves. Thunder? No – it was too regular. Faint, far-off – a dull booming, ever-quickening, was borne to us on the back of the night wind. Drums.... That's what it was. Indian drums. Somewhere beyond those mysterious, black ridges Indians were dancing their war dances, working themselves up to a high pitch of frenzy. How secure they must have felt – how sure of their prey. The rumbling increased. Thudding... thudding ... like the pulse beat of this untamed earth. We listened, trembling in spite of ourselves. The sound reached far back to something primal in our own natures, setting teeth on edge and starting the sweat on our brows.

And somewhere off there to the south where the lightning played, miles away, was rain perhaps, water for parched bodies and throats. Tomorrow, those who lived would see green grass spring up under the miracle of its passage. But here – only the black earth, oven-hot and repellent. Hot earth – and a ring of forty-five men facing great odds. I felt as if every nerve and sinew in my body were as taut as a string about to break; and then the creed

of the trapper touched me like a quiet hand: you did the best that
you could against any odds, and in the end you died like a white
man. . . .

The drums had ceased. No sound now, but the lowing of the
thirsty cattle, the stamp of many hoofs restive within the confines
of the corral. Familiar sounds and reassuring. The ring of wagons
was in closest formation, with tongue overlapping tail gate. All
chinks and crevices had been filled with saddles and bales and
anything available. There were men under the wagons, lying flat
on their stomachs in the black shadows, thumbs on guncock, waiting . . . waiting. . . .

Once again Pierre was circling the corral. I heard him pause,
and saw his dim outline as it bent toward me in the darkness.
"That you, Starbuck?" he questioned.

"Yes."

"How are you making out, lad? Scared?"

I heard my voice answering, "Hardly."

"Good lad!" He clapped me on the back. As he turned away, I
heard him ask, "Where are Bannock and Bailey?"

"Dunno," came Sandy's gruff reply. "They ain't been seen much
fer the last half hour."

"Bannock!" Pierre shouted. "Bannock!"

"What do you want?" a muffled voice answered him.

"Where are you?"

Black Jack was in his wagon. "Just getting another round of
ammunition," he explained curtly.

"I suppose Bailey needs some, too?" The scout's voice had an
edge like a blade.

"Yes, he does," came the sullen response.

"Are you sure you've both got enough now?"

Again came the curt affirmative.

"All right, Bannock," Pierre rasped. "Come on out, both of you!"

The two men appeared in the darkness and Pierre confronted
them. "Listen, you two," he grated. "Stay out here and fight like
men. You *squaw!*"

"Damn you, Leroux!" Black Jack hissed. "I'll bore you for that!"

I heard the click of Bannock's guncock, heard Leroux's foot, lightning swift, lift to kick the pistol from his hand. The gun struck the ground but a foot from my face.

"I knew you were a skunk," Pierre threw at him, "but I didn't know you were a yellow coward as well!"

"Curse you!" Black Jack shouted. "If I was armed, you wouldn't dare to say that!"

"Tomorrow I'll say it again when you *are* armed — if there's any of us here tomorrow. But there's more important things than wasting ammunition on a coyote like you tonight." Be wheeled about, leaving the two men muttering in thwarted rage.

Finally Black Jack picked up his gun and threw himself on his stomach under a wagon. I determined to keep an eye upon him as far as possible, for I knew that if Leroux turned his back upon the man, he would be shot down without compunction. Bailey melted into the shadows and vanished from sight.

Silence settled in again.... Gunlocks were rapped to settle the priming. Men examined their flint and pan for the hundredth time, loosened the knives at their belts for instant action. I lifted Old Chief Thrower up to my cheek and the stock felt still warm from the day's heat.... "Old Chief Thrower, live up to your name," I whispered. "Make 'em come!"

Through a rent in the clouds I caught a glimpse of the Great Dipper, and the angle of its handle proclaimed that dawn was not far off. A figure dropped to the ground beside me. It was Pierre. The barrel of his two-shoot gun gleamed dully.

"Listen!" he muttered suddenly.

Every nerve in my body tensed. "What do you hear?" I whispered back.

"Sounded like a stone rattling."

"It's — it's about dawn, isn't it?"

"Yes. Listen — hear that?"

"Hoot owl, wasn't it?"

"Yes. Good job — for a Kiowa!"

"I wish something would happen," I complained.

"When you hear a gray wolf howl, something will," came the cryptic answer.

Almost before he had finished speaking, it came. The deep, slowly rising bay of the wolf, long-drawn, splintering the darkness.

"The old Kiowa signal," Pierre muttered. "Hoot owl talks to the gray wolf. Hell's going to pop now, son!"

False dawn was lighting the sky, rubbing off the darkness.

"Look thar!" Sandy Smith's voice whispering near me.

From our vantage point against the earth, every moving object must be silhouetted against the sky. Suddenly the outer half-light was alive with racing figures. There came a prolonged yell high-pitched and strident. The Kiowa war cry.

"*Injuns!*" shouted Sandy. "Hyar's doin's! Give 'em Green River, boys, fer hoss an' beaver!"

Bang! went his rifle. *Bang! Bang!* White stabs of flame in the gloom. The air was filled with a terrible uproar. Leroux's gun, vomiting whitely, all but split my eardrums. A scream of pain.... "One down!" he exulted. "*Ow-owgh! Ow-owgh!*"

Men shouted. Rifles spat. Arrows whirred about us. They struck the wood of the wagons with a quivering thud, once heard, never to be forgotten. Out of the din and clamor came the screeching of the Indian riders as they circled our corral, and above all, the shrill neighing of our terrified horses; the high scream of a wounded mule; the lowing of the oxen. *Bang! Bang!* An unremitting din. The sharp crack of rifles; the duller boom of the smoothbores.... the dawn diabolic with shrill war cries, the hoarse shouts of the wagoners, the taunts of the savages.

"*Ow-owgh!* Yere's doin's! Throwed him cold!"

"Green River and into 'em, boys!"

"*Whoo-oop!* Hyar's topknot!" Sandy Smith's shrill cry jarred the air, and when he whooped, he whooped center.

With a dull, quivering thud, an arrow buried itself in the wagon body a few inches above my head. A ripping sound and a tug at my shoulder — an arrow had torn its way through my buckskins, grazing the flesh. Blood — hot and sticky.... Then I saw red. I loaded Old Chief Thrower like a flash and pulled the trigger.... "*Ow-owgh!*" I shouted, "*Ow-owgh!*"

It was lighter now. Out beyond the corralled wagons dark mounds lay still. But sinewy, painted riders circled, circled, the dawn made hideous with their cries. Some darted in to carry off their dead. Shaft and ball spattered in from the half light. Suddenly I heard a groan and turned. Sandy's voice was saying, "Quit this arrer from my meat bag, will ye?"

Pierre leaped to Sandy's side. I heard the old trapper's voice again, fainter now, "Gawd, I'm bleedin'!"

From somewhere a man shouted: "Whew! Reckon that arrer sliced off a lock o' my ha'r!"

"Won't leave so much fer 'em to git hold of," came an answering cry.

All about, dark shape of madness. *Pinnnng* of feathered shaft. Belch of rifles. And out in the paling dawn the ever-narrowing circle of savages — darting, swooping, shifting forward. A rattle of missiles, like hail, against wheel and hub. Sand spattering up into our faces. Sweat running into our eyes.

There was a dark shape crawling toward me over the earth, drawing closer to the corral. . . . An Indian. I heard the man's grunting breath; saw a hand upraised with tomahawk, not two feet from Sandy's recumbent figure. I pressed the trigger. Old Chief Thrower barked. A body fell across Sandy's prostrate form — lay silent.

"Thanks — young 'un."

"Are you all right, Sandy?" I shouted back.

Silence. . . . I groped my way toward him. Then I heard his voice saying, faintly, "The arrer ain't feathered — that — kin stop this coon."

Suddenly cutting across the chaos, I heard Pierre's cry, wild-pitched and ringing clear: "We're trouncing 'em, boys! Give it to 'em, for hoss and ha'r!"

Unbelievably the ranks of the savages were thinning. They had all but disappeared with the light of dawn. Our corral and rifles had proved too strong for their hail of arrows. Why lose warriors in such a costly victory when they had only to wait. They knew well our water ration. Another twenty-four hours and we would be forced to break camp or face stampede of our stock. The Indians could afford to keep just beyond our deadly range-waiting. . . .

With the dawn we saw angry clouds, slate gray, hanging low overhead. And with the coming of light this nightmare seemed less terrible. It was easier to face a foe that you could see and take aim at. Then our hot eyes saw a glow. The red of sunrise. But — that glow came not from the east. *It came from the west!*

"They've fired the grass!" The cry swept through the corral. "Ah, God!"

Thwarted in their attack, the Kiowas had set fire to the grama grass, tinder dry, to burn us out.

Half a mile off they'd started it going, giving the early morning wind full chance to fan it to a conflagration. We watched for a second, stunned. Little fires, like scouts of an advancing army, danced toward us with every playful wind puff. Just the other side of those flames, advancing with them, the Kiowas lurked and darted. What the fire didn't destroy, they would.

Already our cattle had caught the whiff of smoke. It was all they needed after the clamor of the night to set them going.

"We've gone beaver!" came a man's despairing cry.

And so it seemed. The fire was rushing at us, fanned by the piling wind. Yellow smoke rolled above it. There was no time to hitch the oxen to the wagons. The flames would have outstripped them. All that was left us was to leap on our horses and ride for life and scalp — ride straight into the lances of the expectant Kiowas, who, without doubt, had circled the fire and were waiting to receive us.

Oxen and mules, terrified by now, milled and piled within the small corral. We'd be trampled to death if we didn't get out.

"Every man a-horse!" came Pierre's shout.

"But my wagons!" The words were wrung from Black Jack's tortured spirit, even in the shadow of death.

"You won't need 'em where you're going," Pierre flung out. He wheeled Black Knight and shouted again, "A-horse, you fools!"

Men fell upon their mounts. Fingers fought with stubborn hobbles. The stock had gone mad, screaming, braying, bellowing, climbing one another in their hope of escape.

"Break the corral!" came the shout from somewhere.

"Not yet!" Pierre's voice sang out above the turmoil, clarion strong. "Look there!"

His tense hand pointed at the low-hanging clouds, ripped

through by lightning's sudden flash. "If there's a prayer left in any of you, pray for rain, and do it fast!"

But the men heeded not. Bereft of their senses, they were straining to break an opening in the corral. In danger of being crushed by the plunging cattle, they fought to loose tail gate from tongue and make an opening wedge in the ring of wagons. In vain Pierre shouted at them — leaped from his horse into their midst, to throw them right and left. But an opening had been made. Through it the cattle poured out; the first of them trampled under the pressure of those behind, forming a bridge for those that followed. Out they flooded, like an unapposable tide. No stemming it — no turning it. Eyes rolling, horns clashing, tongues lolling, hoofs gouging in wild instinct for escape.

There came an ear-splitting burst of thunder. A single drop of rain touched my forehead. Rain.... *Water!* My fingers found the collar of my buckskin shirt — yanked it open. I couldn't breathe.

Floodgates of the sky opened. Rain descended. Stinging, life-giving. All about us the fire disappeared in clouds of hissing steam, quenched by this flood from heaven.

But through the opening in the corral the fear-maddened animals still poured in wild stampede.

Pierre's shout cut across the clamor, "I want volunteers to help round up!" No man answered.

"It's sure death out there," one of the rivermen muttered at last, sullenly. "Round up? Not this coon!"

"Zenas Kent!" Pierre shouted. "Zenas — how about you?"

"He's dead," came a man's voice.

"It's shore death out there, pardner," spoke up another man.

"It's sure death if you're set afoot, you fool!" Pierre thundered.

"Mebbe we kin hold 'em off," the man retaliated with stubborn insistence.

Black Jack stepped forward, his face white and pinched. "Leroux's right, men," he declaimed unexpectedly. "We can't afford to lose our stock."

"All right — *you* go then," the riverman rumbled.

"How about it, Bannock?" Pierre demanded. "Do you want to come with me?"

"My place as captain is here with my train," came the man's hasty answer.

"I thought so!" Pierre laughed scornfully. "Maybe Bailey would like to join me?"

But Bailey was nowhere to be found.

"How about me?" I called out.

The scout wheeled toward me, his eyes ablaze.

"All right, Starbuck — off with us!"

He swung Black Knight toward the opening in the corral. I leaped to Hawk Eye's back, Old Chief Thrower close in my grip. Together we raced through the break, out into the dawn's gray light, after the vanishing cattle.

CHAPTER XIV

THE JOURNEY OF DEATH

THE HERD was thundering in full stampede. Up ahead, Pierre raced toward the leaders, ghostly in the half-light. Hawk Eye stretched out her neck and we sped along the stream of running cattle. I bent low in the saddle, trusting to this animal's instinct for sure footing. All about me a sea of black and brindle, brown and white; a sea crested with wide-sweeping horns, bluish in the lightning flashes, eyes glass-green in the weird glow. The clamor from the rear gave warning that the herd was sweeping in behind me. I'd be caught in a pocket. There would be no escape. If Hawk Eye should stumble. . . . An instinct for flight swept me, for escape from this welter of plunging horns and hoofs.

"Head 'em off to the south!" Pierre's voice came singing above the tumult, steadying me. "If they go west, we're lost!"

But even as he spoke, it was evident that despite all his efforts the herd was swinging to the west. Somehow I must get to the head of the column and try to turn the tide. A second before Pierre had been just ahead of me. Now he had vanished. Where was he? Had Black Knight stumbled? I pushed the thought from my mind. Low over Hawk Eye's neck I leaned, urging her on to greater speed.

Imperceptibly the little mare's stride lengthened till she had reached her top speed. She couldn't hold it for long. But we were gaining on the head of the column. Heaving backs glistened with sweat in the murky dawn. The animals in the rear plunged blind-

ly after their leaders. *Crack!* Lightning again in brilliant glare, its unearthly blue merging with the coppery haze, picking out each detail with supernatural precision. There was Pierre, still ahead, riding like the wind itself, trying to turn the column to the south. His pistol barked and I saw the white belch of its fire.

The next second Hawk Eye and I were in the thick of the herd, swept along like chips on a millrace. We caught up with Pierre. Neck and neck we raced to reach the ox that formed the apex of the stampede, working desperately into position to turn him. If only we could swing the leader, the rest would follow blindly.

I spurred my pony toward the animal, so close that my moccasin struck its heaving ribs. Then leaning forward in the saddle, I fired my pistol almost into the beast's eye. I felt, rather than saw, that he was giving way. Would we win? I hardly dared to hope.

Then abruptly, without hint of warning, the whole herd swung of single impulse back toward the west! There was no turning them now. Nothing to do but run with them, run for hide and dear life.

Gradually I let them pull ahead, sweeping me on both sides, their horns raking my legs as they passed. Where was Pierre? There he was — a full fifty yards away, seen dimly through the haze of dust. We dropped back together.

"No use," he panted, his body sagging as he looked after the vanishing cattle. "Those critters are headed straight into Comanche country. We'll kill our horses trying to turn 'em and put our heads into a wolf trap besides."

We pulled up and drew to a halt, our horses breathing gustily, Pierre and I both shaken with our wild ride. How many miles we had come from the wagon camp, I had not the slightest idea. And the fact that we had evaded the besieging Kiowas was naught but a miracle of good fortune. The sun was coming up like a clap of thunder, greeting a new day with red anger. Pierre threw up his head and shook the hair out of his eyes.

"What a brace of fools we are," he laughed. "Here we've been worrying about keeping Bannock and his wagons from reaching Santa Fe before Kearny, wondering how we were going to manage it. He won't get there now, my lad." He listened intently for a

second. From far off to the rear we heard intermittent rifle shots. "The Kiowas will take care of that," he concluded with a grim smile. "Bannock has enough water to stand 'em off for another day. After that—"

"It's — it's too bad to leave Sandy," I muttered

"Sandy was paunch-shot, son. He can't last till noon. Zenas went out in the night. The rest of the pack – they can look to themselves. And that's what we're going to do. We're going to find Kearny!"

"Kearny—" I echoed stupidly.

He nodded. "He's somewhere outside of Bent's Fort waiting to get word from me. You didn't know I was as important as that, did you? But first – where's your water flask?"

I looked for the flask of treated bladder that was tied always to the cantle. Somehow, in the stampede, it had been torn off. Pierre took up his own, shook it to his ear and listened. His lips compressed into a line.

"Empty?" I faltered.

"No – not quite," he returned briefly. "We'll have to find more."

"But—"

"Never say die, lad. We'll strike in a wide circle around the wagon camp and the Kiowas. Then head for the Arkansas. Somewhere on this side of the river, between the Crossing and Bent's Fort, there's a creek – Lost Creek. We can find the river all right, but we'll have to trust to God's grace to find Lost Creek first. If we don't—"

There was no need to finish that sentence. We sat silent for a moment, giving our tired horses a chance to catch their wind. The seriousness of what lay ahead placed its hand upon us both, a sense of brooding hostility that pressed upon our hearts and spirits with a crushing weight. *Jornada del Muerto*, the Journey of Death. No picturesque figure of Latin speech, but an insistent reality. For the first time the true nature of this land struck at me. It was a land that seemed soaked in all the memories of man's fruitless efforts to conquer it, shimmering under its spell of hate and thirst, of ragged nerves and thumping heart and wasted flesh.

We rode on, wordless, tongueless.

Over this lonely, secret earth, something everlasting and unchanging brooded there, as it had brooded since time began. The earliest savages, the conquering Spaniards, the wide-ranging Indians, the trappers, the wagon trains, the armies of the *Tejanos* — all these had scratched at its surface and left no more trace of their passage than cloud shadows moving across the land for an instant — then gone. And for a moment something of its grandeur, its inescapable majesty gripped my heart with cold fingers and fevered my blood. Out of the chaos, the blind confusions and cross-purposes of a million lives, some terrible essence had been distilled, made up of time and space and the murmur of the voices of lost men and forlorn hopes.

We turned our horses north and west. They pulled forward, tired, reluctant, with drooping heads, their feet sinking fetlock deep into the sand.

Long hours passed.... The sun climbed the tall sky. It struck down at us like a flashing sword, beating us into the earth, invading our bodies, drawing out all moisture from our tissues. The sand threw back the heat, intensified a thousandfold, stifling our breath, scorching our nostrils, and burning as it filtered into our lungs.

I could feel Hawk Eye trembling beneath me.... "Mebbe so she's gittin' along some in years...." Lanky's words. How long ago. Like something remembered out of another age. What a stroke of ironic fitness that Hawk Eye, Comanche pony, should return to her native range to die. The blind fortuity of chance.

"How — how far is it to the Arkansas, Pierre?"

The scout swallowed before speaking. "We'll reach it tomorrow, son."

Tomorrow. There was blood in my pony's nostrils. Black Knight walked with drooping head, his fine pride humbled. I stole a glance at Pierre. He had withdrawn within himself as though storing up his strength against need still to be met, his eyes, red-rimmed, peering out through the gray dust that masked him. The earth pulled at us, drew us down to its bosom, claimed every hoofbeat that fell and reached upward for the next to come.

The sun struck its zenith and began its relentless westward march. We rode on, wordless, tongueless in the isolation of this vast and hostile world. As the long hours passed, it seemed to me that every atom of my flesh was wrung dry. Dizzy, trembling, I wondered where the strength to tremble came from. I had been thirsty before, but always with the knowledge that I could drink. Now thirst was a mounting torture. My lips cracked. My throat constricted. I remembered the brook behind the cabin in the clearing, running fresh and cool over the stones, leaping out over the ledges — how lightly I had held it. I thought of the yellow waters of the Big Muddy, tons of water rushing away to wanton waste. I saw again the reeking moisture of the buffalo wallows, from which I had turned with repugnance, wondering how the Mexican mule-skinners could slake their thirst on such vile stuff. Water — all these. Water. . . .

As if I had spoken aloud my thought, Pierre warned: "Put it out of your mind, lad." His voice was hoarse.

I heard my own voice, like a stranger's, asking, "Would it be all right — a small — drink?"

Silently Pierre held out his flask, removed the stopper. "Drink, son."

I held the container eagerly to my lips, fighting the impulse to drain it at a gulp. I steadied myself — felt the water's life-giving magic moisten my lips, trickle down my swollen throat, steal through my body. Pulling the flask away, I offered it to Pierre. He shook his head and carefully replaced the stopper with fingers that trembled.

On we plodded through the blinding hours, through this land naked and accursed, like blighted atoms, having no place either in the world of the living or of the dead. Desiccated, numb, hollow as a shell, we plodded through an unreality of silence that was neither dream nor sleep nor waking vision. And the sun burned into us like an inescapable eye.

Somewhere out beyond this inferno, a world of men and events followed accepted laws. Or was that, too, illusion — a spirit mirage to mock us with false promise.? Against the far-off dunes

there was a lake rippling in the breeze, its surface creaming with little wavelets.... Green trees dotted its rim. I blinked, and brushed my hand eagerly across my eyes. An involuntary cry broke from me. "Water!"

"Mirage." Pierre's voice was hoarse to hear.

The day wore on....

I thought that I must have reached the limit of human endurance; then found that the hours could be met somehow, new reserves plumbed for, drawn upon. We quivered like bow cords drawn to utmost limit, held taut and trembling, waiting the second of release.

Perhaps, I thought dully, at the very end we would kill our horses and drink their blood, and then go on afoot, closer, ever closer to the desert that would claim us with its ultimate grip. Would it be so horrible, that last choking agony? Perhaps Nature, in final gesture of mercy, dulled the mind; the body writhed but the brain recorded not. Perhaps. . .

"Drink!"

Once more Pierre offered the flask.

"You first." It was all that I could manage. I would not drink again until he had drunk first. He understood, held the flask to his lips, drank slowly, then passed it to me.

"Finish it!" he commanded.

I looked at him, dull, wondering. He nodded, his cracked lips reiterating the words but no sound came. I realized then that I couldn't see very well and wondered if I were going blind. It was only the night's darkness descending with blessed relief upon this land of the sun.

The day had passed – all sense of time was as blurred as the eye's vision in this timeless immensity of space.

"We'll rest – for awhile."

There came a few hours of fitful, choking slumber, a growing agony of thirst that those last remaining drops of water had but served to intensify. Our animals were bony scarecrows of their former sleek selves. I had no sense of the night being long or short. Somehow it passed, leaving only this one reality: thirst.

The air was luminous with promise of another day. Out of the sultry shadows the earth emerged slowly, brown and violent, weighting our hearts with its terrible certainty. And with the coming of this new day, fear raised its ugly head. It gripped my heart with clammy fingers, tightened my throat, slithered and crawled at my feet like a boneless shape. Lost Creek — did it really exist, or was it...

I must have cried out then, for suddenly Pierre had seized me by both shoulders and was shaking me till my teeth rattled.

"Steady!" he shouted hoarsely. "Get hold of yourself!"

His voice, all but unrecognizable as it was, quieted the panic that gripped me. I learned in that instant that when a man reaches his final limit of endurance, when he sees his whole world tumbling about him in chaos, there is still some kernel of stored-up strength, some hidden miracle of reserve, unsuspected until this extremity calls it forth. That knowledge and its certainty were to stand always at my elbow from that moment on. Silently I turned toward Hawk Eye, pulled myself somehow into the saddle, and waited for Pierre to give the signal.

The man was watching the progress of the sun, turning to scan the north anxiously. The horses pulled forward setting down one foot, then another, and I tried to concentrate upon their movements, dulling my mind to the hours that lay ahead. Perhaps that is why I was suddenly conscious that they were quickening their pace, all but imperceptibly at first. I looked up. Nothing could I see   still the same measureless land breaking into rolling swells. But Hawk Eye and Black Knight had raised their heads with fresh alertness, sniffing at the still air. Then I was aroused to keen awareness by Pierre's shout:

"Lost Creek!"

I remember trying to speak, to give voice to the terrible joy that welled up in me, tearing at my swollen throat. Lost Creek — my eyes sought it out eagerly. There it was! Just a narrow gully writhing over the parched earth through low hills of sand. Dry as a bone it looked to my glazed sight. The horses neighed and trotted swiftly down the slope.

Pierre sprang out of saddle and half ran, half stumbled toward the dry creek bed. "We'll dig," he cried thickly. "There's water — under the sand."

I all but fell from the saddle, spurred to new energy. Dropping down at the creek's edge, we dug feverishly with our knives. Then — miracle of miracles! Moisture seeping upward, coloring the dun earth with precious spots of darkness, life coming to us from the breast of this terrible land. We pressed our mouths against it, felt its magic seep into our veins. The horses were nuzzling at our side, pawing at the damp sand, but we heeded them not. There was only our own extremity, the satisfaction of our final need. We drank and drank, somehow filtering out the sand and restoring our strength with its damp moisture.

As we bent there at the creek, there came a shrill. scream from Hawk Eye. Uncomprehending at first, still dazed, we half rose to our knees, staggered to our feet. Then I saw — saw but couldn't believe.... An arrow, meant for me, had pierced through Hawk Eye's neck. Blood poured from her mouth and nose. With a choking gasp she fell forward, eyes rolling in her head. On the opposite bank of the creek, two bronze shadows flashed away in the sunlight with high-pitched yells.

"*Comanches!*"

Pierre swept his rifle to his shoulder. Its spiteful bark rang out. Then, as I watched, I saw him stagger. He half fell to his knees. With a wild-pitched whoop, the two Indians raced for cover behind the dunes, the fleet heels of their mounts throwing up a dust to hide their night. I fired after them, blindly, a chance shot. One Comanche threw up a hand — and rallied. They were gone.

Flinging down my rifle, I dropped to my knees beside Pierre, numb, tongueless, all strength draining out of me. An arrow, feather-tipped and deep-driven, quivered just under his heart.

"Good — shot," he muttered.

With icy fingers I cut away his buckskin shirt.... Push it on through; cut off the shaft.... The words came to me, remembered from some limbo of forgotten things. But the shaft would not push on through, and the arrowhead wouldn't come free.

"You'll have to butcher it out, young 'un," Pierre's voice was quiet and strangely clear. It was hopeless and he knew it.

With a blind, mechanical precision I took out my knife, wiped the blade across my knee. Then I cut deep into the flesh, just above the shaft. Still the arrow wouldn't pull free. Fighting the nausea that gripped my vitals, I cut once again. Blood spurted from the wound, pouring out over my hands, drenching the sand. A terrible wound — Pierre's life flowing to quench the thirsty *Jornada*. The shaft came loose at last, but not the head.

"No use — Starbuck."

I tore off a strip of my shirt, bound it to the wound. As well try to stem a tide. With a nameless dread choking me, I scooped up a handful of damp sand, pressed it to his lips. Pierre — so vibrant with life — how could he die? How could he cease to be? Black Knight moved close, nickering softly. The dying man seemed to gather strength by superhuman effort. He struggled to raise himself upon one elbow.

"Listen — lad.... Take — off my moccasins."

Scarce knowing what I did, I obeyed.

"Put them on!" His voice held something of its old note of command.

I removed my own and put on his. What was this madness striking us down? Surely it was all a delirium, a fever born of this land of sun and sand and thirst, a nightmare from which we would wake with another day.

Pierre's lips were moving, his voice fainter. I leaned close to hear his words: "The left moccasin — a letter — between two soles. For — Kearny. He'll be waiting for it. Find him!"

"I will," I vowed. "I will Pierre!" The words were wrung out of me from the bottom of my despair.

"Good lad," he whispered, his fingers tightening on my arm, "Tell Kearny—"

"Tell him what, Pierre?"

"Tell him—"

I had to press my ear to his lips to catch his words.

Shadows shortened over the land as the sun climbed. A man's

life shortened too. A red sun, life-giving, life-taking, flooded the wide earth with its glow. Pierre opened his eyes, searched me with a look that seemed to probe the innermost reaches of my spirit. I nodded my head, bereft of speech, my mind number to emptiness. a corner of his mouth quirked. His shoulders quivered under my arm, then were still. I felt, rather than thought, it is over. Lost Creek? Leroux Creek now.

...."Men following our trail fifty years hence will wonder where this creek got its name..."

With my rifle butt I dug a grave there beside the creek's bed. And when it was all over, I dragged heavy stones upon the grave and smoothed the sand. And then I straightened up, and the red sun swam, and my hands gripped at my throat to stop its hot burning. Black Knight nuzzled at my shoulder, finding the end of my endurance.

"Black Knight!" I cried. "Black Knight—"

And then I could say no more. I set my foot on the stirrup and turned the horse's head north of the sun's passage. The whole world seemed painted in blood. Even the shadows of the long dunes were red. Kearny — he was somewhere over there beyond the Arkansas, and I must find him. I must. We climbed the weary rise. I looked back for a second at Leroux Creek.... "Sleep your long sleep, here on the desert where you belong. The Buffalo will thunder over your head ten thousand strong, and perhaps you'll hear. The stars will look down, remote but friendly, and perhaps you'll know—"

Then Black Knight and I rode down the slope toward the shadowy dunes, turning our backs on the creek forever. As we rode, the shadows leaped and lengthened. Shadows? No. Horses were streaming down over the dunes toward me. Dozens, hundreds it seemed to my dazed sight. Lean riders bent low, while high and raucous sounded their cries. Red demons out of darkness. The hosts of hell.

Comanches!

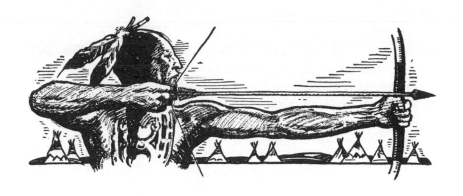

CHAPTER XV

CAPTURED

BLACK KNIGHT wheeled on his haunches and leaped forward in response to quirt and rowel; ears flat, head extended, nostrils wide. Good old Black Knight — how valiantly he tried. But thirst had sapped his strength. The Indian ponies were gaining on us. High whoops shrilled in my ears like trumpet calls of doom.

A backward glance showed me two Comanches pulling ahead of the others — chiefs, probably, on the fastest horses. My stallion, pounds heavier than their ponies, was laboring in the deep sand. Escape was beyond hope. A kind of mad joy possessed me. Nothing that happened to me seemed to matter, with Pierre in his shallow grave, Hawk Eye food for the buzzards. My teeth clamped shut, my eyes misted over with red. "It's a wise man who saves his last shot for himself." Who had said that? Sandy? Pierre?

Old Chief Thrower — primed and ready with his single shot, That shot must count, but it wouldn't be for me! The Indian in the lead was but a few yards away, cutting directly across my path. Behind him, racing the wind, his companion fitted an arrow to the bow. With every sense alert I saw that the leading Indian carried an old fusil. He raised it, taking running aim. I whipped Old Chief Thrower to my shoulder and pressed the trigger with silent prayer. At the same second the savage's fusil cracked. I swayed in the saddle, gripped with my knees. Not the impact of a bullet: it was the arrow of the second Comanche slicing the flesh across my fore-

head. I felt the rasp of the feathers. Something hot and sticky ran down onto my eyes. I couldn't see.

I dashed my hand across my face. The Indian I had shot lay prone in the sand. The second Indian was whipping another arrow to the cord. This one would get me. I knew it, as I knew that the sun shone and was hot. There was no time for me to reload. My rifle had said its say. Only one thing left to do. I yanked at the bit and hauled the stallion to a right-angle turn, then drove the rowels into his ribs and bore down upon the surprised Indian. Too late the savage saw his peril. I whipped my knife from my belt and in the same instant saw the flash of a blade in the Indian's hand. The next second, our two horses had come together with a crash.

My knife ripped across the man's chest. I felt the stab of a blade in my shoulder, hot as a branding iron. But the Comanche pony fell before the weight of Black Knight and sprawled its length in the sand, pulling its rider to the ground.

My right-angle turn had enabled the other Indians to close in. I knew then that the game was up. I had lost the hand. I was surrounded. Shaking the blood out of my eyes, I looked around at the circle of savage faces, heaving horses, and glittering eyes. Twenty fusils covered my every movement. A dozen bowstrings quivered with arrows drawn to the head. One Comanche rode a pace toward me and said, in Spanish:

"The knife – drop it!"

The blade fell from my nerveless fingers. Then the Indian rode up to me and seized Old Chief Thrower from my grasp, and struck me across the face with his quirt. I felt myself swaying in the saddle, motes of light dancing in the blackness before my eyes. I was falling ... falling I threw out my hands with the blind instinct for self-preservation. And then I knew no more.

A series of disconnected fragments, flashes of returning consciousness cutting through a delirium: the exquisite torture of a trotting horse; lying on my stomach across a saddle, my arms

The Comanche pony fell...

bound behind me; the ache of thirst; and then (surely it was only a dream) the horses were splashing through a stream, throwing up slivers of silver light. Wet drops spattering against my face. Men laughing, talking in harsh gutturals some language that was strange to my ears. The sun shining hot on the horned lodges of the Comanche village. Spots of bright color. Dogs snapping and snarling at our heels. Squaws hurling invectives at me as we rode into the encampment. Then the lodge of the chief emblazoned with buffalo horns. Dimly I sensed the sullen, watchful hostility of the warriors around me.

Some of these things I can piece together again now, sights and sounds and actions which assailed ear and retina, stored away in the secret hiding places of the subconscious, to come seeping through hours, days, weeks later.

They yanked me out of the saddle. As I fell to the ground, a foot kicked at me. I remember the stunning impact against my ribs. I tried to rise, my cracked lips forming the words: *"Agua!* Water — water!" A deep voice gave a guttural command, and then, O God be thanked! There was water, a gourd full and brimming. The bright sparkle of it brought tears to my eyes. At another command, the thongs that bound my hands were slit, but my fingers shook so that they were like to spill the precious liquid as I conveyed it to my lips. But some instinct greater even than my own extremity prompted me to drink slowly after the first wild gulp. The water stole down my throat, easing its ache, and I felt its magic permeating my body, restoring life, power, and the will to live.

As fuller consciousness revived, I looked about me with mounting interest. At first the gloom of the lodge seemed impenetrable after the glare of the desert. Then figures emerged from the gloom, savage figures, half naked, painted and feathered and silent. Beyond the triangle of white light that formed the door of the lodge, faces crowded the opening, staring.... At a harsh command, the faces disappeared. This then was the lodge of the Chief of Chiefs, and the thick-set savage in the center of the circle, he who uttered the command, must be the chief himself. I struggled to rise, but still lacked the strength and so fell back. In the center of the lodge a small fire burned brightly under an iron kettle, and

smoke was rising in a thin column toward the hole which served as a vent at the lodge's peak, some ten feet above. Within the kettle something bubbled lustily and sent forth a tantalizing odor of boiling meat. Stabbing pangs of hunger reminded me that I hadn't eaten for two, three, how many days?

The chief spoke again, and an ancient squaw, fat and wrinkled beyond belief, hobbled out of the shadows and fished a piece of meat from the pot. She set it down before me and disappeared. I fell upon the steaming meat and devoured it as an animal. Then as the mists began to clear from my brain with the satisfaction of this animal need, I found myself wondering at such treatment from Comanches. Indians did not take prisoners except to torture them.

My eyes traveled around the circle of warriors and came to rest again upon the chief. All the men had half of their heads shaved, the locks on the opposite side reaching almost to the floor. Although the chief varied little from the others in outward physical aspect, there was a suggestion of great power about him which signaled him out from the others. He was rather short, as were all the Comanches, as if his legs had been stunted in growth from a life spent, since childhood, upon horseback. But his upper body was strong and muscular. His face beaked like a hawk's; high-cheeked; a broad, even noble, brow with a thin, cruel line of mouth to contradict it. Keenly intelligent, utterly savage. Eyes black and opaque as obsidian, giving forth nothing beyond a dull luster — neither hate nor anger. They seemed devoid of all human emotion, impenetrable, fathomless. Looking into them was like looking into the eyes of Fate itself, and involuntarily I drew back, with the feeling of an animal caught in a trap. But some instinct far back in my blood (something, I believe, of the spirit which must have made the white race persist to prevail) warned me against any show of fear. I willed myself to quietness, thrust my hands behind me to hide their trembling, and looked around once again at the circle of savage faces, searching them one by one. Red-brown in color, richly hued as the earth itself, tight-lipped, unreadable. Beads and ornaments lay heavily on scarred chests; war bonnets bristled with cresting feathers.

From one face to another I looked, searching for I knew not

what. Each pair of eyes was a blank, repellent wall. Of a sudden I felt a shock of swift surprise. From under the low rim of a feathered headdress, one pair of eyes looked back into mine; level, inscrutable. But my breath caught in my throat and my heart began to thump madly, for the eyes...

"White dog!"

"It was the chief's voice claiming my attention, bringing me back with a start. He was speaking in a thick Spanish. "There is Comanche blood upon your hands. What have you to say before you die?" His dark eyes were emotionless.

Still reeling with what I had seen, I fought for time. "I have nothing to say," I parried.

An evil smile hooked the savage's lips. "You will be long in dying," he promised. "You will have time to think of much. Who are you and whence do you come?" The question darted at me like a snake.

I caught at my wits, trying to match this crafty brain and boring eye. Kearny – somehow I must win through and get to Kearny.... The least sign of fear, of indecision, would be fatal. Only through boldness could I hope to succeed.

"I come from Independence to find Colonel Kearny," I ventured, watching for the effect of my words.

"Who is Kearny?" the chief temporized.

"You know who he is!" I answered boldly. "He is the great War Chief of the white warriors. He has three thousand braves at his command, and many rifles."

"Such as this one?" The chief raised a rifle in his hands and I saw that it was Old Chief Thrower. Involuntarily I leaned forward, then caught myself. Old Chief Thrower...

"Better by far than that, O Chief," I made answer. "Rifles that can fire two shots. Pistols that can fire six times without reloading. You can kill me if you like, but when the white warriors come, they will wipe out the whole Comanche nation with their fine rifles."

The chief's eyes sparked balefully. "You lie," he returned. "You talk to White Buffalo, the Chief of Chiefs. The Comanche fears not the whole white nation. He wears his scalp-lock long, that he may take it who dares! There is war between the Americano and the

Mexicano. The Comanche is the Mexicano's friend. I read your thoughts, white youth; you're like a frightened coyote, doubling your tracks to gain time. I am not deceived."

"When Kearny's men come, you will crawl in the dust and cry to him to spare your women and children," I promised with a boldness I was far from feeling.

"You will not be here to see," came his retort charged with venom. He laid Old Chief Thrower beside him on the buffalo robe. "This will kill no more Comanches!"

"There are other guns," I retaliated. "Your lodges will be darkened with their smoke."

His thin lips folded back from his long teeth in a smile of derision. "Coyote! You snap your teeth while your tail hangs low. You have not come this far alone. Where is the wagon train you came with, and who owned it?"

There was nothing to lose by the truth. "It belonged to Black Jack Bannock, and—"

If a keg of gunpowder had exploded within the lodge, the effect could have been no greater than that of my words.

"Bannock!" The chief half rose to his feet, his voice mounting on the name. The sound echoed from the lips of his braves in tones incredulous and wondering. My own surprise was as great as theirs. What could these savages know of Black Jack Bannock? How could his name have reached this remote fastness, lost in the desert of the Cimarron?

The chief leaned forward and gripped me by one arm, his fingers biting into my flesh while his eyes fixed me with their glare. "Dog!" he hissed. "If you have spoken the truth, you shall live — for what does a coward prize more than his life? Where is Bannock?"

"The train was attacked by the Kiowas the second day after Cimarron Crossing," I answered breathlessly. "The cattle stampeded. Leroux and I—"

The chief waited to hear no more. He leaped to his feet, harsh orders jarring the air. The whole camp was thrown into an uproar. Outside I could hear the women screaming, children crying, the sounds of horses being brought in from the corral, the clatter of weapons. Past the door opening, figures streamed, children scur-

rying like frightened rabbits. Drums began to beat. One by one
the warriors faded out through the opening, until only one of
them was left besides the chief; a young warrior this, straight as a
sapling, standing half hidden in the shadows.

Then the chief stepped up to me and flung a final word in my
face: "You may eat and drink. None will harm you unless you try
to escape. We go to Bannock. But if you have lied—"

There was no need to finish the sentence. The threat hooked to
the end of it carried its own message of doom. The chief stooped
and disappeared out through the door opening. The young warrior who had been standing in the shadows followed at his heels,
but ere he too had disappeared, he turned, and once again his
eyes met mine, Yes – I had been right.

His eyes were blue!

As he vanished into the light, the sun threw back a gleam of
gold from under the feathered headdress: it was the lock of hair,
yellow as corn silk in midsummer....

And then I knew. This blue-eyed Indian was Tim Cooper.

The drums were beating in ever-rising crescendo, the chanting of the women merging with the drumbeats. As I lay there on the hard earth floor of the Comanche lodge, I tried to piece together into a lucid whole some of the fragmentary events of the past hours. "We go to Bannock," White Buffalo had said, indicating, I judged, that the Comanches were riding to his assistance. What could be more probable than that Governor Armijo of New Mexico had negotiated with the Comanche chief to give Bannock and his valuable cargo safe convoy on its hazardous crossing of the *Jornada?* The Kiowas were hereditary enemies of the Comanches; in going thus to Black Jack's assistance, they could carry out Armijo's commission and deal a blow at their enemies at the same time.

But such speculations were idle. And dwarfing all else was the discovery that Tim Cooper was alive, and that I had seen him but a few moments since. I couldn't fathom the meaning of the look that he had thrown at me as he left the lodge, but I would stake my life that he would help me to escape. Doubtless he had been compelled to go forth to battle with the other warriors, but surely, surely he would work out some plan. Even though he had lived for seven years among this wild tribe, becoming an Indian in his mode of life, in his ways of thought, blood remained thicker than water and he would never see one who had been his friend, done to death.

In the meantime I was in an extremely precarious position. The thought of escape was uppermost in my mind. The warriors of the tribe had gone forth to battle, yes, but their camp would certainly not be left unguarded. There would be a horse-guard of fledgling warriors, and perhaps old men too decrepit to fight but still able to wield a bow in defense of the village. And I was without weapon of any sort and still weak from my ordeal in the *Jornada.*

The ancient squaw who had given me meat moved silently into one corner of the lodge and squatted on her haunches, eyeing me with the unblinking solemnity of a graven image. At the least suspicious move on my part she would raise a hue and cry that would have the entire village about my ears. That much was certain. At my signal she brought another gourd of water, and after I had

slaked my thirst I made motions toward the iron kettle which still bubbled over its low fire. Grumbling and making remarks which were doubtless reflections upon my ancestry even unto the third and fourth generations, she dished another morsel of meat into a wooden bowl and set it down before me. Her eyes, almost buried in folds of flesh, sparked with a ferret-like glitter.

Lying there on the buffalo robes, I ate slowly, making no waste motions, trying to hoard my returning strength. If, by some miracle, the chance of escape should present itself, I would need all the reserves at my command.

The afternoon waned and the shadows deepened in the lodge. I heard the women and children about the cook fires, laughing as they prepared the evening meal. The old squaw helped herself from the iron kettle and squatted on her haunches as she ate, never taking her eyes from me as she ground up the antelope meat with her toothless gums. I lay down on the robes, pretending sleep, and after a while I saw that she, too, was dozing fitfully in her corner, waking up with a start from time to time to dart a quick look at me. I had no intention of falling asleep. If ever I should be able to effect an escape from the Comanche stronghold, it must be tonight, under cover of darkness. There was no telling what the morrow might bring. If only I could find a weapon. . . . Surreptitiously I glanced around the lodge. But there was no sign of gun or pistol or knife. Not even a stick of wood for a club. Old Chief Thrower — with a start I realized that my rifle had been in Tim Cooper's hands as he vanished through the door behind White Buffalo!

The old squaw roused herself and peered at me through the gathering gloom. I closed my eyes and simulated a deep and regular breathing. Then the strain of the past days, the long hours in the saddle, my deep exhaustion in the desert, overcame me. Before I knew it, I was sound asleep.

With a start I waked, tense in every nerve. The lodge was in pitch darkness. Not a sound did I hear throughout the village. Far off a wolf howled and another answered. I had no idea how long I had slept, but I felt refreshed and strong. I listened for the

breathing of the old squaw. Yes — she slept. Then I was conscious of a faint, scuffling noise, a breath choked off as if by the grip of a hand. Then silence.

Straining every sense, I listened. — Something — yes — something was slithering toward me across the dark floor. Sweat broke out on my forehead, drenched my body with sudden terror. What was it? I gathered myself to spring. . . . Someone was there in the darkness, crawling toward me! Was this to be the end — to die like a rat in a Comanche's grip?

There came a sibilant whisper: "Starbuck!"

I swallowed violently. Had I gone daft here in this cursed desert, touched by the sun, stricken down by the madness that overtook men in these sandy wastes?

"Starbuck—" came the whisper again. "It's me. Tim Cooper."

I wanted to laugh, to shout, to yell. Instead I put out my hand and a warm one gripped it.

"Not a sound," came the warning whisper. "I've gagged and tied the old squaw. "We've got to escape while the men are gone, before they find that I deserted them."

"But how— "

"No questions now," he answered swiftly. "I've two rifles. There's horses tethered at the foot of the village with none to guard them but old men. Come!"

He gripped my arm, pulling me down to the earth, and drew me toward the door-opening of the lodge. The night itself was scarcely less dark than the lodge's interior and only a triangular patch of stars marked our exit. We crawled on our bellies toward the opening, out into the square of the village, hugging the shadows. Then like moving shadows ourselves we threaded our way through the silent lodges. I could see nothing, but Tim's knowledge and instinct were better than any eyes. With his guiding hand we fled swiftly. Somewhere a child cried in its sleep. A dog barked, and Tim hissed a word of Comanche. The animal hushed its noise. But within the lodge someone moved and a head peered out. We drew back into the black shadows, and I felt that the pounding of my heart must surely be heard, for it sounded in my

ears like the crack of doom. But the head disappeared and on we fled toward the horse corral.

The guard dozed at its labors. Thrusting a rifle into my hands, Tim swung himself up to a pony's back. And then a horse neighed loudly. I knew that sound – Black Knight! The animal had caught my scent and trotted up to me, making a great to-do. Tim cursed and I leaped up to the stallion's back.

The horse guard waked from its dozing with shouts that echoed throughout the village. In a second every r lodge had sprung to life and action. Old men were running: through the village spreading the word. Somewhere a rifle barked. Tim gripped the jaw thong of Black Knight and swiftly he guided us out through the milling horses.

Darkness covered our flight. Torches were being lighted. An arrow whirred by, a random shot...

"Come on!" Tim shouted. "Trust your horse to follow mine!"

Then we were fleeing blindly, and the wind of freedom rushed forward to greet us.

CHAPTER XVI

THE LONG ARM OF ARMIJO

DURING the two days which followed, only Tim's training as
an Indian could have saved us from death by thirst, hunger,
or arrow. Striking an old Indian trail known to the red men alone,
we followed a little feeding stream of the Cimarron, skirting along
it in a northwesterly direction, headed back once again toward the
Arkansas and Bent's Fort.

It rained hard that first night, drenching us to the skin and
turning the brook into a miniature torrent. The valley was strewn
with boulders and cacti, and how Tim managed to find his way
along the trail in the darkness will ever remain a mystery to me.
But we dared not pause. We knew that the Comanches would pur-
sue us, and we pushed ahead all night and into the following
morning before we drew rein. At noon Tim shot a black-tailed
deer with his bow. We built a fire of stunted cedar which gave
forth no telltale smoke to reveal us to our enemies. While the meat
roasted and the horses grazed at picket, Tim and I had our first
opportunity to get reacquainted. He was filled with eagerness to
know all about Independence, and to have news of people whom
he had known there. There were still Cooper relatives in the little
Missouri town and he could scarcely credit the fact that soon, if
the gods were kind, he might see them once again. As the years
had passed, he had almost given up hope of escape from the

Comanches. And he had been so long in the tribe, living a wild and savage life, that of late he had begun to doubt whether he could ever again fit into a white man's community if the opportunity should present itself. He didn't know, until I told him, that Colonel Bent had tried to ransom him and that old Chief Bald Head had claimed that the boy was dead.

Haltingly at first, the story of his captivity began to be told. Not once in all those years had he spoken to another white man, and his mother tongue had grown rusty with disuse and fell awkwardly from his lips. Without his feathered headdress he looked much like the old Tim that I remembered, though much bigger, of course. As he squatted there on the ground beside the roasting meat, flat on his heels like a savage, his smooth-rippling muscles spoke of long years spent in the saddle, and his blue eyes blazed startlingly against the deep bronze of his skin. I saw that his features had taken on something of the impassivity of the Indian, and, as he talked, they were slow to relax, and he seldom smiled.

The Comanches had treated him well, for he had developed into a clever warrior and a fine horseman. We tallied on and on, and finally he related how Governor Armijo had bought the friendship of the Comanche chiefs with presents and fine promises, inciting them to warfare against the Americans.

"I made up my mind then to escape, first chance I got," Tim explained. "When we — the tribe, I mean — made raids on the border towns, or on the *ciboleros*, it seemed all right to me; for the Comanches had brought me up to it. But when it came to attacking my own people, I — I couldn't," he concluded lamely.

"And it was Armijo who had planned to have Bannock's wagons given safe escort by the Comanches across the *Jornada?*" I demanded.

"Of course! But we weren't looking for Bannock for another two weeks," he answered. "Armijo promised White Buffalo two hundred rifles and twenty kegs of powder."

"How did you manage to give them the slip when they rode to Bannock's aid?" I asked.

He smiled slowly. "When we'd ridden for a couple of hours, I

lamed my horse and told them I was putting back for a fresh one. Ordinarily it wouldn't have worked, and I thought sure they'd smell a rat, but they were so plumb excited over the chance to fight the Kiowas, and the fact that Bannock was already in the *Jornada*, that no one paid any attention to me."

The venison roasted on its spit and the savory odor heightened the pangs of hunger that gnawed at our young vitals. When we fell to the feast, the meat was scarcely more than half done, but so famished were we by that time that we ate our fill. Then we mounted again, from the right side, as Indians, and rode on until midnight. Having neither saddle nor robe, we lay down on the springy earth beside the brook and were asleep on the instant, secure in the knowledge that no Plains Indian ever ranged abroad on the dark of the moon.

It was an instinct with Tim to awake two hours before dawn. He aroused me; and being caked with dust and sweat and grime, I felt that here was a long-awaited chance for a bath. No telling when I'd have another!

When I had finished my ablutions, Tim commented on my carelessness. "You've left sign an Injun could read with his eyes shut," he scoffed.

"How?" I questioned.

"Well — first you splash water all over the bank, then you get dressed and you plant hoof in the mud; and your moccasins are a white man's. You'd better take 'em off and use mine. I don't mind going barefoot."

Take off Pierre's moccasins. . . . "No thanks," I answered briefly. "I'll be more careful."

I didn't explain about the message for Kearny that was concealed between two soles in the left moccasin. It was not any lack of confidence in Tim Cooper which prompted me to silence. I couldn't have explained it, exactly, but it was compounded of native caution and the feeling that Pierre's last words were a charge meant for my ears alone: a solemn charge laid upon me by a dying man, which somehow I must carry through to completion. Tim had been satisfied with my explanation that at Bent's Fort we

could join up with a caravan going to Santa Fe, or even returning to Independence. I made no mention of Kearny, but prayed that he would still be near Bent's Fort.

"All right," Tim was saying, breaking in on my thought, "but remember that from now on, until you reach the settlements, you're an Injun. Every camp we make is an Injun camp." He smoothed over the earth where we had sat at the camp fire, and then stuffed the bones of our meal into the mouth of a prairie-dog hole. He straightened up and voiced the thought that was upper-most in his mind, "Once White Buffalo learns we're gone, he'll move heaven and earth to find us, and if he does— "

A shadow clouded his face, and I knew that the thought of the fate which would be ours if we should fall into Comanche hands was enough to make the soul turn sick. Who should have known better than Tim the limits of cruelty which the Comanche could achieve? With his own eyes he had seen them riddle his father with arrows and split open his mother's skull with a tomahawk. The seven years that had passed since that fateful day could only have deepened the horror of its recollection. Stories that I had heard of Indian revenge and torture passed through my mind, trooping from a child's shadowy storehouse of remembered tales.... Involuntarily I shuddered and looked down at Old Chief Thrower — for this was the rifle which Tim had thrust into my hands the night of our flight. I remembered that commonplace of trapper advice: "It's a wise man who saves his last bullet for himself."

"But we've got a long head-start on White Buffalo's men," I sug-gested. "And they'll have their hands full with the Kiowas."

He nodded his assent. "But there's plenty of other Injuns round about this country, don't forget that. And Mexican cavalry scouts, too — Armijo's men. There wouldn't be much choice between 'em and we can't afford to be getting careless. Maybe Injuns can't read books," he went on, "but we — *they*, I mean — can read 'sign' like it was a printed page. Yesterday we passed sign, and you were so busy looking around that you never even noticed it!"

Abashed, I demanded, "What sign?"

"Kiowa," he came back at me. "Three days old."

"How do you know it was?"

He grinned good-naturedly at my discomfiture. "Because the bank of the brook was muddy when they were there, and it takes three days for mud to dry that hard," he explained patiently. "The shape of their moccasins showed that they were Kiowas. A family party — 'cause there were children's tracks too, and so there must have been women. You'd know that, even if you hadn't seen the marks of the pony-travois poles."

"How — how many were there?" I asked, struck anew with this evidence of the tenderfoot's ignorance of the wilderness.

"The ashes of four campfires, so at least that many families," came Tim's answer. "They were probably some squaws and old men of the outfit that attacked Bannock; maybe on their way to some village on the Canadian."

He explained all these things with patience, but not without a certain friendly scorn. I had to remember that the years he had spent with his Comanche captors had blurred his recollections of a more civilized mode of life; he had forgotten that men who lived in the white settlements had no need to know these things which were the "sign" by which a savage was enabled to keep ahead of his enemies in the relentless struggle for survival. The sudden snapping of a twig, a leaf floating downstream, the imprint of a foot in the mud, the uneasiness of a horse, a roiled brook, the hoot of an owl — these were the signs which often spelled life or death to the inhabitant of the wilderness. They were messages to be read, as clear to the eye that was trained in such things as the pages of a book to a man who could read.

But that night it was not the knowledge of Indian ways, or lack of caution, which proved our undoing. We had picketed our horses close at hand in a sheltered pocket of the valley, handy to water and a bit of grass. We made no fire and ate some of the meat we had smoked at noon. Tim scouted around the camp site and appeared satisfied that we were not being trailed. Then we lay down on the earth, to snatch a few hours of slumber before moving on. We fell instantly asleep.

But while Plains Indians do not prowl at dark of night, white

men frequently do. I was aroused by a sudden shout. I leaped to my feet, reaching automatically for Old Chief Thrower. The rifle was not there! I could see nothing. The sounds of a struggle and Tim's panting voice struck my ear.

Then a strange voice cried: "*Por Dios!* but he is strong! Quick, the *reata!*"

Mexicans!

I leaped in the direction of the struggle. Two pair of arms seized me from behind. I twisted madly to free myself. In vain. As I fell heavily, the edge of a binding cord cut into my wrists. I lashed out with my feet. Within a moment they, too, were prisoned. I was helpless.

All this happened so suddenly that, waking from a deep sleep, I had had no chance even to hazard what it all might mean. I heard a despairing groan from Tim; then a smooth Latin laugh. A spark of light caught my eye as a fire was kindled with flint and steel. A stick of greasewood flared up brightly, lighting the scene. Swept with consternation and dismay, I took in our plight at a glance. There was Tim, trussed up hand and foot, even as I. Four Mexican soldiers dressed in ragged splendor stood over us. The firelight glinted on tarnished gold braid, on their flashing teeth, and on their musket barrels.

One of the men, who cut a more imposing figure than the others, smiled at us good-naturedly, his fingers playing with the hilt of the saber that dangled from his belt. He swept off his hat with mocking regality and cried:

"*Hola, muchachos!*"

"What — what's this all mean?" I managed to gulp out.

The man's smooth laughter rang out in the darkness. "You have the honor of being prisoners of his Excellency, *El Gobernador* Don Manuel Armijo," came his answer. "*Viva Armijo! Viva Mejico!*"

"*Viva Mejico!*" came the answering shout from the other three soldiers.

I looked across the fire at Tim and our eyes met. Prisoners of Armijo....

How would I ever reach Kearny now?

CHAPTER XVII

MAGOFFIN'S GOLD

SANTA FE. The ancient City of the Holy Faith of Saint Francis. As we rode down its narrow streets in the early morning, the peaks of the Sangre de Cristo – the Mountains of the Blood of Christ – were somber against the pearly sky. Adobe houses built of the earth itself, into the earth, looked as changeless as the mountains, as enduring as the sky. Through the narrow streets the scent of *piñon* smoke and roasting coffee mingled with more elemental smells. Women in black *rebozos* peered from the doorways at the sound of our horses' hoofs, stared wide-eyed at me and Tim Cooper and at our dusty escort.

"*Americanos!*"

The word was caught up in excited chatter. Children scurried to look, then broke to run and spread the news. Our soldier guard, impressed now with the dignity of their position, rode in haughty silence, glancing neither to right nor left, flanking Tim and me on both sides.

We had been disarmed, of course, and during the four days since our capture the vigilance of our guard had left no loophole for escape. The soldiers, we had found, were part of the New Mexican cavalry which Armijo periodically sent out against marauding Apaches and Navajos. They had proved friendly

enough with us over the camp fires in the desert, and inquired jokingly as to Kearny's whereabouts, and asked when they might expect to see him enter Santa Fe. They made no bones of their innate contempt for the former sheep stealer who had lifted himself to power as Governor of New Mexico; and I began to believe that some of the rumors which had reached my ears might be true: that Armijo wasn't above listening to the alluring clink of gold. I remembered what Pierre had told me of James Magoffin's mission on behalf of President Polk. Sometimes money spoke more forcibly than gunpowder and was cheaper in the end.

We rode into the *Plaza* where arcaded buildings formed shadowy recesses from the sun's bright glare. We saw Pueblo Indians whose heavy brown faces emerged from white blankets; Mexican *ricos* in tight-fitting trousers slashed at the bottoms; bold-eyed girls, barefoot and arresting. Before the *casas de comidas* men lingered over their morning coffee to pass the time of day. They broke off as we passed, to breathe the word: "*Americanos!*" Santa Fe, drowsing in the sun; a golden city where time stood still and people moved to the music of cathedral bells.

On we rode, past the *Palacio* of the Governor, past the barracks, to stop before a high-grilled gate: the dreaded *calabozo*. One of our escort called out a command. Within the *patio* we heard musket butts rattle on the cobbles. Then the doors swung open on their heavy hinges. Tim and I, with our dusty guard, rode through the opening and the gates clanged shut behind us. Something about the sound of those great locks falling into place brought an acute realization of our plight. There was finality in the sound, making it hard to believe that we would ever live to see those gates swing open again. Soldiers sprang toward us as we dismounted. The Captain of the Guard detailed two men to take charge of us and we were led away.

"Good-by, Tim!" I called after his vanishing figure.

He threw me a rueful grin. "Good-by, Johnny."

"Give my respects to His Excellency, if you see him first!"

We had to joke, Tim and I, for it was the only way we could keep up our faltering courage. Then the guards led us to separate

corridors and I lost sight of my friend's slim figure and wondered if I should ever see him again. During these past days in the desert, we had come to know one another better than we could have during a lifetime spent in civilized surroundings; bound together by a common danger and the certainty of a terrible fate if caught by White Buffalo's braves. The desert strips a man clean, until the thing that he *is*, is the only thing that is left; he sheds the shams of civilization like an outgrown shirt. Now that we had fallen into the hands of Armijo, who could say what would happen to us? For was not Armijo himself a friend and patron of the Comanche tribe?

The cell in the *cárcel* where I was thrown may have been ten feet long. Certainly it was no wider than six. I could cross it in two strides. Innocent of all furnishings, even the most primitive, its floor was the earth itself; its walls adobe mud; the rugged *vigas* of the ceiling I could reach with my hands. A heavy door, dark with age and stained with all the misery this prison had nourished, formed the fourth wall of the cell. The very sight of that massive door with its great iron lock was enough to plunge me into blackest despair. Surely it would never swing open again to release me to the world of sun and air!

Through a narrow, heavily barred grille high in the door, I could catch a square of sunlight out in the *patio* of the *calabozo*. A shadow moved across it every now and then — the wide-brimmed *sombrero* of the guard on his rounds.

I have no words to describe the terrible dejection which settled upon my spirit. Somewhere to the southeast Kearny was waiting for word from Pierre Leroux. . . . My head throbbed unmercifully. The wound in my shoulder (which had never properly healed) burned now and was sore to the touch. The damp, fetid air of the *cárcel* was poisonous to breathe; only by standing close to the little opening, could I draw a full breath into my lungs. But I was too tired and too weak long to remain on my feet, and so I lay down on the floor wondering what was to happen next.

The door swung on its creaking hinges at last and two soldiers entered. One of them was resplendent with gold braid and cock-

aded hat. Not being familiar with Mexican military insignia, I judged the man to be at least a brigadier-general. He proved but the corporal of the guard.

"Search him!" this fine man commanded.

I stripped off my buckskins and passed them over for inspection. The Mountain Man's costume, built without pockets of any sort, was not designed to harbor contraband, and the inspection was soon over. Would they remember the moccasins?

"When may I see His Excellency, the Governor"

I asked, hoping to divert the attention of the corporal.

He ignored the question. "Your moccasins—" he snapped. "Take them off!"

I held my breath as the man's avid fingers closed about them, peered into them, felt the flaps of their sides. Whoever had made them, had worked well. They held their secret. I put them on again, trying to mask my elation and relief.

The soldiers disappeared and a fat Mexican jailer entered. He grinned at me from toothless gums, set down a jug of water and a soggy *tortilla*, and motioned me to drink and eat, then watched with hands crossed on his fat paunch. I avoided the *tortilla* and lifted the jug to drink – set it down again, repulsed by the ill-smelling water.

The Mexican laughed hugely, and said, "It will taste better to you tomorrow, *muchacho!*"

"I suppose so," I assented, trying to draw him into conversation. "And perhaps even better the day after tomorrow."

He shrugged expressive shoulders. "*Por Dios!* Maybe there will be no after-tomorrow for you!" He laughed loudly again, as one who has uttered a profound witticism, and his belly shook with his mirth.

I controlled myself and answered as quietly as possible,

"When will I see His Excellency, the Governor?"

Again he shrugged. "*Quien sabe?* Soon enough, gringo!"

With that he disappeared and the heavy lock clicked as the key turned. Somehow the long hours passed. How quickly the sense of time is lost when there are no outer events to mark its passage!

I slept on the earth floor; woke to the feeling of something clammy crossing my face; sat up with a start. Rats.... The barred rectangular opening in the door framed a strip of starlight. It was night.

I slept again. When next I awoke, a thin bar of gold filtered through the grille and fell across the earth floor. That band of honey-colored light somehow restored me to new hope, brought me some assurance that outside this dungeon, old, warm, familiar things still persisted, unchanged. I felt better after my night's sleep, fitful though it had been. The hard floor was no privation for one whose only bed for many long weeks had been the ground. Once again I lifted the jug, and this time (just as the jailer had prophesied) I drank. Digging my toes into the door and gripping the bars of the grating, I pulled myself up until I could catch a glimpse of the *patio.* Under the wide roof of the arcade, a ring of shadowy doors met my eyes, but there was no sight or sound of Tim. Two soldiers kept careless guard beneath the shade of a box elder. I fell back once more, trying to throw off my feeling of despondence. How long — how long might this imprisonment last? I couldn't free my mind of the thought of the Yankee trader who had been thrown into jail in Chihuahua, there to rot for nine long years. Events trooped through my tired mind. To what wretched hands had Old Chief Thrower passed? What Mexican *peon* might now be in possession of Black Knight, to break his spirit and hitch him to a plow. But always my thoughts returned to escape....

Guards could be bought with money but not with promises, and the few dollars which had been in my possible sack had been confiscated by the Mexican soldiers with the sack itself. The long hours wore on and the guards joked and laughed in the *patio.* From outside, street noises filtered through, muted by the thick walls of mud. Voices reached me like a deep, droning hum in which all words were indistinguishable. But once it seemed to me that I heard a shout, a cry taken up out there in the Plaza by other voices. It sounded like, *"Los carros! Los carros!"* That would mean "The wagons!"

The guards heard it, too, for their *sombreros* flashed by the grille, and I thought I heard one of them mutter: *"Americanos!"*

Kearny? It couldn't be — and yet.... why not? Kearny would be out there somewhere. He wouldn't wait forever to hear from Pierre Leroux. As nearly as I could figure the calendar by checking off past events, August was at hand, and the Army of the West must strike and strike soon. I grew weary of thinking — thinking — always in circles. Feeling like a drowning rat going round and round in a tub, I fell asleep on the floor again, while the flies buzzed around my ears in the hot air.

The creaking of the door wakened me. How long had I slept? Still dazed with the weight of my slumber, I saw the resplendent corporal of the guard standing in the opening.

"On your feet, gringo!" he barked. "You have the honor of going to see His Excellency, Don Manuel Armijo!"

My heart began to thump. What would I find to say to this Mexican tyrant? What would the next hours, nay, minutes, bring? Would my ears be added to the collection of the ears of his enemies, which were strung on strings along his walls? The corporal led me out into the sunlight and involuntarily I shut my eyes against the glare; blinding after the gloom of the *cárcel.* I must have stumbled, for with the butt of his musket he shoved me toward a wide stair.

Then we were crossing a long corridor, at the end of which a soldier stood guard before a pair of tall carved doors. The corporal exchanged words with him. The doors swung open. I passed through and paused for a second in amazement at the spaciousness of the chamber. At the far end of the room, opposite the door by which I had entered, two other doors rose high and black against the white adobe walls.

A man was seated at a table before those doors. A ponderous man, handsome in a brutish way, his heavy, blue jowls overflowing the collar of his magnificent uniform. I had a confused impression of green velvet and gold braid, of general's epaulettes and a crimson sash; of a cocked hat with tall plumes lying on the table, and the gleam of a saber at the man's side.

The Corporal prodded me again. "Go ahead, you fool!" he hissed.

I compelled Armijo's eyes with my own.

I crossed the room slowly, my gaze fixed upon the dramatic figure seated at the table. Manuel Armijo, Governor of New Mexico.
He was looking back at me as I advanced, and I saw that his eyes
were close-set and piggish, glittering from under heavy brows.

He surveyed me silently for a moment, then spoke. "Does the
young *señor* enjoy his accommodations?" he inquired with heavy
sarcasm. "The guests of Armijo seldom complain of his hospitali-
ty." The voice was thick, guttural; the voice of the peasant sheep
stealer that he was reputed to have been.

With a rush of wonder I realized that I was not afraid of this
fat hulk, this peasant who dressed himself in velvet and gold
braid. Something warned me that he was like a child who whistles
in the dark to keep up his wavering courage. Behind his bombast
the soul of a coward lurked.

I compelled his eyes with my own. "Perhaps you will have the
opportunity of enjoying the same accommodations, Your
Excellency, when Kearny comes," I answered.

His face purpled and he banged his fist on the table till the
green quill in the silver inkstand rattled with the motion. "Kearny
will not live to reach Santa Fe, my smart young spy!" he thundered. "My forces are strong, my men are loyal — *muy valeroso!*
One hundred men can hold Apache Canyon against ten thousand
Yanquis!"

"There's nothing to prevent Kearny's men from crossing the
passes to the north and entering Santa Fe by the Taos road," I shot
back. "Fremont has taken California, and Wool occupies Chihuahua.
Your country has fallen, *señor*. You can kill me, and every American
in Santa Fe, too, but you might as well try to stem the Rio Grande
at flood as to hold back the Army of the West!"

Armijo's little eyes probed into mine, seeking to read-what?
When he spoke, his voice was quieter. "Is he so well equipped
then, this Kearny?"

"He has three thousand dragoons at his command," I invented
hastily — "and a whole battalion of artillery: six-pounders and
twelve-pounders, too."

The heavy figure slumped for a second behind the great
Spanish table and thick hands fumbled for the decanter — poured

out a glass of ruby wine. Every Governor since Oñate had sat at this table. Doubtless it had been brought by toiling slaves a thousand miles from Old Mexico, and the hand-wrought silver candlesticks, too, and the crystal-and-silver chandeliers. And in the midst of this splendor sat this swinish Mexican, this upstart cattle thief, trying to ape the dress and manner of a Spanish grandee. There was something pathetic in the attempt, as well as in the ugly fear that sagged his jowls: the fear of Kearny's army almost at the gates of his city, bringing to an end this childish charade.

The Governor cleared his throat. "And you think that I — Don Manuel Armijo — have no fine equipment ready to do my command?"

"The Mexican army is ill-trained and without proper arms," I answered. "That is known to everyone."

Armijo half rose to his feet, his hands closing about a slim bamboo cane that lay across the table's top. For a second I thought that he would strike me with it. Then a crafty smile crossed his face and he sank back in his chair. The smile spread up to his eyes and his face took on the look of a man who holds the last trump and is reluctant to terminate his own pleasure by playing it. "What," he asked softly, "was the name of your brother spy?"

"If you knew that I had a brother spy, as you call him, then surely you must know his name, Your Excellency," I answered. But now I was beset with misgivings. How had Armijo known about Pierre Leroux? How much did he know?

"Perhaps I know much more than you are aware of," he answered, as if he had read my thought. He whispered to the corporal. The corporal disappeared. The Governor lifted the crystal goblet and drank, wiping his thick lips on the velvet of his sleeve. His yellow, jagged teeth showed in a leering smile. "Armijo is not so ill-prepared as you imagine, my smart stripling. You shall see——"

The tall doors behind his chair swung silently open. I stared into the opening, scarce able to credit what my eyes beheld. I felt that I was suffocating — my heart racing to sudden tumult.

In the doorway stood Black Jack Bannock and Jake Bailey. Their eyes sparked with their triumph.

"I believe——" Armijo's hand swept from me toward the two

men in a gracious gesture, "that you have had the pleasure of meeting these gentlemen before, *non?*"

I swallowed, beyond speech.... White Buffalo had found Bannock in the desert and guided his accursed wagons to the border.... That cry I had heard in the streets, *"Los carros!"* had been Bannock's wagons rumbling into town with their precious cargo.

"We know each other very well, Your Excellency," Black Jack responded easily. He stepped into the room with Bailey following at his heels, as a mongrel follows his master, and they both lounged at the Governor's elbow, enjoying to the full my stupefaction.

Bannock drew on a Mexican cigar and blew a ring of smoke toward the ceiling, then shot a question at me like a barb: "Where's Leroux?" And his eyes were like pieces of ice on fire.

"He's – dead," I managed.

The man laughed harshly. "I wish I could believe that!" he flashed. Then swinging toward Armijo, he cried: "Your Excellency, this boy and Leroux left me to the Kiowas in the Cimarron. Leroux is one of Polk's men. He knows too much for everyone's good. Send out scouts for him. If he ever gets to Kearny—"

"*Amigo,* he will not get to Kearny," the Governor promised blandly. "My scouts are combing the desert. "Nor will this *muchacho* get to Kearny, either." Armijo leaned toward me across the table, and his voice when he spoke had a saber's edge. "Tomorrow morning, *Señor* Spy, when the sun lifts above the Mountains of the Blood of Christ, you will find that my soldiers are not so poorly equipped. They will have bullets enough to riddle your carcass!" He made a sign to the corporal.

"But Your Excellency—" I began.

"Take him out!" the Governor shouted, The corporal gripped me by the arm and led me toward the door, and as I crossed the wide chamber, Bannock's laughter mingled with Bailey's, reverberating in my ears like a chorus of doom.

Back in my cell once again I gave myself over to despair. The game was up now. It was up for me before I had had a chance to play out my hand. Tomorrow morning, when the sun rose above the Mountains of the Blood of Christ, this little comedy would be

ended. And all the fine hopes that I had set forth with, the dreams I'd dreamed, the achievements my father had wanted for me, would be laid in dust. "Find Kearny," Pierre had whispered with his last breath, and I had vowed that I would. And now....

I sprang up from the floor, swept by a fury of impotent rage, and leaped against the door, the bars of the iron grating cutting into my hooked fingers.

"Let me out!" I shouted wildly. "Let me out!" The guards sauntered across the *patio* and laughed up at me. This was the way condemned men always acted.... It broke the monotony of a guard's long days. The men raised their rifles and took mock aim at me as I clung there. Then laughed and laughed again, till their sides shook with their mirth.

I dropped back from the door and threw myself on the floor, my bleeding fingers gripping at the earth while sobs wracked my body.

How long I lay there I do not know. The bells from the cathedral sounded across the air. Twilight.... I grew calmer and raised myself up, to lean against the wall. Outside in the *patio* a guitar was tinkling and the voices of the guards were lifted in boisterous song. Doubtless one of them had smuggled in a bottle of *aguardiente* to help pass away the hours.

The door of my cell opened at length and the jailer entered to set down a jug of water and a pannikin of red *frijoles*.

"Eat, *muchacho*," he invited slyly. "You will need strength tomorrow morning. Strength to face the rifles!"

I hurled the jug at him and it crashed against the door jamb, shattering behind his retreating figure. His high-pitched cackle floated through the grille.

There was one thing that I must do before tomorrow morning: destroy the letter which Pierre had given me for Kearny. It must not be found upon me after, after — I couldn't complete the thought.

Quietly I took off my moccasins. It was growing dark by now and the guards were not likely to come again to my cell. Out in the *patio* the guitar still tinkled and the voices rose louder and more abandoned. *Aguardiente* loosened men's tongues and fogged

their thoughts. The left moccasin — carefully I examined its inner sole. It had been sewn with minute stitches of elk sinew. It seemed hopeless at first to break those stitches with naught but finger nail and tooth to serve the purpose. Every few moments I raised my head to listen, for I must not be surprised at this task. The letter could be torn into small pieces, a hole dug in the earth floor, the letter buried and the earth pounded back into place. Soon the dampness would finish the final disintegration. Moving close up to the door, I took advantage of the little light remaining. One by one the stitches came free around the heel of the moccasin. When the opening was large enough, I thrust in my fingers. There! They came in contact with something soft and pliable. My hands trembled as they extracted an envelope encased in oiled silk. That rectangle of paper shone luminous in the gloom, and a red official seal glowed in one corner like a splotch of blood. Bold, black handwriting scrawled a message across the envelope's face. Leaning close to the grille, I could just make out the words. They spelled:

Pass bearer, without question, under any circumstances.
                       (Signed) W. L. Marcy, Secretary of War.

Had I the right to destroy this envelope? I had no knowledge of its contents. The man to whom it had been intrusted was dead, and perhaps its importance had died with him. And tomorrow by dawn I should be dead, too. But one thing was certain: this message to Kearny must not fall into Armijo's hands. My fingers gripped the envelope. Then, in the very second of tearing it across, some instinctive warning — call it what you will — bade me pause. I threw up my head.

Outside, a man was singing softly, scarcely to be heard through the roistering shouts of the drunken guards. I listened, and cold sweat broke out on my brow. There it was again! Closer this time. That voice—

Chico! Moro! Zaino!
Vamos pingo por favor!

The Wagoner's Song. Manuel. . . . It was Manuel! The boy who had vanished at Little Arkansas!

My hands shook so that I could scarcely thrust the letter back into my moccasin.

A dark shape shadowed the grille, while a low, sibilant hiss struck my ear. I leaped across the cell as the door swung just wide enough for a figure to enter.

"Manuel!" I breathed.

"Shhhh!" his voice came to me in warning whisper. "They are drunk, but have care. I brought the *aguardiente* to my uncle. It is he who is your jailer. I took his keys, and he didn't even notice. Quick! There is no time to lose. Put on this *sombrero!*"

His wide-brimmed hat fitted my head as if it had been made for me, and its enveloping shadow would be as protective at night as a mask.

"Here – *this serape! Por Dios,* but hurry!"

The long, enveloping folds of a heavy *serape* were flung over my shoulders. "Now follow me," the boy breathed, "and pray to the Mother of God."

We slipped silently out through the door and into the dark arcade, hugging the shadows, black pools of refuge. The lock clicked behind me as Manuel turned the key. Across the *patio,* where a lantern gleamed brightly, we saw that the guards were having a drunken altercation with the jailer. Their noisy dispute covered our flight. We slipped past them like ghosts. At the outer gate Manuel thrust his head through a small opening and said to the guard on the outside:

"Here's a *peso.* My uncle says he'll give you a drink if you'll run over to the *cantiña* and get another bottle of *aguardiente.*"

"But—" came the guard's hesitant protest. "I'll watch the gate for you," Manuel offered. "Here – give me your rifle!"

The *peso* and the rifle changed hands. The guard's footsteps disappeared in the direction of the *cantiña.* Then the heavy outer gate swung open and Manuel and I stole through it like shadows. A throng of people sauntered around the *Plaza,* listening to a group of musicians. We melted into the crowd. I kept my head well

lowered and my chin sunk into the folds of the *serape.* No one glanced at us as we passed.

Slipping down a side street, we gained the entrance of a dark alley. Manuel's hand drew me into the shadow and we paused, trying to catch our breath. The pounding of my heart sounded in my ears lie a roll of drums.

The Mexican boy leaned toward me and his voice whispered: "There is a horse at the alley's end. Take it and ride swiftly. This street leads to the Las Vegas road – to Kearny! Carry this message to your gringo commander: The pig Armijo was a trader before he was a soldier. Gold has bought him. There will be no soldiers to oppose the *Americanos* at Apache Pass. Ride – and tell him to come!"

I gripped his hand to whisper my thanks, but he tore it from my grasp and hissed: "It is not for you that I do this, *Americano! Non!* It is to foil *his* plan!"

"His plan?" I faltered. "*Whose* plan?"

The boy leaned forward till a gleam of light, filtering through a shuttered window, fell across his face. A terrible smile twisted his young lips.

"*El Señor* Bannock," he breathed. "Look!" He raised one corner of a dirty bandage that covered his eye. I felt my flesh crawl at the sight revealed. That scene on the banks of the Little Arkansas flashed into my mind. The crack of Bannock's lash across Manuel's face sounded again in my ears.... I understood.

Manuel thrust the guard's rifle into my hands. "Take this and go!" he whispered fiercely. "*Vaya con Dios!*"

Then he had vanished.

At the end of the alley a horse was tethered. I leaped to its back. The music from the *Plaza* struck my ears like music from another sphere. Here the streets were deserted. I spurred my mount to a gallop.

Straight ahead the road to Las Vegas lay like a ribbon under the stars; and somewhere – somewhere out there Kearny was encamped, waiting for Pierre Leroux.

CHAPTER XVIII

VICTORY

THE MARE was a good one and she held to a swift pace, eating up the miles. We cantered through dark, silent villages where no lights gleamed and even the dogs held their peace. Then on, into the open, lonely country of New Mexico. Rugged and forbidding it seemed in the night, the dark shapes of the *piñons* looming against the sky like monsters about to spring.

At any moment I expected the challenging cry of Armijo's men to halt my progress, but I dared not leave the highway. In the hills I should have been hopelessly lost. I would have to trust to the grace of God to get through somehow. Silently I thanked Manuel for the rifle in my hands. Had he, I wondered, spoken the truth? Could it be that the shadowy James Magoffin had succeeded in buying off Armijo? Was Kearny really in camp somewhere along the Las Vegas road? I had to believe that he was, for I knew that if I should fail to reach him now, I would never have another chance.

The little mare thundered on. I had no knowledge of the miles we traversed, or the hours that passed, but almost before I knew it, the position of Orion proclaimed that the night was well along. On I rode, straight up and over Apache Pass, on toward the hamlet of Vernal. Would Kearny — I scarcely dared to hope. Then descending a bend in the steep-falling road, I saw the plain below dotted with dark houses. No, not houses — triangular shapes. . . . *Tents!* I wanted to shout and sing, I wanted. . .

"Halt! Who goes there!"

So suddenly did the cry spring out of darkness that the little mare shied and reared, almost unseating me. The next second, before I could control her, she had plunged ahead. There came a rifle's report almost in my ear, the white flash of fire cutting the darkness. My mare gave a scream of pain and crashed to the

ground, catapulting me over her head. I struck with shattering impact, and consciousness snuffed out, like a candle in the wind.

There was a light burning in the tent, flickering in the draught. Shadows danced grotesquely on the canvas walls. A thin man in a shabby, blue uniform was standing beside the cot where I lay.

"He's coming around, sir," I heard his voice saying. "Struck his head when the sentry shot his horse. Got a lump as big as an egg ... He's no Mexican, in spite of the *serape*."

I looked up and saw a strong, kindly face with concern written in the eyes. A second man stood behind this one, a thick about man with sandy hair and jutting jaw. Soldiers both, in worn, blue uniforms. I remember trying to rise from the cot, mumbling the word: "Kearny—" My head ached unmercifully and my senses were slow in returning.

The thin man pushed me back again. "Take it easy, lad. What do you want with Kearny?" he asked.

"I've – I've a message—"

"Here, drink this!" A cup of brandy and water was held to my lips and I gasped as the fiery liquid burned its way down my throat.

The sandy-haired man stepped closer and his eyes bored into mine. "Who's the message from?" he demanded.

"Pierre Leroux," I answered.

An exclamation ripped from the man's lips. "Leroux! Where is he?"

Weak as I was, I was caught up by the excitement behind his words. "He's – dead." I whispered.

The man grabbed me by the arm and shook me. "I'm Kearny!" he cried. "Tell me!"

Kearny. He was here, just a foot away. I had found him. For a

second I couldn't trust myself to speak. I looked back into the two faces which were bent toward me, faces worn and tired and anxious. The lives of fifteen hundred men lay in the hands of these two officers, and their decisions might change the course of America's history. I struggled to clear the mists from my brain.

"Tell me about Leroux!" Kearny was reiterating.

"He — gave me a letter," I managed.

"Where is it? Quick, boy!"

"In — my left — moccasin."

Eager fingers had the moccasin off within a second's time. There came a brittle crack of paper as the envelope was slit with a sword. I watched the man's face as his eyes raced across the written page. His expression changed from disappointment to swift bitterness. He handed the letter to his companion.

"Look at this, Doniphan!" he grated. "Marcy thinks that war can be waged from an armchair in Washington!"

Andrew Doniphan glanced over the letter, reading it half to himself, half aloud. I strained to catch the words as they fell. . . . " 'Advance on Santa Fe upon receipt of this order, provided Pierre Leroux, the bearer, deems it the proper moment. . .' "

There was more to the message, but that was all that I could catch. Doniphan looked up, the sheet of paper quivering in his fingers. "Provided Leroux deems it—" he mused. A thought struck him and his eyes flashed. "But this boy must have ridden through Apache Pass, sir!"

Kearny turned to me and demanded, "How did you get through the lines, boy?"

"The lines?" I echoed stupidly.

He made an impatient gesture. "Apache Pass is heavily fortified. I've had word there are six hundred men holding it. *One* hundred could hold it against a battalion! How did you get through?"

I struggled to rise. "Colonel Kearny," I shouted hoarsely, "there isn't a soldier in Apache Pass!"

"What are you saying?" he thundered.

"It's true!" I cried. "I rode through the Pass tonight. It's deserted. The road to Santa Fe is clear!"

Andrew Doniphan gave an exultant cry. "Magoffin's gold!

Armijo's been bought off, sir, just as we'd hoped! We're only five miles from the Pass, and twenty-five from Santa Fe——"

Kearny ripped: "Give orders to march at once! Let your scouts ride in advance as usual, and fall back on the main body if they sight the enemy. Armijo may have a trick up his sleeve yet."

Doniphan yanked open the flap of the tent and rushed into the dark. His voice came back through the thin canvas, hurling orders right and left. In a second the camp was in an uproar, fifteen hundred men making ready to march forth to conquer.

Kearny stood with arms folded across his chest. His eyes burned in the light of the guttering candle and a grim smile carved his lips. A cavalryman from head to spurs. He walked toward the tent flap, paused, turned back toward me.

"You'll be all right when you get your wind, son," he said. "And you're going to ride into Santa Fe with the Army of the West!"

He disappeared through the opening. With the sound of his words in my ears, I knew a sudden smarting on my eyelids and shut my eyes tight and thought, "It's all right now, Pierre. It's all right."

The rest is history. Everyone knows how Kearny marched through Apache Pass without a shot being fired or a Mexican soldier to oppose him. Armijo's elaborate fortifications proved a myth, and the Governor's proud boasting had been but hollow words. The road to Santa Fe was clear. Armijo, listening to the clink of Magoffin's gold, had sold out his country to *Los Americanos* and fled toward El Paso. Only Juan Bautista Vigil, lieutenant-governor, was left to receive the conqueror in the *Palacio* of the ancient City of the Holy Faith of Saint Francis.

Fifteen hundred victorious dragoons, dusty and triumphant, swept into the streets of the city, singing at the top of their lusty lungs. Above the rolling thunder of the drums came the high squealing of the fifes and the rumble of many boots. The red, white, and green flag of Mexico came down on the run as a dull boom of cannon reverberated across the *Plaza:* the first shot of a thirteen-gun salute. The Stars and Stripes, faded and tattered by their long journey from Fort Leavenworth, floated above the Rio Grande, and an era that dated back to Coronado was at an end.

These events, as I have said, are history. But there are a few

points of lesser importance (in the sight of historians!) which possibly have been slighted. What, you ask, happened to Black Jack Bannock and Jake Bailey? Well, as might have been expected of Armijo, when he betrayed his country and fled to El Paso, he abandoned his two accomplices to their fate. They and their twelve wagons of precious firearms were left to the mercy of Kearny. In less time than it takes to tell, Black Jack and his henchman were tried as traitors and sentenced to die upon the gallows.

When all the excitement had simmered down, an order from Headquarters brought me to the *Palacio* for the second and last time. In place of Armijo's Corporal of the Guard, a lean-ribbed dragoon from Jackson County was my escort.

"How, thar, young cub," he grinned at me. "Ye're a regular ring-tailed hero, ain't ye? I reckon the General's fixin' to pin a medal on yer chest!"

He clapped me on the back good-naturedly and opened the great doors of Armijo's chamber and pushed me unceremoniously into the room. I stumbled and lost my coon-skin cap; then grew red about the ears as I reached to retrieve it.

On the other side of the great Spanish table where, but a few days ago, Armijo had slouched in splendor as he sentenced me to death, Stephen Watts Kearny sat in sober dragoon-blue. He had been raised from colonel to brigadier, and the single star of his new rank glistened on his shoulder straps.

I stood at attention and the man rose from the table, came around it, and gripped my hand.

"How are you, Starbuck?"

"Fine, sir, thank you."

"Charlie Bent's outfitting a train to make the trip back to the Missouri, as you probably have heard. Would you like to go back with it?"

For a second I hesitated. Events had crowded in upon me so thick and fast these past days that I had made no plans and had given scarce a thought to the future. And then an idea that must have lain fallow in the back of my mind for a long time rose unbidden, and I was voicing it.

"No, sir, thank you," I heard myself make answer. "You see —

California's only a thousand miles west of the Rio Grande. I'd —
I'd sort of like to see it, General."

His laugh rang through the room. "Go to it, son!" he cried.
"And if there's anything I can do for you—"

"There's one thing, sir," I put in.

"And that?"

"A friend of mine — Tim Cooper — was thrown into jail by
Armijo—"

"He was released this afternoon," came the man's reply, "along
with all the other American prisoners who've been rotting in
Armijo's *calabozo*. Anything else?"

There was something else — but it was like looking for a needle
in a hayloft. "There was a rifle, sir," I began. "A flintlock. My father
gave it to me. Dan'l Boone made it. It was taken from me by
Armijo's men. I'd like to find it, if possible, before I go."

"Is that the one?" The general pointed to a rifle standing
against the wall. "It was found here in this room. Even Armijo
must have known it for a beauty!"

Old Chief Thrower....The sunlight slanting through the deep
window fell across the octagonal barrel, gleamed on the warm
maple of its stock and glistened like a star on the silver patch box.
My heart was full as I lifted it up and felt once more its homely
familiarity in my hands. Then I clicked my spurs in as military a
fashion as I could manage and saluted. Gravely the General returned the salute, and his face broke into a smile.

"Good luck to you, lad, and good-by!"

As I started through the door, his voice called me back:
"Starbuck?"

"Yes, sir"

"You'll find your friend Cooper at the Barracks. Oh — and there's
a stallion that he says belongs to you. A fine animal named Black
Knight—"

I waited to hear no more.

THE END

TRAIL TALK

A Guide for the Greenhorn

*The conversation of the Mountain Man was well nigh unintelligible
to the greenhorn. Spanish, French, English, and Indian words rubbed
elbows and mingled freely in the racy dialect of the American frontier.
The author has tried to preserve something of the flavor of this speech;
and in the following list to clarify it for the unaccustomed ear.*

amigo (ä-mē′gō), friend; comrade.
aparejo (ä-pär-ā′hō), a packsaddle of stuffed leather.
apishamore (ä-pĭsh-à-mōr′à), a saddle blanket of buffalo calfskin.
Blue Ruin, liquor, usually of a bad quality.
boudins, sections of buffalo intestines, roasted and relished by the
  Mountain Men.
buffalo chips, the dried dung of the buffalo, used for fuel.
bullwhacker, the driver of the oxen.
calabozo (cäl-à-bōth′ō), a jail.
cárcel (cär′thel), prison, cell.
casas de comidas (cä′sàs dā cŏ-mē′dà), eating houses.
cavvyard, a Plains corruption of the Spanish word *caballada* (cä-
  bál-yäh′dà); a herder of the loose stock.
cibolero (thī-bō-la′rŏ), A Mexican buffalo hunter.
concha (cŏn′tchä), silver ornaments, for bridle and saddle decorations.

dearborn, a light four-wheeled carriage with a top, and curtains at the side.

escopeta (es-cō-pä′tȧ), a short rifle.

fâché (fä′tchā), angry.

fofarraw (fō-fä′rŏ), the Mountain Man's expression of contempt for anything fancy or civilized; a corruption of the French *fanfarron.*

Galeny pill, a bullet of Galena lead.

¿habla Español? (ä′blä ȧs-pǎn-yōl′?) Do you speak Spanish?

"Hola, muchacho!" (ō′lȧ mōō-thcǎ′tchŏ) "Hello, boy!"

hog-tie, to tie by binding the four feet together.

Lift ha'r, the Plainsman's term for scalping.

lodgepoling, to beat, with an Indian lodgepole.

meatbag, the stomach.

muleskinner, mule herder, or driver.

muy valeroso (mōō′ē väl-ä-rō′sō), very brave.

¿no es verdad? (nō äs vīr-däd′), "Is it not so?"

nooning-it, Plains expression of the midday camp.

osnaburg (ŏz′nȧ-bûrg), at kind of coarse cotton fabric, originally made in Osnabruck, Germany; used as covers for the covered wagons.

parflêche (pär-flāsh′), a container, or saddlebag of buffalo hide.

piñon (pē′nyōn), a low-growing pine of North America and Mexico.

plew (plū), a beaver pelt.

possibles, contents of the pack-sack; the answer to possible need.

¿Quien sabe? (kē-än′ sä′bä), who knows?

reata (rā-ä′tȧ), lariat of plaited rawhide.

rebozo (rā-bōth′ō), a plain, or embroidered scarf.

rico (rē′kō) the wealthy class.

serape (sẽr-ä′pȧ), an enveloping blanket, worn over the shoulders.

"That shines!" the Mountain Man's exclamation of unqualified praise.

tortilla (târ-tē′lyä), a thin, flat cake.

viga (vē′gȧ), a rafter, or beam.

whangs, rawhide thongs for repairing saddles, moccasins, etc.

WAGONS WESTWARD

has been set in a digital version of Berthold AG's Bodoni Old Face, a type based on the designs of Giambattista Bodoni (1740–1813). The son of a Piedmontese printer, Bodoni first gained experience and earned renown as superintendent of the Press of Propagation of the Faith in Rome. In 1768 he was named head of the ducal printing house in Parma, where he carried out his most important work as printer and typographer. An innovator in type design and printing, Bodoni's books are known for their opulence and generous margins, and his types, considered the first "modern" faces, with their pronounced contrasts of thicks and thins and their fine serifs, are known for their openness and delicacy.

Design, typesetting, and digital imaging by
Carl W. Scarbrough